Escape from Coolville

a novel

Sherman Sutherland

Platen Press
Washington, D.C.

For all the L.J. Davenports of the world.

Published by
Platen Press
Washington, D.C.

This book is a work of fiction. Names, characters, businesses, organizations, places, events, and incidents either are the product of the author's imagination or are used fictitiously. Any resemblance to actual persons, living or dead, events, or locales is entirely coincidental.

Library of Congress Control Number: 2012910208
Cataloging-in-Publication Data
Sutherland, Sherman.
    Escape from coolville : a novel / Sherman Sutherland.—1st ed.
        p. cm.
    ISBN: 978-0-9857501-0-7
    1. Autobiography—Authorship—Fiction. 2. Karma—Fiction. 3. Humor.
4. Psychic readings—Fiction. 5. Revenge—Fiction. 6. Telemarketing—
Fiction. I. Title
PS3566.U84 E83 2012
813'.54—dc21   2012910208

Book design: Tara Hsiao
Images: L.T. Wang

www.PlatenBooks.com

Printed in the United States of America

10 9 8 7 6 5 4 3 2 1

舍利弗。若有善男子善女人。聞說阿彌陀佛。執持名號。若一日。若二日。若三日。若四日。若五日。若六日。若七日。一心不亂。其人臨命終時。阿彌陀佛。與諸聖眾。現在其前。是人終時。心不顛倒。即得往生阿彌陀佛極樂國土。

—Amitabha Sutra

Escape from Coolville

June 5

I barely got a chance to say, "Thanks for calling your psychic adviser," before the guy started freaking out in my headset: "You're going to hell, Antonio, if that's your real name. You're going to hell!"

He spent his whole twenty minutes reading me Bible verses and telling me how evil I am for daring to divine God's will, or some crap like that. On and on and on and on.

"Woe unto the foolish prophets, that follow their own spirit, and have seen nothing."

What is that even supposed to mean?

I used to love it when the callers did all the talking. You don't have to worry about saying the right thing to keep them on the line, or the wrong thing that'll make them hang up. All you have to do is kick back and say, "Mmm hmm, mmm hmm," every few minutes while you space off about unicorns or whatever. But now, not so much.

I tried to tell Angry Bible Guy that it's just a job and, besides, it says FOR ENTERTAINMENT ONLY on the bottom of all the ads, but that just made him more pissed. How dare I use that as an excuse? That's what the Nazis did. That's what those idiots in Washington are doing.

The only time he shut up is when he thought I went to look for my Bible. I told him I was going to mark down all those passages as soon as we hung up and he was like, "Why don't you do it now?"

"It might take me a while to find it."

He said, "I can wait," which is the absolute worst thing to say to somebody whose job is to keep you on the phone for as long as possible.

Like a dumbass, I said, "Really?" which is negative, instead of, "Okay," which is affirmative.

But he still said, "Of course, son. I'm tryin' to save yer soul."

The last thing I really wanted to do was defend Appalachian TeleServices, but, I mean, what did that guy expect? It's not like I can quit my job and forget about my credit card bills and my student loans and my rent and everything else. I'm already buying the cheap bags of fake cereal and the generic Toaster Pastries because I can't afford the real Frosted Flakes and the real Pop Tarts. If I could find another job that paid me eleven bucks an hour to sit on my ass all day, I'd take it. But it's not like people are pounding on my door every day, telling me, "L.J! We need you to come answer the phones for us at NASA!"

So, yeah, I'm pretty much stuck here being an abomination unto the Lord. Taking verbal abuse from religious jerkoffs who say they want to save me from God's everlasting reproach and perpetual shame.

By the way, dude, here's a tip: if you really want to save somebody's soul, try being something other than a complete ass about it.

About fifteen minutes into my next call, or maybe it was the call after that, Smeagol put my phone on MAKE BUSY—ATS code for, "Come back to my office after this call."

So I was all psyched, right? All I could think about was how he was going to tell me he liked the way I handled that angry caller, following the LEF steps—Listen, Empathize, Fraternize—and now he was ready to make me the new Floor Supervisor. All those months of clocking in on time and laughing at his stupid jokes and pretending to care about soccer have finally paid off. Before I know it, they'll move me up to QA. A few months after that, they'll make me a trainer and, maybe a year or two after that, I can be a Floor Manager and then an Operations Manager. I totally had this little I'm-going-to-get-promoted happy dance going on in my head.

When I got back to his office, though, Smeagol didn't want to talk about the Floor Supervisor job.

He started in with the twenty questions: "Lucas, how long have you worked here? Are you still in college? Are you planning to go back and finish? What made you decide on Antonio as your telephone alias?"

I was just like, "It'll be a year next week.

"No.

"Yes.

"I guess Antonio just sounded more psychic-y than L.J. or Lucas."

Then Smeagol was like, "The reason I called you in here is to discuss your performance on the call floor."

So I was thinking, *All right, here it comes! Two more dollars an hour and no more taking crap from callers all night.*

But then he said, "Your score on this last Quality Assurance evaluation is well below the standard we expect from our TSRs."

I was just like, "What? Seriously?" I figured he must've been joking, but when I looked up, he was still all serious.

I said, "But I always have good AHTs."

"I believe your average handle times have been more than adequate, but you just scored a forty-eight on this last QA. You received PINs for Greeting, Verification and Sincerity."

Okay, first of all: "more than adequate"? What's that about? I had the top AHT of the whole entire floor last month, and I've been in the top five almost every week since I started working here. Out of two hundred people, I'd say that's way better than "more than adequate." That kind of pisses me off, the more I think about it.

But I didn't say anything. I just sat there like an idiot while he read my whole DAF all the way through.

"Lucas J. Davenport, the purpose of this Disciplinary Action Form is to advise you, as a Telephone Sales Representative of Appalachian TeleServices, that you have been assessed either three Step One or two Step Two Professional Improvement Notifications within one consecutive sixty-day period, blah blah blah." Like I wouldn't be able to read my own pink copy on my own time. And then he made me initial the little line on my DAF every single time he finished a paragraph.

When he finally finished, he asked if I had any questions.

I said, more to myself than anything, "I don't understand how I could've scored so low. I thought I was doing good."

Like a total douche, he read the whole paragraph about Sincerity again.

But why is Sincerity even one of the PIN options, anyway? That's my question. I mean, we read people their Tarot cards over the phone for $5.99 or $Whatever-they-charge-in-Canada.99 a minute. There's nothing about this job that's sincere. They're always telling us that we're not supposed to "impede the illusion" that we're sitting alone in a candlelit room in front of our crystal ball or whatever, but downstairs, we've got people selling the ShamWow and the Shake Weight and doing tech support for DirecTV.

What's sincere about that?

"Sincerity," Smeagol said, "refers to your tone of voice. According to your evaluation, you were PINed for "sarcasm during your close.""

How is that even possible? Seriously, how can anybody sarcastically say, "That beep you just heard is to advise us that this call is about to end. Company policy requires that these calls not last longer than twenty minutes and we're almost there"?

And now that I think about it, I didn't even have a close on that call. I remember I heard the beep and I kept trying to do my close, but that guy wouldn't shut up with his Ezekiel this and his Ecclesiastes that. So how could I have been sarcastic when I didn't even say anything? And I couldn't interrupt him—interrupting the caller is an automatic Step Two—so I don't know what they expect me to do.

Then I asked what the problem with my greeting was.

Smeagol sighed like it was some big annoying question. "The correct opening is, 'Thank you for calling your psychic advisor. This is'—and then you give your name. Then you say, 'May I have your first name and date of birth, please?' When they give you that, then you ask, 'And may I have your age, please?'"

"Yeah," I said. "I do that. Every call."

"According to this, you asked for their age before their date of birth."

Seriously?

Seriously.

First of all, when you do it with the date of birth first, as soon as you ask the caller their age, they always say, "You're the psychic, you tell me," like instant subtraction is an essential psychic skill. They're always total dicks about it, too. "You're the psychic, you tell me." "You're the psychic, you tell me." After hearing that for the eighteen millionth time, you can't help but give somebody a reading that involves an exploding apartment or a career in porn or whatever.

But when you ask them their age first, they just tell you their date of birth, no problem, and then you move right into a normal call. Which is why every single person on the floor does it that way.

I tried to explain all that to Smeagol, how it's better for hold times to do it my way, and then I said, "What difference does it make, anyway?"

"Exactly," he said. "What difference indeed?" like that was the end of the conversation.

I just sat there like an idiot.

After a while, he was like, "Is that it?"

I wanted to ask him about the Verification PIN, but it seemed like he was getting sick of talking to me. I mean, I understand that we're supposed to verify that the callers are at least eighteen before we give them a reading, but they told us in training that we can still talk to them if they're not old enough—there's no law against that—we just can't give them a reading. If we hung up right away on every fourteen-year-old girl who called, our AHTs would suck.

And it's not like I didn't try to get that guy's information, anyway. When I asked him his name, he was like, "Why do you need my name when you've already got all that information on the big computer in North Dakota?"

I need it because I'm supposed to address you by name at least three times, buttface.

Smeagol told me, out of the goodness of his heart, apparently, that he'd give me the option to go back to training. Two weeks in the classroom and then one week of on-the-job training. Or maybe it was one week in the classroom and two of OJT.

I'd get to spend some of that time sitting next to "more-qualified TSRs," double-jacked into their phones, listening to their calls and looking like a total douche who can't do the easiest job in the whole entire world. Or I can stay on the call floor and make sure I don't get another Step Two PIN for the next two months.

Then he told me, if I choose training, my pay rate will go back down to the eight dollars an hour they pay trainees.

"Can I have some time to think about it?"

"Of course," he said. "Next training class starts Monday. Just make sure you don't get any PINs in the meantime."

Fucktard.

That's been my day so far. In twenty minutes, I went from being the perfect employee to being one wrong inflection away from getting fired.

Oh, and the worst part—I almost forgot: Smeagol gave the Floor Supervisor job to Liz. Liz! What the hell? She's never had an AHT above twelve minutes since she's been here. I'd be surprised if she's even had one call longer than twelve minutes. Seriously. If I would've known I'd have to stoop to her level of brownnosing to get the job, I never would've gotten my hopes up in the first place.

It doesn't matter. I'm probably going to get fired after this call, anyway. This lady on the phone now still hasn't given me her age or date of birth. When she finally told me her name, I was like, "And, Samantha, how old are you?"

"Samantha, let me get your age and date of birth."

"Samantha, can you tell me your age and date of birth so I can mark it down on my sheet here?"

Instead of answering, she just keeps talking talking talking about how my advice last year saved her life and how she thought I was crazy when I told her she needed to pack up all her stuff and move across the country that night, but she did it because I sounded so serious and so worried about her and, when she saw her ex on the news the next day, talking about the big gas explosion that blew up their apartment, she knew I was the most awesome telephone psychic ever and she's been trying to call me back ever since and when it was always somebody else who answered, she started to think that I wasn't real, that I was an angel or something, especially after she did some research on Tarot cards and found out that all the supposed experts said that the Star card represents hope and inspiration, not danger like I said, but now she's really talking to me and I'm really real and now she can really thank me, for real.

Normally I'd be all about a call like this—Look! in that tiny cubicle!

It's a bird!

It's a plane!

It's Superpsychic!

Unintentionally saving people's lives one phone call at a time.

But right now I'm too paranoid to enjoy it, wondering if the QA's listening, all prepared to give me another verification PIN.

I totally liked this job earlier today, too. I mean, it wasn't like I was all thinking, *Golly gee, I can't wait to spend the next eight hours in this two-foot box, telling people what to do with their lives*, but I rushed to work to make sure I clocked in on time. That's got to mean something.

What sucks is, if I would've logged into my phone just thirty seconds later, I would've been deeper down in the queue and somebody else would've gotten that call from Angry Bible Guy and I would've gotten a caller who would've given me their name and age and date of birth.

I totally had my chance to get here later, too.

When I stopped by the Cool Spot to get my CornNuts, this gorgeous girl—dark hair up in a librarian bun thing, tight black business-y dress that went down to her knees, designer-type sunglasses—parked right beside me and walked in right behind me. I could hear her walking behind me and I wanted to turn around and get a better look at her but I didn't. Then, when I got to the door, I opened it and turned around and looked right at her as I turned around—but I didn't let her go first—and she looked at me through those big-ass sunglasses.

By the time I got up to the checkout line with my Corn-Nuts and my Sobe Green Tea—which they moved all the way down to the other end of the cooler—the girl was right in front of me. And she had a bag of CornNuts, too.

I totally could've, I don't know, talked to her or something. At least said, "Hey. CornNuts. Yeah," or something.

But no-o-o-o-o.

I was all worried about clocking in by three o'clock. All so I can keep getting that awesome quarter-an-hour perfect attendance bonus.

I'm such an idiot.

Samantha's still talking. She's starting to worry about her ex. She wishes he could talk to me. He used to be so into his job, especially the data analysis part, but now, when she calls him, he sounds weirder and weirder all the time, talking about righting wrongs and putting the universe in balance.

"Like Batman?" I ask.

"Huh?"

"Nothing."

Mike leans around the cubicle partition and whispers in my ear, "I know what you're thinking: from this angle, those vertical blinds look just like prison bars."

They sort of do, when you think about it.

June 6

CHEW
MAIL POUCH
TOBACCO
TREAT YOURSELF TO THE BEST
* * *

Welcome To
WEST VIRGINIA
Wild and Wonderful
* * *

Virginia
Welcomes You
* * *

I don't even know how I ended up here, wherever *here* is. Under a buzzing orange light in the last parking space at some rest area on I-77. In Virginia, I think. Maybe North Carolina.

The last thing I remember, I was driving to work and I was listening to Radiohead—"Idioteque"—and I was in a hurry and worried about being late, and I still wasn't sure what I was going to tell Smeagol—was I going back to training, or not—and the weather was really really beautiful for the first time in a long time (actually, everybody's been saying for a month how nice it is, but this was the first time I noticed).

The sky was perfectly sky blue and not that hazy blah color that it usually is, and the temperature was just perfect and it was just humid enough without being too humid, and it smelled like everybody between Athens and Coolville had just mowed their lawns and it seemed like everywhere there were these purple blooming bushes and white blooming trees and yellow blooming dandelions and birds were flittering from tree to tree and people were waving and I was really really high.

But I was still planning to go to work. Seriously.

I had my business casual blue shirt already tucked into my business casual khakis, which matched my business casual tan socks. I'd even had my business casual brown shoes tied and my business casual reversible belt flipped over to the brown side.

I wouldn't have gone to all that trouble if I'd never planned to go to work. But *Maury* had the fat kids on today, which made me totally hungry for a grilled cheese sandwich and, before I even got the cheese goo tongue-rubbed out of my teeth, it was like, *Holy crap, I'm late!*

When I unlocked my car door, I noticed that the key didn't stick like it has every day for the last however-many months and the door didn't squeak when I opened it.

Then there was this wall, like, of warm vanilla air that washed across my face when I leaned in. And the car didn't make that normal squonking noise when I sat down.

And the door shut easy and the window rolled all the way down without sticking and the engine started on the first try and the gearshift actually slid into reverse without having to push down and yank on it and I could hear the gravel crunching under my tires when I backed up and then when I plugged in my iPod, the song that started playing right away was "Idioteque" and I couldn't help but think, *This is going to be a good day.*

I was still planning to go to work then, though, too.

I missed every single pothole on Carpenter—even that super-bumpy part at Court Street—and I even hit the green light at Stimson, which never happens. And then I didn't see one cop on the whole entire highway, so I could drive eighty all the way to where the road splits to Coolville or Pomeroy. It was like the whole universe was working together to get me to work on time.

When I got to that "Abortion Stops a Beating" billboard, I remember thinking, *God, I wish I didn't have to go to work today*, but I didn't notice it being any different than my normal *God, I wish I didn't have to go to work today* feeling.

And somewhere in there I was trying to figure in my head how much I pay for rent, plus the electric bill, plus groceries, plus all my credit cards, plus whatever else, and trying to figure out, if I made eight dollars an hour instead of eleven, if I'd have enough to pay my bills and still get schwasted every now and then.

And then I slowed down as I got to Dixon Road—I had my turn signal on, I remember that—and I looked at my watch and I was thinking, *Okay, it says 3:26, but it's actually forty-three minutes fast, so that means it's actually 2:54, which means I've got eight minutes to get from Dixon Road to Dogwood to Buckeye. I bet I can still make it if I sprint across the parking lot and up the stairs, as long as Security Guard Gary isn't flirting with the girls at the front desk so he can let me in the door right away and as long as there's no dumbass at the time clock trying to swipe their card backwards a million times, saying, "Why won't this stupid thing ever work?"*

So I was thinking all that as I came up to the turn and I just . . . kept driving. I don't even know why.

I just kind of stared at the little green street sign—Dixon Rd—and I drove on past.

Then I drove across the Hocking River right there, and then past that little rest area and then I was in Belpre, then Parkersburg and on the I-77 onramp and, before I even really knew what was going on, I'd driven past Ripley and Charleston and some town with a bunch of strip clubs, and then another town and then I drove through this long tunnel and when I came out the other side, there was this "Virginia Welcomes You" sign.

Weird.

The thing it reminded me of more than anything was in fifth grade when we had to fill out those surveys.

"Don't put your name on it," they kept telling us. "These are anonymous. We want to know what you really think."

When it got to the question, "What do you like least about school?" I wrote, "Bitchy teachers."

Even though I wrote it in different handwriting, I was still scared they'd know it was me. And when I handed it in, I felt the same way as I did today when I watched myself drive past the turn onto Dixon Road. Kind of giddy and relieved and nervous and scared all at the same time.

Hopefully Mom and Dad won't be waiting for me whenever I get back home. That would suck.

At least in fifth grade, I could say, "But that's really what I like least about school!"

Now, all I'd be able to say is, "Uh, Radiohead was playing. And the song wasn't over. And I was really really high."

They'd bitch slap me into next week.

* * *

Rules and Regulations of Waysides and Rest Areas that I either plan to, hope to, or expect to break:

#3: When posted, parking shall be limited to the two-hour period specified.

#4: No overnight parking will be permitted.

#7: No vehicle shall be parked in such a manner as to occupy more than one marked parking space.

#9: No person shall pick any flowers, foliage or fruit; or cut, break, dig up, or in any way mutilate or injure any tree, shrub, plant, grass turf, railing, seat, fence, structure, or anything within this area or cut, carve, paint, mark or paste on any tree, stone, fence, wall, building, monument or other object therein any bill, advertisement or inscription whatsoever.

#12: No threatening, abusive, boisterous, insulting or indecent language, gesture or behavior shall be used or performed within this area. Nor shall any oration or other public demonstration be made, unless by special authority of the Commissioner.

* * *

Cast

(in order of appearance)

ME: Twenty-two-year-old bundle of telephone psychic awesomeness who's currently confused about his present job situation, among other things.

THE OTHER ME: The person in my head I talk to when I talk to myself in my head.

SCENE ONE

Driver's seat of my car, parked in the second-to-last spot at the Rocky Gap Rest Area in Virginia. It's late night-early morning. An orange street light/sidewalk light/rest area light shines in through my windshield so I can see to write. Outside, a stranger sits on a picnic table nearby. Every few seconds, a truck or an occasional car can be heard speeding past on the nearby interstate. Closer, but less frequently—every several minutes, maybe—a car passes slowly behind before it picks up speed on the nearby interstate onramp. On the other side of the rest area and welcome center building, a truck's airbrakes will make that squonking truck airbrake sound. Sometimes people talk on their phones or to each other as they walk to the restroom, but never loud enough to make out their conversation through the car window that's rolled down just an inch to let out the cigarette smoke. Me is talking to Other Me, but the conversation is taking place entirely in my head while Me does his best to dictate the conversation verbatim.

ME: Thanks for visiting your psychic advisor in the front seat of my car. This is Antonio. May I have your first name and—

OTHER ME: Why are you talking to yourself?

ME: I'm not talking to myself. I'm thinking to myself.

OTHER ME: Whatever. Why are you thinking to yourself?

ME: I'm trying to make this feel like a real reading. I figure maybe it'll work better that way. I give people advice all day, so I—

OTHER ME: That's scary.

ME: Do you want to do this or not?

OTHER ME: You know you're not really a psychic, right?

ME: All of us are born with inherent psychic abilities. It's just that some of us were raised in an environment where—

OTHER ME: Cut the crap. You don't even believe in this.

ME: I sort of do. Sometimes. There's Irene, at work, she's totally psychic.

OTHER ME: Maybe she's just better at lying than you are.

ME: Okay, but what about when I have those nights at work when the cards are exactly right on every single call?

OTHER ME: That's just the law of averages. When you do twenty or thirty readings a night for a year, the cards are bound to be right every now and then.

ME: You don't believe that. You think, at the very least, that there's some subconscious Rainman part of our brain that knows the answers and is shuffling the cards just right to show us what those answers are. Otherwise, we wouldn't be having this conversation.

OTHER ME: Just shut up and deal the cards.

ME: Okay. I need you to quiet your mind as you think of your question.

OTHER ME: What's my question?

ME: You want to know if you should go back to training

or not. On the one hand, if you go back to training, you won't have to worry about getting fired. On the other hand, you'll make three dollars less an hour, which sucks, because you can barely pay your bills now. On the other other hand, training is boring, and it'd be super boring the second time. But it'll also be easy, so you'll get paid to do basically nothing, which would be nice. On the other other other hand, everybody will think you're an idiot for going back to training, but since when do you care about what everybody else thinks anyway, especially everybody else at ATS? On the other other other other other hand, training is at nine in the morning, every morning—for three whole unholy weeks—but you'd also have normal weekends for a change, instead of Tuesdays and Wednesdays off, when all the bars have their stupid Eighties Night or Lady Gaga Night or Drink This Crap We Found Under the Sink Night.

OTHER ME: Whoa! How do you know all that? Maybe you really are psychic.

ME: See? Maybe this will work after all. Now quiet your mind and tell me when you feel I should stop shuffling the cards.

OTHER ME: What's that noise? Is somebody chanting in the restroom?

ME: No. That's me. My landlady's been playing this crazy music nonstop since yesterday morning and I can't get it out of my head.

OTHER ME: E-jean boo lawn chi wren ling Ming John she ah me toe foe you chew shin John Zen's eye Cheech in she wren John she zing booed yen Dow gee duh wan shin ah me toe foe gee lug whoa two—

ME: Please stop. I can hear it just fine without you singing along. Just ignore it and tell me when to stop shuffling the cards.

OTHER ME: Stop.

ME: Okay, a lot of cup cards, a lot of swords. From the looks of these cards, I'd say you have an active love life.

OTHER ME: Dude, you totally suck at this.

ME: You don't have to be a butthead. I'm just reading your cards.

OTHER ME: What's up with the Death card in my first position?

ME: We like to call it the card of transition.

OTHER ME: That's just so your callers won't hang up on you right away.

ME: True. But if you look at the picture on the card, you see a guy swinging his scythe in the middle of a burned field. Farmers do that all the time so their crops will grow better in the spring. I'm more interested in this Queen of Swords in your second position. It suggests a quick-witted woman in your life. Plus you have three different Cup cards. Cups are the cards of love—

OTHER ME: Yeah, yeah. And Swords are the cards of the mind, and Coins are money and Wands are strength. I know all that. But I don't have any kind of love life at all.

ME: But this inverted Four of Cups in your sixth position. A new, loving relationship in your future—

OTHER ME: Dude, I'm telling you, I've only had sex once in the whole last year. Remember? two months ago? after I got kicked out of that stupid Halfway to Halloween party? Catwoman? the bushes behind Konneker Hall? How could you forget that?

ME: As I recall, that was followed by a campus police escort to my dorm, where they saw my Hawaiian themed room and all those plastic plants I borrowed from Shively Hall.

OTHER ME: Yeah, that part sucked. Catwoman was fun, though. But that's as close as I've been to a girlfriend since Ashley.

ME: Maybe there's somebody else. Somebody you don't know about.

OTHER ME: How could I not know about it?

ME: Your eighth position represents the people around you, and the Two of Cups is one of the clearest signs of love in the Tarot deck. As you look at it, you see—

OTHER ME: As you look at it, you see there's another card stuck to it, Mr. Psychic: an upside-down Knight of Cups. What's that supposed to mean?

ME: The inverted Knight of Cups here suggests that you also have a romantic rival, somebody sneaky and distrustful. Who do you think that is?

OTHER ME: Dude, seriously, I don't have a love life.

ME: The rest of these cards look right, though: transition in your first position. The Three of Coins representing your recent past. The Hanged Man in your seventh position—you feel like you're in limbo right now, right? The Knight of Swords in your ninth position says you hope to act bravely when the need arises.

OTHER ME: You could say that about anybody. Just tell me if I should go back to training or not.

ME: Often the answers to such questions are already inside of us.

OTHER ME: Isn't that a line from *The Matrix*? Could you please just answer my question?

ME: Which question?

OTHER ME: Should I go back to training or not?

ME: In your tenth position, you have the Chariot, inverted: defeat, stagnation. If you stay on your current path, you have that to look forward to.

OTHER ME: But that's just it: I don't know what my current path is. I'm in the parking lot of some rest area in Virginia at three in the morning. Does that mean that the path I'm on now is to a beach in Florida, or am I actually just here for the night and I'm actually headed back to work to-morrow? I don't know. It's like I'm in the middle of this big forest with all these trees and no path whatsoever. I don't even know which direction I'm supposed to go to find a path, or which direction I want to go, or which direction I can go. It's like *The Blair Witch Project* inside my head, except without the witch and the shaky camera and that super annoying chick who should've died before the movie even started.

ME: The Six of Swords here in your fifth posit—

OTHER ME: God, you're annoying. How do you get people to stay on the phone with you so long?

ME: That's a very good question. What I try to do first is empathize with the caller. Let them know I understand what they're feeling. For example, you feel like somebody else is always in charge of everything you do: Go to school. Get out of our school. Do what we tell you to do when we tell you to do it. Say what we tell you to say when we tell you to say it. You don't feel like a real person, but more like a puppet on a string or a video game character that somebody else is always controlling. When you were little, you used to picture what your life would be like when you were twenty-two. This isn't what you'd imagined. Sometimes you wish the earth was flat so you could just drive off the end and float into peaceful nothingness. Sound about right?

OTHER ME: Yeah, I guess.

ME: I can also keep people on the phone by going off on a lot of tangents. Make them think we're just having a normal conversation. Time goes a lot faster that way. Open-ended questions help a lot, too. Half the time, they already know the answer to whatever question they have; they just need to hear it out loud. The main thing, though, is to never let the conversation stop. Always keep it moving, moving, moving, and you too can be an excellent telephone psychic.

OTHER ME: If you're so great why are you on probation at work?

ME: Let's not talk about me. We're here to help you.

OTHER ME: Which you still haven't done, by the way.

ME: What is it you really want?

OTHER ME: I want to be like Matt—remember? freshman year? Used the last of his money to buy a plane ticket to California without knowing a single solitary person in the whole entire state, met those Bud Light or Miller Lite models on the plane, they hooked him up with a landscaping job for, like, twenty-five bucks an hour, and now he's got it made. I wish I had the balls to do that.

ME: Yeah, you are a wimp. I don't need to be psychic to see that. Maybe you can start small. What can you do besides flying to California and hoping for a job?

OTHER ME: I don't know.

ME: What would you like to do right now?

OTHER ME: I'd kind of like to get out of here before that weird guy at the picnic table comes over here and does something.

ME: What's he going to do?

OTHER ME: I don't know. Something crazy. Can we just leave?

ME: I guess. Where are we going?

OTHER ME: That's what you're supposed to tell me. Where *should* we go?

ME: How the hell should I know?

June 7

I can't get these two monster truck announcers out of my head:

"Forget everything you thought you hated about PowerPoint."

Forget it all.

"ATS training will make you hate PowerPoint like never before."

Like never before.

"Phrases flying in."

One painful word at a time.

"Lame sound effects!"

Whoosh!

"We've got that and more!"

So much more!

"Graphs and charts!"

Red and blue!

"Venn diagrams!"

Shaded!

"More clip art than you ever knew existed!"

The only smiley face you'll see will be on the screen!

"But we don't stop there!"

We make it suck even more!

"Trainer Tim reads everything on the screen word for word!"

Word for word!

"If he misses one, he goes back and rereads the whole line!"

The whole entire line!

"Company policies!"

Boring.

"Telephone etiquette!"
Common sense.
"Rules and regulations!"
Stupid.
"Monday, Monday, Monday!"
That's right! Three straight Mondays!
"Thru Friday, Friday, Friday!"
Eight hours a day!
"With a half hour for lunch!"
And two fifteen-minute breaks!
"Appalachian—"
whoosh
"TeleServices—"
whoosh
"Telephone—"
whoosh
"Sales—"
whoosh
"Representative—"
whoosh
"Orientation—"
whoosh
"and—"
whoosh
"Training—"
whoosh-oosh-oosh.
"You'll curse Bill Gates."
Or whatever evil assface invented PowerPoint.
"You'll question your life choices."
Why are you here?
"You'll beg for death"
Kill me, please.
"Monday, Monday, Monday!"
Thru Friday, Friday, Friday.

"You'll be here!"

Nine a.m.

"Because you need the money!"

Rent! Credit cards! Student loans! You've got it all!

"You're screwed, screwed, screwed."

Bend over!

* * *

Why is it that, in every single classroom in the whole entire world, there has to be at least one person who asks the most incredibly stupid, obvious, off-topic, waste-of-time questions the world has ever known? Is there some super-secret underground society of stupid question askers that I don't know about? Like the Masons for dumbasses?

Today there's two of them somewhere behind me—Douche One and Douche Two—and I swear they're competing for the grand prize of stupid question asking.

Everything started off okay. We did the introductions. Welcome to ATS. What brings you to ATS? That sort of thing.

Nobody was saying much, which was good, because hopefully we'll be done faster.

Then Tim asked if any of us or anybody we know ever called a telephone psychic, and that got a couple people talking.

Some lady said, "I call one once a month," like she was totally proud of it, and then some guy said, "My ex-fiancée used to call one all the time," and then a couple other people might have said something. I kind of tuned out for a while, or maybe I fell asleep.

Then Tim went through the PowerPoint with all the company policies, which make the job sound like it's the most awesome job in the whole entire universe.

You get to set your own hours, Yea!

You can take your breaks and lunch whenever you want,

Yea!

We have an Open Door Policy (whatever that means), Yea!

We offer tuition assistance to qualified employees, Yea!

We pay cash rewards for your suggestions that we use, Yea!

Multiple absences for the same illness only count as one absence, Yea!

Then he started in on the "Please wear your I.D. badge at all times" stuff, and "Use the East entrance since you work on the third floor. Emergency exits are located at the North and South ends of the building."

Then, about half-way through the dress code, Douche One says, "What if you don't wear socks?"

Tim was just like, "Excuse me?"

"What if you don't wear socks? I never wear socks—shoes, either—they're oppressive to the feet."

So Tim read again what he'd just read: "Socks must be worn at all times."

"Why?"

"What?"

"Why do we have to wear socks at all times?"

"I don't know. I think it's probably a health issue."

And then Douche Two's like, "But your feet are actually less healthy when you wear shoes and socks. They did a study that found that the Zulu people in Africa had the healthiest feet in the world. Better circulation, stronger toes, no flat—"

"I'm just telling you what the policy says," Tim said.

"I know that's what it *says*," Douche One says, "but what if I don't wear them?"

"If you don't follow the dress code, you won't be allowed to clock in and you'll incur any absence or attendance points associated with you not clocking in."

"So if I forget to wear socks when I come in to work, and

I have to go out to my car or to a store somewhere to get some socks, and then I clock in late because of that, I'll get two attendance points?"

"Only if it takes you more than fifteen minutes. Remember, you only get one attendance point if you're tardy, which is less than fifteen minutes late, two points if you're *late* late or if you leave early, four if you're absent but you call the front desk to let them know you'll be absent, and eight if you're absent and you don't call."

"So if I have to go buy socks, I can only do that eight times before you fire me?"

"I'm not sure I understand."

Then Douche Two takes over again and he talks real annoyingly slow, like Tim is the one who's the idiot, and he says, "If he has to buy socks before work and, as a result, he clocks in more than fifteen minutes late—resulting in two attendance points, correct?—he can only do that eight times every ninety days, otherwise he's fired?"

"Actually, he can only do it seven times. Once you accumulate sixteen attendance points during an attendance quarter, you're automatically terminated."

"*Daaaaaamn!*" Douche One said, like it's some super-oppressive policy that must've been concocted by Stalin or somebody.

"ATS recognizes the need for an occasional absence or tardy," Tim said. "But, keep in mind: you were hired to fulfill a need and so they expect you to be here when you're scheduled."

I totally wanted to say, "if you think the attendance policy sucks, wait till they give you a PIN for asking somebody their age before their date of birth."

But I didn't.

We all figured that was the end of it and we'd be able to take our break soon, since Tim said he'd give us a break after we finished the Dress Code policies. But then Tim got to the line about how we can't wear jeans and Douche Two was like, "What about black pants that are made of denim material?"

Everybody in the room let out a big, loud *shut-the-hell-up* sigh, which made Douche Two more determined than ever to win the stupid-question contest. "Black denim pants aren't technically jeans. 'Jeans' is from the French term, *bleu de Genes*, which translates to 'the blue of Genoa.'"

Somebody said, "Who cares?"

"Black is a completely different color than blue," he said, like we're all idiots who didn't already know that.

Then somebody was like, "Dude, it says right on the screen, 'Denim or "jeans" of any kind or any color is considered inappropriate attire.'"

Tim said, "Maybe it's time we took a break. Anybody have any questions before we go?"

"Yeah," Douche One said. "What do you mean by 'worn out or torn attire'? Because I have to buy all my clothes at Goodwill, and they already come worn out and torn up."

First of all, that's a bunch of crap. I buy pretty much everything except for socks and boxers at Goodwill and none of it's torn up. I mean, yeah, it's hard to find your size, and a lot of it was out of style twenty years ago, but it's not like all their clothes have big ginormous holes in them.

I'd love to bust him on it, but I don't want everybody to know that I shop at Goodwill.

But, even if I *was* going to bust him on it, I never would've gotten the chance because Douche One made Tim describe in excruciating detail exactly how the Tuition Reimbursement Plan works.

So we figured that would be the end of it, but then Tim asked if there were any more questions before the break.

Everybody knew that was a mistake.

Douche Two said, "Why does everyone at a funeral say,

'He's in a better place'? If they really believed that, they shouldn't be sad, right? When somebody is in Hawaii on vacation, you don't hear their friends saying, 'Boo-hoo, he's in a better place.'"

And the winner of the stupid question contest is . . . Douche Two!

*   *   *

Back from break for round two.

While Tim took everybody on a tour of the break room—"this is a vending machine; you put this stuff called money in this slot and a whole bunch of unhealthy, barely edible crap comes out"—so I figured that was a good time for me to sneak outside and grab a smoke.

Just as I was about to light up, though, Derek came up behind me like, "What're you doing here?"

Now that he knows I'm in training, too, he's got this whole big conspiracy theory thing about us failing our QAs.

He said, "Dude, think about it: we both started at the same time; we were in the same training class a year ago. You think that's a coincidence?"

"You think the moon landing was a conspiracy."

He gave up after that and we spent the rest of the break making fun of the new trainees.

There's the lady who's so glad for the opportunity to finally have a job; she's been looking everywhere, and the lady who's so excited for the chance to finally hone her psychic abilities—"she'll be disappointed when she actually starts working here," Derek said. "All these people must be escaped mental patients or something. And what kind of guy answers 'revenge' when somebody asks why you're working here? A total douchebag, that's who."

That was pretty much my whole entire break. Now it's time for more PowerPoints, aka naptime.

*   *   *

Douche Two and Douche One
won't shut up, won't shut down.
So many stupid questions,
says Trainer Tim's frown.
We all wish they'd shut up,
we do, we do, we do.
Oh, please shut the hell up
Douchebag One and Douche Two.

*   *   *

Overheard in the Break room:

Douche Two (aka Viking Boy): "There's no way a samurai could beat a Viking."

Some other trainee: "I'm just telling you I saw it on Hulu."

Douche Two: "I'm telling you it's bullshit. The katana could never get through the Viking's chain mail and the Viking's battle axe would chop the samurai in two."

Other trainee: "Whatever."

Douche Two: "It wasn't at all realistic. They had the Viking fighting on his knees. Why would he fight on his knees?"

Other trainee: "Because Vikings liked to suck cock."

Douche Two: "You're a racist."

Other trainee: "How is that racist?"

Douche Two: "I have Viking in my blood."

June 8

I came in to work today, bright and early at nine a.m. for the second day in a row, and I plopped into my uncomfortable ATS armless office chair, preparing my pens for another major doodlefest—Doodlepalooza? Doodlaroo?—when in walked the girl of my dreams.

She smiled and said "Hi" as she sat down right beside me. I think I smiled back—I hope I smiled back—and I accidentally did one of those things where you move your mouth like you're saying "Hi," but no actual sound comes out. If I would've left it at that, it probably would've been okay. She probably would've thought I'm some kind of badass who's too cool to pronounce words. But something in my brain was determined to say something.

I was trying super quick to figure if it'd be better to say, "I'm happy to see you," or to ask, "How are you?" But before I did, it occurred to me that both of those would make it sound like I remembered her, and I didn't want that, in case she didn't remember me, so at the last second, I decided to say, "How do you do?" which would've been perfect in that situation.

What actually came out of my mouth, though, was, "How do I do you?"

It's times like this that I wish I didn't smoke so much weed.

The worst part was, I just sat there with probably the stupidest smile on my face while she looked at me wondering if I really said what she thought I just said.

Yes, hot girl with the super-long hair. Yes I did.

She pretended she didn't notice, though, so that was nice of her. It makes her kind of more sexy, too, if you ask me.

I still don't know if she remembers me. I met her at Lucky's a couple weeks ago. Mike and I were playing darts against these two douchebags who thought they were God's gift to darts and I'd just hit the twenty and then the bull with my first two darts and we started celebrating because those guys were dicks. Then they were like, "You still need to hit double-bull. That's how you play Around the Clock: bull, double-bull."

So I threw my next dart and, *bam*, right in the center. Just as I started in on my happy dance, she was right there, probably walking back from the restroom, and as she tried to squeeze through, I grabbed her hands and we started sort of dancing. I don't know what it's called, but we did that thing where she comes close on one side and then on the other side and then she did that little twirl thing in front of me and then she smiled and went back to wherever it was she was sitting. She never said anything and I never said anything; we just had this brief little amazing moment.

I didn't think I'd ever see her again, but here she is, sitting in the cubicle right beside me. How awesome is that? I'll tell you how awesome: it's pretty damn awesome. It'd be even more awesome if I hadn't just made her think I'm mentally deficient or something.

So now I've got my head buried in my cubicle trying to think of any legitimate-sounding reason whatsoever to say something not stupid to her.

First of all, if she doesn't remember me and I'm all like, "Hey, remember me? I'm the guy who danced with you for almost five whole seconds almost a month ago," then she'll think I'm a freak.

If she does remember, she still might think it's weird that I would remember, too.

But if I act like I don't remember, would she think that I just don't care? Or that I'm some disease-ridden male slut who does that kind of crazy, super-confident stuff with every girl I see?

I've still got to come up with something to say.

Possible things to say:

> Do you come here often?
>
> Do you want to go to my apartment after work and read each other's Tarot cards?
>
> You look familiar; have we met before?

Things not to say:

> You've got some long-ass hair! Does it make you horny when it tickles your butt crack?
>
> If I was a moon, I'd circle Uranus.
>
> I like to think about you when I masturbate.

* * *

How did I not notice her yesterday? That's what I want to know. I mean, she had to have been here, didn't she? You can't just skip the first day of training, can you?

If you can, I want to know how. And can I skip the next two weeks?

* * *

I was in the vending machine line behind the hot girl who sits beside me and she was like, "Oh, man," and she turned around and said to me, "If you buy the Barbeque CornNuts, I'll trade you the ranch flavor."

The dumbass vending machine guy put them both in the same slot again.

I said, "Sounds sure yeah CornNuts."

"What?"

"Yeah," I said. "Okay."

For some reason, I could form real sentences again after I got my CornNuts. We started kind of sort of having a conversation. She's got this happy, warm cocoa voice that makes you feel like a big soft teddy bear is hugging you from the inside. I was trying to figure out, without saying anything, if she remembered me from Lucky's, or if that moment we had was all just my imagination.

I'm still not sure.

I don't know what we talked about, exactly, because I kept trying to figure out where the black center part of her eyeballs ended and the dark sexy outside part began, but somehow it came out that she was standing next to me in line at the Cool Spot last Friday afternoon. And apparently she was here for training yesterday, too.

She said, "You're not very observant, are you?"

She said it in kind of a good, mind-tickling sort of way—like, she doesn't know me well enough that she can reach out and actually start for-real tickling me, so she just kind of teased me like that instead. That's how I took it, anyway.

Now that I think about it, though, maybe she was talking about our Lucky's moment. Like, she doesn't think I remember. I don't know.

Pretty soon, we were talking about CornNuts again.

She's all about the barbeque flavor, which surprised me for some reason. Don't get me wrong, barbeque flavor's awesome for road trips, or when you're alone, but Barbeque CornNuts take a commitment because, when you eat them, you have that mushy cottony skunk mouth until the next time you brush your teeth.

You can chew some gum and drink a Sobe Green Tea to sort of get rid of the skunk mouth, but every time you talk, it always feels like you just inhaled a big balloon of nitrous, except without the uncontrollable gigglies. That's why they're bad to eat at work.

I didn't mention the nitrous part because I'm not sure if she parties or not, but, other than that, we were having, like, kind of an okay conversation. As okay a conversation as you can have when you're talking about CornNuts.

I was right at the point where I was like, *Screw it, I'm just going to come right out and say, "You know what? I hate to sound like a jerk, but I don't know if I ever got your name. I'm L.J., by the way."*

But right as I get to "You know what?" Adam comes back to the break room and he's all like, "L.J.! Dude, I heard you quit! What're you doing here in the morning? Did you come to see if there are any hot snatches in the new training class?"

I tried to look at the girl with one of those, *I hardly know this guy* faces, but he was standing way too close and acting way too friendly for that.

I asked him, "Is that why you're here?"

"Dude, ever since the cops made that big bust in Meigs county, my weed's been costing me a fortune—and then the more hours I work, the more weed I need to smoke. It's a vicious cycle," and then he said to the girl, "You know what I mean?"

She scrunched her eyebrows together like she was superserious and she nodded and said, "Oh, yeah—absolutely," real sarcastically. It was kind of cute and funny and sexy all at the same time.

He didn't notice. He said, "I just got a call from this crazy bitch who wanted me to take the voodoo spell off her exboyfriend. I go, 'Ma'am, that's not really what I do. My specialty is Tarot cards,' just like that. So she was ready to hang up right away, right? So I said, 'But I can use the cards to try to determine what your next steps should be,'" then Adam looked at me and then he looked at the girl and he was like, "I know, right? Great line. I learned it from this guy," and he put his arm around my shoulder and pulled me in real hard and he said, "Give this guy a deck of Tarot cards and he'll make you believe anything."

Then he said, "So I give this stupid bitch her reading.

Nothing special. But it only takes us to eleven minutes. I tell her not to do anything crazy—yeah right, right? Long story short, I convinced her to hum into the phone to take the voodoo spell away. She's still humming. L.J., man, I knew you'd love that. I'm going to grab a quick smoke while she's still humming."

After he left, the hot girl was like, "I couldn't imagine doing something like that to a caller."

I was just like, "Uh, yeah. Me neither."

Then I figured, okay, now's my chance to ask her name, but then Derek came over and he starts going on and on about how he just registered for classes at Hocking College because—wasn't I listening?—ATS will pay your tuition after you've worked here a year and, as of yesterday, he has been here exactly one year.

He doesn't even care what classes he's taking; he just wants to screw ATS out of his tuition money. Now all he has to do is maintain a B average, and how tough can that be at Hocking College?

So I figured, okay, maybe that's the end of it, but then he started complaining about his girlfriend/baby mama. He was like, "Every time I look in the cupboard, I swear she's preparing for the apocalypse. We've got at least six jars of salsa, about ten cans of corn and ten cans of beans, five boxes of Fiber One cereal and five bottles of mouthwash. Why would anybody need five bottles of mouthwash?"

Hot Girl said, "Maybe she's trying to tell you something."

I like her more and more all the time.

*   *   *

Bannister, Caroline
Davenport, Lucas
Gillette, William
Folsom, Margaret

Harrington, Jeffrey
Hemingford, Amy
Joseph, Tanha
Kinsley, Bridget
Lackey, Katrina
Marshall, Helen
Mosely, Peter
Newton, Rhonda
Preston, Paul
Reynolds, Derek
Schwartz, Thomas
Stevens, Larissa
Thomas, Andrea
Valentine, Jeanette
Vaughn, Anthony
Washington, Leon

She's in there somewhere. Helen? Andrea? Caroline? I bet it's Caroline. She looks like a Caroline. With that voice like warm cocoa, and her smile that's like springtime and the way she smells like—actually, she smells like springtime, so maybe her smile is more like sunshine. Her voice is definitely warm cocoa, though, for sure. Just like a Caroline.

Or maybe Larissa. Larissa is like a name for somebody uniquely perfect. I bet that's it.

I think about it and it's like, I should just ask her what her name is. But I've been trying to. I mean, what should I do? Just lean over and say, "Hey, hot quiet chick with the super-long dark hair and the big, sexy Jessica Alba lips, what's your name"

That's not how smooth, suave, sophisticated guys do it, is it?

But how do smooth, suave, sophisticated guys do it? That's what I want to know.

By the way, I wonder how long it'll take Tim to realize

the roster from his training class is missing.
    My guess: two days, if ever.

June 9

I had today all perfectly planned out.

I got up two hours early so I could drive the forty-five minutes to Parkersburg (which was more like an hour because of the construction) and find the only Tim Hortons in the whole entire town, I think (which was on the complete other side of town, too, by the way) and then drive the thirty minutes back to Coolville (which was more like forty-five, because of that same construction) and to wonderful Appalachia TeleServices, just so I could hang out in the break room with my Tim Hortons Iced Cappuccino (Chocolate Brownie Supreme, I think the flavor was called) and wait for the hot girl who sits next to me to come in and see my Tim Horton's cup there and say, "Tim Hortons! I love Tim Hortons!"

And then I'd pretend like I didn't hear her say that to another chick in our training class yesterday, and I'd play it all cool and say, "Really? Yeah, me too."

And then she'd be like, "Wow, we have so much in common."

So I figured the Tim Hortons would finally give me the opening to say, "Would you like to sit down?"

And then, as she was sitting, I'd hold out my hand and say, all debonair like, "My name's L.J. by the way."

She'd shake my hand real gentle and her hand would be all soft and she'd say, "I'm _____" whatever her name is.

And I'd be like, "Ah, I've always loved that name," or maybe, "Oh, that's such a nice name," or, if I was feeling really confident from the caffeine, something like, "Such a beautiful name for such a beautiful young woman."

And then maybe she'd giggle and blush or something.

I also had a backup plan in case she was already there

when I got there: I'd go into the break room and she'd be sitting there reading whatever book she'd be reading and I'd drop my drink on the table, loud enough that she'd look up—but not so loud that it'd be annoying—and she'd say, "You went to Tim Hortons? I love Tim Hortons!" etc.

But because the road construction sucked so bad, and because Tim Hortons took me forever to find because Google Maps hates me, and because it took me about twenty minutes to order once I got there because there were about eighteen million cars ahead of me and I didn't know what the hell I was ordering besides, by the time I got to work, it was already nine o'clock (8:58:36 on the time clock when I swiped my badge) and I had to throw away what was left of my stupid iced cappuccino since we can't take drinks into the training room unless they have an ATS-approved spill-proof lid, which the Tim Hortons Iced Cappuccino definitely does not have, with its ginormous hole in the top.

So that didn't work.

It was probably just as well, though, because it occurs to me now that I wouldn't have known what to say when she asked me why I was in Parkersburg because, as far as I know, the only reason to go to Parkersburg is to go to the strip clubs and they're probably not open at eight in the morning and, even if they were, I don't think I'd want to tell her that's why I drove all the way to Parkersburg before work, so, yeah. . . .

* * *

After work, I got stuck giving a ride to the barefoot guy from our training class. I thought he just wanted a ride home, but he had me stop by Bobcat Pawn Shop on the way.

As soon as I parked, he said, "I need you to go in before me and ask to look at the guns."

"What?"

"Just check out the handguns. I'll be in right behind you."

It all seemed kind of sketchy, but he promised he wouldn't rob them or anything, so I didn't really have a reason not to.

I don't know crap about guns. The guy behind the counter was like, "You looking for a twenty-two? A forty-five? Nine-millimeter?"

"Nine-millimeter, I guess."

"Nines are down here. Are there any you want to take a closer look at?"

"How about that one?"

"This is a Springfield XD. It's factory ported. I don't know why. There's not much recoil in a nine-millimeter to begin with. The porting won't do much more than increase the report."

That's pretty much all I remember. I had no idea what he was talking about and I'm pretty sure he could tell. Now I know the difference between a semi-automatic and a revolver, but that's about it.

When I get back out to my car, the barefoot guy is dialing a number on what looked like the most humongous cell phone I'd ever seen in my life. It turns out that it was one of the cordless landlines from inside the pawn shop.

I said, "I thought you said you weren't going to rob them."

"I didn't. To rob them, I'd have to go in there with a gun and say, 'Give me your money!' All I did was grabbed this phone off the counter. And I'm not keeping it, anyway. I'm just making a call."

Apparently, the number he called was some weather service in Australia. The reason he called it was because he went to that pawn shop a couple weeks ago to sell an engagement ring. They told him they needed to keep the ring overnight and have somebody look at it the next day and, when he went back, they told him the ring was only worth two hundred dollars and when he wanted his ring back, he says they gave him a completely different ring and kicked him out of the store when he complained.

I asked him if he called the police. Did he file a police report? Did he call a lawyer? Calling some long-distance number and hiding their phone under their dumpster won't help anything.

"It'll help them," he said.

"What? How? Why?"

"I'm a karmic rejuvenation therapist—a karmic enforc-er—whatever you want to call it. I help people improve their karma."

"Karma Police?" I asked. He looked at me like I was an idiot. "Radiohead? *OK Computer*?" Still nothing. "Seriously?" I said. "If you've never heard that song, where'd you get the idea? *My Name is Earl* reruns in Bizarro World?"

"I don't know what that is. I've employed these same techniques for hundreds of years, over many lifetimes."

"You've been making long-distance calls on people's phones for hundreds of years?"

"Providing karmic adjustments," he said. "It's different today—we don't have the same student-master relation-ships—so I've had to adapt. I help more people this way, but the help I provide isn't as significant."

I was like, "All you're doing is getting revenge on people who piss you off."

"It probably seems like that to the untrained eye. It's not revenge, though. It's a service. I provide them with unsolicit-ed spiritual renovation."

"You should put that on business cards."

"Yeah, maybe."

I still don't know if he was messing with me, or if he re-ally believes what he was saying. He seemed pretty excited about the whole phone thing, though, until I told him the pawn shop would just call the phone company and dispute the charges.

"Some people make it hard for me to help them," he said.

So, yeah, he's a freak.

He gave me ten bucks for gas, though, so I'll probably give him a ride again if he needs it.

June 10

Tanha. Her name's Tanha.
Tanha Tanha Tanha.
Let's hook up mañana,
you can ride on my iguana,
I'll take you to nirvana,
better than marijuana,
my flora in your fauna,
you know you really wanna,
so tell me, are we gonna?
Taa-a-a-a-a-a-n-ha-a-a-a.

* * *

Here's how today began: Tim said, "Okay, we'll take a break from PowerPoints for a while—"

We all cheered.

Then Tim got all pissy, like, "I didn't make the PowerPoints, okay? I just have to read them."

After we all shut up, he was like, "As I was saying, we're going to take a break from the PowerPoints and do some mock readings.

"Get together with the person next to you and take turns reading each other's cards. Use the ten-card spread that we talked about yesterday."

Viking Boy asked, "What if we prefer the fifteen-card Romany?"

"While we're in training and OJT, we'll all use the same ten-card spread that we taught you, okay?"

"But the fifteen-card Romany is more accurate for general readings."

"Once you're out on the call floor, you can use whatever spread gives you the best handle times. Until then, we'll all use the same ten-card spread, okay?

"And remember, you want to practice like it's an actual call, so use your scripted greeting and close."

Then Tim said, "Any questions?"

As soon as he asked, you could tell he regretted it.

Viking Boy asked, "Don't you think it's ironic that the majority of viruses on your computer come from pictures of women who probably have all kinds of real life viruses?"

Tim was just like, "Um, I don't—"

"And is the universe eternal or transient, or both—or neither?

"Just pair up and start your readings, okay?"

The girl of my dreams turned and said to me, "Do you want to be my partner?"

"Sure."

Before I got the chance to say, "I'm L.J., by the way"—and I was totally ready to say it this time, too; I'm pretty sure I would've said it, anyway, but she beat me to it—she held out her hand and said, "I'm Tanha," and she started one of those super-long hand sandwich handshakes that'd feel totally uncomfortable if it was a guy doing it.

Her hands were so soft and warm and perfect and my hand was just sitting in between there all happy like, *yeah.*

Finally I said, "I'm L.J."

"I know," she said.

That's a good sign, isn't it? That she knows my name. I think it's a good sign. I don't know how it could not be a good sign, so I'll keep thinking that it's a good sign.

I said, "We actually met a couple months ago. At Lucky's. I was playing darts and—"

"You remembered!" she said. "I was starting to think I must not have made much of an impression."

That's totally a good sign.

And now I know her name. Tanha.

I didn't learn too much more about her during our mock readings. She had the inverted King of Swords in her eighth position and the moon card in her sixth position, so apparently there's somebody close to her who's immature and, if she keeps going in the same direction, somebody will deceive her in some way, but that's about it.

I had the moon card in my eighth position; that's never good. Apparently there's somebody lying to me right now.

* * *

Another thing that sucks about training is that we all take our lunch break at the same time, so it kind of limits my opportunities for one on one time with Tanha.

Tanha Tanha Tanha.

I figured if I sat at this empty table in the back, maybe eventually she would see me and come back here and say, "Hey, do you mind if I sit here?"

But instead, Viking Boy came and sat down right next to me—or, actually, right next to the chair I've got my feet on—and now he won't . . . stop . . . talking. Seriously.

I thought if I took my notebook out and started writing, he'd eventually get the hint, but so far it hasn't worked. I mean, I've been writing for the last—what? two minutes? five minutes? ten minutes?—and he's been talking the whole time. I don't even know what about.

Right now, he's saying that he's usually shy, if you can believe that, but the medication he takes makes him more outgoing and he's not sure if he likes it because the old him is inside there somewhere and the old him can see the new him and he's not sure if the old him likes the new him and what's wrong with being the shy version of himself, anyway, because that's the real version of himself, even though the doctor said this is an improved version of himself, but it doesn't feel like the real version of himself and why should he have to accommodate what society wants him to be, anyway? Why can't he just be the real himself? He wasn't hurting anyone. And on and on.

Holy crap.

Everybody else in the whole break room is completely quiet. They're probably waiting to hear what kind of bizarre weirdness he'll blurt out next. This morning, he spent pretty much the whole fifteen-minute break telling some pregnant lady why momma dogs eat the afterbirth after they have their puppies.

I'm guessing that's why nobody else has sat down at this table.

Normally I'd just get up and leave, but I don't want everybody to think I'm a jerk for abandoning him. I'm pretty sure everybody's staring at us. I don't want to look up because that'll just encourage him—kind of like, you know, how you're supposed to not look at homeless people and pretend like you don't notice them. That's the strategy I'm going with now, anyway.

It's not working.

I keep thinking he's about to run out of things to say because he'll pause for a couple seconds, but it'll just be to take a breath. Then he's right back at it. "Reverend Marpa said you carry your notebook around all the time because you had panic attacks when you were in grade school. Is that true?

"Writing therapy didn't work for me because it made my shyness worse.

"Do you think he really is a reincarnation of the real Marpa? I guess he could be. The original Marpa brought Naropa's teachings to Tibet. That's what he's most known for. Marpa the translator. But he also helped Milarepa purify his karma—he made him build and tear down three towers. That's kind of what Reverend Marpa's doing now, so I guess they could be the same person."

Have a guy build some towers, make a long-distance call

to Australia . . . yeah, that sounds like the same thing.

"Hey! are you writing this down? You just wrote that down, didn't you? Maybe you did, I can't tell. Your handwriting is even worse than mine."

Pretty soon, I'll have to look up and ask, "I'm sorry. Did you say something?" Not yet, though. Not yet. I'm still holding out hope that Tanha will come over and say Hi.

* * *

King of the Hill is on and it's the one where Bobby keeps yelling, "That's my purse!" before he kicks someone else in the kiwis. It's probably the best episode ever. It's even funny when you're only listening to it.

But Viking Boy just slapped me on the leg, and that pretty much ruined the moment for me. He played it off like it was just a harmless, doesn't-mean-anything, guy-on-guy leg slap, and so I pretended it was nothing, too. But still.

He'd been holding up his hand for a high-five, and I pretended like I didn't see it—which was kind of hard, considering he kept waving it in front of my face—but then, just as I was about to look up and say, "What?" he went for my leg instead.

I mean, granted, it's a funny episode, but I've never thought something was funny enough to slap someone else on the leg. Unless it'd be hot Tanha with her super long hair. Pretty much anything would make me laugh hard enough to touch her on the leg. I could be watching *C.S.I.* or some other super-unfunny show and I'd be like, "Ha-ha, hot Tanha with the super-long hair, isn't that funny?" *slap, slap.*

Tickle, tickle. Rub, rub. Kiss, kiss. Squeeze, squeeze. Unzip. Unsnap. Lick, lick. Nibble, nibble. Pull, pull. Thrust, thrust. Yes.

Nice image. But I didn't want Viking Boy to be like that with me.

I'm going outside to smoke.

June 11

Apparently Trainer Tim was pissed at me for not paying attention during his awesome PowerPoints, so to punish me or teach me a lesson or whatever, he got a tape of the call I got all my PINs on. He didn't mention any of this at the time; he just said, "Okay, as promised, we're going to listen to a few actual calls."

It took me a while to realize it was me, because I wasn't really paying attention, for one, but mainly because I sound way totally more dorkish than I realized.

When we took our break, Tim was like, "L.J., could I talk to you for a second?"

And then he went into this whole thing about how he was trying to teach me a lesson since I'm never listening and everything and how he was planning to play the call and then tell everyone, "Okay, that's what you're not supposed to do on your calls."

But then he was like, "I don't know how you scored so low on that call. I used to be in QA, as you probably know, and I don't see how you could've scored lower than a ninety-seven. I've got your QA tally sheet right here—Greeting, Verification, Sincerity—those were all good on this call. I'll talk to Daniel to see if we can't get you back on the call floor tomorrow, okay?"

But right then, Tanha walked past and she smiled kind of a cute little sexy smile at me, and then I caught a look at her perfect little tight butt as she went out the door and I was like, "That's okay, Tim. Training's not so bad."

"Are you sure?" he asked. "Don't get me wrong. I'd love to have you in here. I get a bonus for everybody who completes training. But you really could be—should be—out on the call floor."

"That's all right," I said. "I really am getting a lot out of your training. I don't always look like I'm listening, but I really am."

I'm turning into as big a perv as Adam.

* * *

God, I hate OU. I just called them to find out about my results from Judiciaries, and they're like, "I'm sorry, I can't give that information out over the phone. If you haven't already received the letter detailing your results, you should probably be getting that in the next few days."

"Can't you just tell me what the results are?"

"I'm sorry, I can't give that information out over the phone."

"I haven't gotten it. Did you send it to my address in Athens, or to my parents' address?"

"I'm sorry, I can't give that information out over the phone."

"Did you send it to my school address or to my home address?"

"I'm sorry. I can't give that information out over the phone."

"How about this? Can I verify my address? Did you send it to Athens, or to Cincinnati?"

"According to this, it was not sent to Athens."

So now I've got to drive all the way to Cincinnati after work tonight just to find out if I'll still be suspended next year or not.

It's a good thing I'm in training. If I would've been working my regular hours, I wouldn't get there until, like, one-thirty in the morning. At least now I can make it there by eight, easy. Maybe I got sent back to training so I could get the letter out of the mail before Mom and Dad open it— one of those, the Lord works in mysterious ways sort of things. Of course, if I never got sent back to training, I could've driven there before work, while Mom and Dad were both at work, and got the letter before they get home from work. So maybe the Lord doesn't work in mysterious ways, after all.

Now I've got to get all ninja and hope Mom and Dad don't catch me going through their mail. Hopefully Mom won't open my letter before I get there. And why did they send it to Mom and Dad's anyway? They're supposed to send stuff like that to me at my local address.

Fucktards.

* * *

I am the ninja, coo coo ca-choo.

Mom and Dad weren't home when I got there, so I got in and out in about ten minutes. It would've been quicker, but they're planting some new something in the back yard, so I had a bunch of muddy footprints to clean up.

The main thing is, I got the letter and got out before I had to deal with any of the "How's school?" "Are you graduating this year?" "Do you have a major, at least?" questions that always lead to the "When I was your age" or "It's time for you to grow up" arguments that never end, or the "Keith did this and Keith did that and why can't you be a big shot investment banker like Keith and worship the almighty Dollar like a normal person" crap that always makes me wish I had the balls to quote that thing from Jesus about how it's easier for a camel to go through a needle than it is for some rich dude to get into heaven.

The letter was basically what I expected: Blah blah blah, blah blah blah, "numerous code of conduct infractions," blah blah, "your best interest," blah blah blah, "your request for academic reinstatement has been denied," blah blah blah, "one academic year," blah blah, "at which time we will review any request for readmission," blah.

At least I got to the letter before Mom opened it. Otherwise I'd still be stuck on the couch in the living room, Dad standing in front of me giving me the disappointed look, while Mom's pacing back and forth behind him, every once in a while saying, "And premarital sex is bad, too," or asking, "Are you on drugs?"

Since I got out of Mom and Dad's house a lot sooner than I expected, I decided to stop by Fitzgerald's for a beer. I just wanted to kind of chill out before I drove back to Athens and, I don't know, think about my life or something now that it was definite that I won't be at OU next year.

Pretty much as soon as I sat down, though, Ernie Ameedo comes up and starts yapping yapping yapping away.

"Lucas Davenport! What brings you here?"

He asks about Keith and Mom and Dad and what I'm up to and he's telling the bartender all about the time I broke my leg when I was five, and about all the crazy stuff he and Keith did in high school. Pretty soon, though, it becomes obvious that what he really wants to talk about is the Grab Bag.

I mean, I understand that he owns the bar now, but that doesn't mean that he needs to be talking weed talk loud enough for pretty much everyone to hear.

He said to the bartender, "Lucas' brother and me had this friend, Charlie, who had an uncle who collected weed. Some people collect stamps, he collected weed. Whenever he got a hold of some primo kind buds, he'd set aside about an eighth of an ounce and keep it in this Crown Royal bag he had. Twenty years worth of the best, red-haired, sticky stuff you ever smoked in your life. He gave it all to Charlie on his eighteenth birthday. I can't tell you how many times I tried to buy it. I offered him three grand, and he still wouldn't sell it. So imagine my surprise when I hear that Charlie's moved out west and sold his Grab Bag to Keith's little brother here."

Then he says to me, "How much did you pay him for it?

I'll give you two grand for it right now. Cash. It's in the back."

I don't know if he thinks I carry a big ginormous Crown Royal bag full of weed around with me all the time or what, but he acted totally shocked when I told him I didn't have it.

"You don't have it with you now, or you don't have it at all?"

"I don't have it now."

He kept going on and on to the bartender about how the Grab Bag is "Hall of Fame of Weed," so I didn't want to tell him that I lost it when I moved. I'd just avoided a lecture about responsibility from Mom and Dad; I didn't want to replace it with one from Keith's high school buddy. So I lied.

"Bring it by when you're ready to sell it," he said. "I'll make sure we're both happy."

Okay.

Then he starts arguing with the bartender because the bartender thought weed was more potent now than it used to be.

Ernie was like, "That's what the cops want you to think so they can buy all their expensive cop crap. Have you seen that tank the police have now? A fucking *tank*. Why the hell do the police need a fucking tank? They don't. But if they scare enough people, they can convince somebody to buy them one."

I sneaked out of there pretty soon after that. Now I'm home.

And bored.

And sober.

One nice thing about the night, though, was that I finally talked to somebody who knows the Grab Bag is real. Every time I try to tell the guys at work about it, they're all like, "Oh, yeah, L.J.'s got this magical bag of weed that's better than anything anybody's ever smoked."

Then I'd say something like, "It's not better than anything ever smoked, because it's been smoked—that's the whole point."

But they'd always be like I totally made it up. Seeing Ernie tonight reminded me that it's real, even though it's lost now.

June 12

I did it. I have officially seen all of the internet. Every stupid joke. Every naked woman. Every episode of *It's Always Sunny in Philadelphia*.

I don't know which hurts worse—my eyes, my ass or my wrist from clicking the mouse all day. My eyes hurt so bad they're sore all the way up inside my head. So probably my eyes.

* * *

On days like today, I wish I was in a coma so I'd have an excuse for not accomplishing anything.

* * *

I saw this thing online called "Cubicles Suck" or something and so I thought, Hey, I should check this out. On his webpage, the guy is sitting there whining about working in his cubicle, but then he's got pictures and it's like this ginormous Taj Mahal of cubicles.

I always thought cubicles, by definition, were the tiny little three-sided boxes that we have at work with not even enough room to turn to the side without conking our knees— two feet wide and two feet deep. This guy online had shelves and filing cabinets and a whole bunch of other crap in there. He even took pictures of himself all stretched out, sleeping on his cubicle desk.

We can't even put our feet up without getting PINed. If I could ever contort myself enough to lie down at work, they'd boot me out of there so fast I'd leave a vapor trail.

I feel totally cheated.

* * *

I also saw this thing about this Heaven's Gate cult from however many years ago. Those people were freaks. Cutting off their junk and wrapping plastic bags around their heads so they could hitch a ride to heaven on some comet. That's hardcore insane.

The thing is, though, I think I'm actually kind of jealous of them. I would love to believe in something—anything—so much that I'd happily cut off Sir Lancelot for it. Even if it is something totally batshit crazy like that. I mean, if you believe in something enough to chop your own balls off, you have to *really* believe in it. And I think that would be awesome. It just seems like life would be so much easier and making decisions would be so much easier and everything would be so much easier if you really really believed in something.

Instead of being constantly worried about money and worried about getting fired and wondering if I'll ever get laid ever again, all I'd have to do is whatever the Great Comet wanted me to do. Every decision I make would be like, *Is this what I should do, knowing that the earth is about to be recycled or whatever?* And I'd actually have the willpower to follow through on it—that'd be awesome, too.

Still, I hope that whatever or whoever I believe in never wants me to chop off my junk. That would suck.

June 13

Resin:
The buzz is good.
The buzz is nice.
The buzz is great
at this low price.

*   *   *

All that talk the other day about the Grab Bag made me totally determined to find it, once and for all, or at least know for sure if some cockmunch actually did steal it.

I still can't believe that somebody could've stolen it even if they wanted to, because I'm sure I would've hidden it someplace where it'd be almost impossible to find. But I can't find it.

I remember one time I hid it in my box of books because I knew nobody would look in there. But it's not in there. I kind of sort of remember hiding it someplace else, but I don't remember where and I've looked everywhere and it's not anywhere, so maybe some shit brained assface did steal it.

When I couldn't find it, that just bummed me out and made me need to get stoned way more than I needed to before I started looking. So I scraped the resin out of every smoking device I could find in the apartment.

For a resin buzz, I'm pretty hi-i-i-i-i-igh.

*   *   *

Then I realized that all I wanted to do was eat some bacon and take a bath (preferably in that order). So now the tub is filling and the oven is heating up and it's totally obvious that the tub will be ready wa-a-ay before the bacon, which is a total drag because right now it seems like the need for bacon is way more urgent than the need for a bath.

*   *   *

If anybody ever dies from eating too many Cheetos, to-night will be the night. My *News of the Weird* obituary will say, "An Athens, Ohio, man died of a heart attack after eating every last Cheeto he had in his apartment. Allegedly his last words were, "I was in the mood for something cheesy.""

*   *   *

It's not too late to take a bath is it? The water filling up is loud as hell. The landlady upstairs will be stomping on the floor in a couple minutes.

(Note to self: never rent a place where the landlady lives upstairs. You may think it's a great place, the rent may be cheap, but you'll never be able to listen to your stereo ever again. She'll stomp on the floor first, so you'll assume she dropped something, but then she'll come down, all pissed, saying she just called the cops again, so you'll get one of those headphone extensions, but it'll always make those little crack-ly noises when you start dancing. Basically, if you want to re-ally jam out to your music, you have to do it in the little six-foot half-circle in front of your stereo, so most of the music you hear is in your head. Or just make sure that your iPod is always charged; it seems like mine never is.)

*   *   *

I've got all these things in my head that need to bust out. It's like my head is this tea kettle and the steam has just been building up inside.

I'm a little teapot, about to explode, there's where my brains'll be, and there, my toes.

*   *   *

But then it's like, the spout just becomes unstuck and the steam can start getting out and I can start to think again. It's like, something in my head just snapped, and I don't mean in an I'm-about-to-go-postal way, but in an I'm-incapable-of-rational-thought way and, up until five minutes ago, I don't know how I was even able to function.

*   *   *

I forgot what I was going to say, but I'm pretty sure it was brilliant. It's like I've got all these brilliant thoughts swirling around in my head, but they're like these slippery fish, and I don't have a net, and I'm trying to catch them like a grizzly catches salmon, only I don't have the claws or the sharp teeth, so I can't catch any of them and they just keep swirling, swirling, swirling.

*   *   *

How cool are these stain rings on the side of your tub from setting down your cup of coffee every day? Does that mean your coffee cup leaks or you dribble when you drink? You should clean those someday.

*   *   *

Your tub's full. While you're waiting for the oven, it's a good time to shut the lights out in the rest of the apartment and light some candles in here, huh? Yeah.

Apparently lighting candles makes you think in second-person.

And sing.

Except the song you've got in your head is Iggy Pop's "Lust for Life," which sucks because the song's ruined because whatever cruise ship company it is *still* plays that song in their commercials. And they totally misrepresent the song, that's what sucks; all they sing in the commercial is "lust for life, lust for life, lust for life," like it was written for families who want to run on beaches and go jet skiing and rock climbing and putt-putt golfing but, in the song, he's singing about liquor and drugs and stripping and a bunch of other stuff that nobody would want their adolescent daughter doing, whether she's on vacation or not. Stupid cruise ship ass munchers.

*   *   *

Is it toxic when you burn all the dust and crap sitting in

the top of the candle?

*   *   *

Note to self: The oven probably heats up faster when you actually turn it on.

*   *   *

That salty residue at the bottom of a bag of chips—I'm thinking specifically of Tostitos Bite-Sized Corn Chips—somebody should totally market that. Just put it in a bag and sell it—call it Salty Residue—I'd totally buy that. Just design some kind of packaging that allows for convenient pouring into one's mouth so you wouldn't have to snorf it all off the front of your shirt like I've been doing for the last couple minutes.

And they'd probably have to sell it at head shops, but that's okay.

*   *   *

Without the water running, it's so quiet that this cockroach crawling up the shower curtain sounds like an elephant. Maybe not an elephant, but definitely something way louder than a cockroach. And then I about had a heart attack when I thought I kicked a snake, but it was the extension cord, so everything's cool because extension cords don't usually bite.

*   *   *

The landlady's playing her music again. Or still. Maybe it's never stopped and I just don't notice it anymore. "Ah Moe ah me toe phone ah Moe ah meat oh phone ah Moe ah me toe phone ah Moe ah meat oh phone ah Moe."

I thought I understood it for a second, but I guess not.

*   *   *

Why do I have an extension cord in the bathroom? It's not like I'm using it for anything. It's just sitting on the floor giving me a heart attack.

*   *   *

I totally forgot what I wanted to remember and all I can

think about is all the stuff that Viking Boy was saying at work the other day. How the goals everyone sets for themselves—to be rich, or famous, or to save the world—are all arbitrary and stupid when you realize that you're living on this tiny mole in the armpit of God, waiting for all the pure energy of the whole entire universe to get simultaneously in synch and make this beautiful white implosion and then explosion and then the big bang and everything starts all over again. It doesn't matter what you do, or how you do it, or who you do it to, because you're just this tiny part of this infinite kaleidoscope that is the universe.

* * *

Replenishes Colored/Permed/Dry/Damaged Hair
Massage into wet hair, lather and rinse thoroughly. For complete revitalization, use Herbal Essences Replenishing Conditioner with Hawafena to enhance the natural health and feel of your hair. Finish with Herbal Essences Styling Products.

* * *

Maybe you have ADD. You've passed—or failed, depending upon how you look at it—all those ADD or ADHD or OPP tests online that say, "If you score where you just scored, you definitely have ADD or AHAD or whatever. You need prescription drugs, man, that's the only thing that'll save you." (Survey courtesy of your caring friends at Glaxo Smith Kline, Merck and Pfizer.)

Ooh, the oven just beeped. Time to put in the bacon.

* * *

Where were you? Oh, yeah. You don't know.

* * *

You're either too stoned or not stoned enough to concentrate; you're going to base your actions on the not-stoned-enough theory.

* * *

Yeah.

* * *

Okay, I just figured out how karma works: say the universe consisted of just the people in this apartment house. The way it is now, if a new guy forgets a box of fabric softener sheets in the laundry room, somebody else will take them, and then the new guy with the fabric softener sheets will assume that's the way the universe works, so he'll keep somebody else's roll of quarters and then the quarters guy will steal my brand-new jug of Mountain Fresh Tide and the first thing I'll think is, *Oh, that's what I get for leaving a brand-new jug of Mountain Fresh Tide in the laundry room where anybody can steal it.*

My question is, Why can't it go the other way? Why can't we get positive karma to go around? What if nobody stole the new guy's box of Bounce? And then he'd leave the quarters and the quarters guy would think, *Hey, somebody left my quarters, so I won't steal this brand-new jug of Mountain Fresh Tide.* And then eventually people would expect to find their stuff where they left it and the landlady could throw away the "Not responsible for lost or stolen articles" sign and everybody would help everybody else find their stuff because that's what we'd want somebody else to do. And I could do laundry a week later and my Mountain Fresh Tide would still be there.

All we need is one person who doesn't steal everybody else's stuff when they leave it in the laundry room.

I'll start as soon as I make up for my Mountain Fresh Tide that some dickface stole.

* * *

Is it just my imagination, or are my eyebrows really growing inside my head?

* * *

And, by the way, what's the deal with mountain climbing? Even if everyone's goals aren't arbitrary and certain stuff actually does matter even though we'll all be dead one day, mountain climbing is the most arbitrary goal of all arbitrary goals in the whole entire universe. It's cold, it's windy, they don't have time to look around and really enjoy the scenery, plus they've got their Sherpas doing all the hard work, anyway, so what do they even accomplish? And they leave their trash all over the side of the mountain. Mountain climbing is stupid.

* * *

There's something about easing into a perfectly warm tub that just . . . feels good.

* * *

There's something that's a drag about realizing, once you get in a perfectly warm tub, that you left your lighter in the kitchen and you have to get out of the perfectly warm tub and drip water all over your apartment until you remember where you left it.

But then you find it balanced on a dirty mixing bowl in the dish drainer and you figure you may as well light another stick of rainforest incense in the kitchen while you're there, since you plan on soaking in the tub until you have to leave for work tomorrow morning.

* * *

I should do the dishes. They're starting to stink. What they smell like is when we had to help Uncle Russell clean up after whatever that river was that flooded. There was that layer of brown, chocolate-pudding-looking mud on everything that didn't smell so bad, but when you stepped in it, there was that other layer underneath that was black and tarry and totally skanky-smelling. That's what it smelled like in the sink just now when I knocked over a bowl.

* * *

I bet Matt has a dishwasher in California.

* * *

Ooh, I forgot about the bacon. It's ready.

* * *

If anybody ever dies from eating bacon, tonight will be the night.

> An Athens, Ohio, man died of a heart attack after eating a half sheet pan of bacon. Apparently his last words were, "I was in the mood for something salty."

Hopefully that won't be my *News of the Weird* obituary.

* * *

It's so quiet I can hear the sizzling of the candle wick.

* * *

Is this moldy black crap on the shower curtain bad?

* * *

Railroad crossing without any cars; can you spell that without any Rs?

* * *

T-h-a-t.

* * *

What if the mountains are alive?

* * *

Maybe to somebody else, our whole universe only lasts as long as a fart bubble in the bathtub.

* * *

Speaking of bubbles, next time I take a bath, I'm totally breaking out the Mr. Bubble. It's packed away somewhere.

* * *

I bet this is what it's like to be in one of those sensory deprivation chambers. I was just kicking back, with my arms back behind my head and it felt like my elbows were touching each other even though they were four or five or however many feet apart. I kept trying to figure out what the feeling was, but I couldn't. Then it felt like there was this big huge fan blowing down on me, holding me in the tub. Then I was flying—I just took off almost immediately. Whoa! He's too high! Slide down. It's bumpy.

WhumpWhumpWhumpWhumpWhump. Then my arms and legs started inflating and before I knew it I was as big as those balloons in the Macy's Easter Parade (or was it Thanksgiving?) Everything inflated except for my hands and my feet and my head. And my penis. And then it was like, Whoa! There goes the penis! It's inflated! God, it's huge! And my face expanded too. I was floating like Underdog—no— Long Dong Silver. I looked down to see who was holding my strings and it was this totally hot chick. I got down closer until I could see down her shirt. Sir Lancelot was so huge he was dragging on the street, knocking over cars—Oops!—and a school bus. The girl looked up and caught me checking her out. But she was smiling. She loved it. Then, Whoa! She flashed me her big bazoombas. I picked her up with my penis and gave her a ride to the roof of a building and she put a tractor tire around the top of my penis so she'd have a place to put her feet. And she rode. I had to get out my binoculars to see her facial expressions since she was twelve stories higher than I was. She was loving it. The volcano was about to erupt, I could tell. Then it came. God, it was incredible. All over her. All over the city. Covering cars; filling up jeeps and convertibles. Tires on pick-ups were exploding from all the extra weight. Then it was like, *We're losing air. Damnit, Scottie, do something! She's going to fall.*

* * *

I think I ate too much bacon.

June 14

Dear water-splashing fucktard,

Dude, what the hell? Seriously. What the hell are you doing in the restroom that you get water all over the whole sink counter and then that huge puddle all over the floor? Unless you've got flippers for hands or you're the Jolly Green fucking Giant washing your hands after you drop a ginormous green deuce, I can't even come close to figuring out how the hell you can get so much water all over the place. Seriously.

I used to think maybe a toilet flooded, or maybe one of the faucets doesn't work, but it's never wet by any of the toilets or urinals, and all the faucets work fine, and none of the pipes are leaking and it's not coming out of the wall because it's always dry by the wall, too. (Yeah, I checked, asshole.) So then I figured that you must be that Muslim guy who does his religious washing thing every day, but when I sneaked in to catch him in the act, he was wiping up whatever water he did splash. While this does explain why we're always out of paper towels, it doesn't address the more urgent question: Who are you, Water Splashing Fucktard? And how do you splash so much water all over the sink and the floor *every single day*? Are you washing your hands, or scrubbing up for surgery? I mean, even if I tried, I couldn't make that big of a mess. That's what I don't get. What is it, exactly, that you're doing?

And why don't you ever wipe it up? There are paper towels in the paper towel thing right now—I checked—so you could have wiped up that big wet mess. But, no, that's not your style. And, thanks to you, water-splashing fucktard, I have a dark wet spot right in the middle of my crotch from when I leaned in to get an eyelash out of my eye. So now it totally looks like I soiled myself, because I'm wearing my light gray cotton pants, so the wet spot is super-dark and right there where no guy wants a giant wet spot to be. And I can't untuck my shirt to cover it up, because then Smeagol would give me a PIN for a dress code violation. I tried to make another wet spot over to the side, thinking that'd make it clear to everyone that it isn't pee on my pants, but that didn't work at all, so now it just looks like my penis was spraying out full force like a fire hose that nobody's got a hold of. Then I was too embarrassed to go into the break room or outside to smoke because I didn't want any more people than necessary to see my huge wet spot. So I couldn't get a cigarette or a Sobe tea or any CornNuts. So now I'm hungry, thirsty and stressed. All because of you, fucktard.

I'll find you, oh yes, and when I do, I'll kick you in the balls so hard that you crumple over right into your own water puddle. Then I'll pee on your face. Until then, I'm going to eat asparagus for every single meal in anticipation of that glorious occasion.

Sincerely,
L.J. Davenport

* * *

Overheard on the ATS call floor
Carl: Why would you try to convince someone she needs to have sex with a midget?
Adam: Why *wouldn't* I?
Carl: Dude, you're the worst psychic ever.
Adam: No I'm not.

* * *

I didn't think there was anything worse than Trainer Tim's PowerPoints, but that was before I got double jacked with Gretchen. After listening to her on the phone for the last—has it seriously only been one hour? holy crap; I figured it was two hours, at least—I've come to the inescapable conclusion that she is:

A few fries short of a Happy Meal.

A few sandwiches short of a picnic.

A few eggs short of an omelet.

A few clowns short of a circus.

A few twists short of a Slinky.

A few paternity tests short of a *Maury* episode.

A few coughs short of the flu.

A few animals short of a zoo.

A few Corn Flakes short of a bowl.

A few steps short of a stroll.

A few wheels short of a car.

A few beers short of a bar.

A few conductors short of a train.

A few synapses short of a brain.

A few ounces short of a pound.

A few thoughts short of profound.

A few pancakes short of a stack.

A few cigarettes short of a pack.

A few cards short of a deck.

A few Canadians short of Quebec.

A few hugs short of a cuddle.

A few drops short of a puddle.

A few ideas short of a plan.

A few guitarists short of a band.

A few drinks short of a drunk.

A few stinks short of a skunk.

If I gave her a penny for her thoughts, I'm pretty sure she'd give me change because she isn't the sharpest knife in the drawer or the quickest horse in the barn.

She couldn't spell *cat* if I spotted her the *c* and the *t*, because she is five gold stars short of a good rating, four score short of eighty years, three corners short of a triangle, two tacos short of a fiesta platter and one finger short of an obscene gesture. Seriously.

I want to go back to the training room.

* * *

God, I am such an idiot. I had a shot with Tanha today, but I totally blew it.

I mean, I don't know how much of a shot I had—maybe it wasn't a shot at all, for me—but somebody who would've known what the hell they were doing would've totally had a shot for sure. I don't know what they would've done or what they could've said, which is part of my problem, I guess, but they would've done something kind of . . . something.

Tanha needed a ride home because her car caught on fire, somehow, while she drove to work. We passed it on the way home and it looked like it'd been firebombed in Iraq.

I asked her how it happened and she was like, "I don't know. I just somehow manage to always burn things."

That would've been a perfect time for me to say something witty like, "Good thing I'm wearing my flame-retardant underwear," but I just sat there like an idiot, without saying anything. Then she started listing all these things that she's accidentally burned and then she went into this long story about how she burned her last apartment. She lit some candles to surprise her boyfriend—ex-boyfriend now; she made that clear, which I figured was a good sign that she made it clear—and the candles somehow caught her curtain on fire and when she tried to put it out, she got water in the light socket and that knocked out the power and she had to wait outside for the fire department wearing only a sexy negligee.

She wouldn't tell me all that if she didn't like me, would she?

She lives out in that trailer park in The Plains where a lot of college students live because it's far enough away that they can get a decent parking pass at OU. Once we got there,

I started to lean in, thinking maybe I had a chance for a kiss—I don't know why—but suddenly I wasn't getting the vibe at all, so I pretended like I was just turning around to get something out from behind my seat.

The problem was, the only thing back there besides McDonalds trash was this big brown grocery sack full of women's panties and crap that Adam left in my car last week. He was like, "Can you hold on to this? It's for my buddy's bachelor party and I don't want my girlfriend to find it."

It wasn't until I already had my hand in the bag that I remembered what it was. I didn't want to pull out a pair of panties, so I just latched on to the first non-panty thing I felt: The Doc Johnson UR3 Mouth Palm Pal. "Super Suck! Slip it in! Get off!" Once I sort of figured out what it was, I tried to imagine in my head how the truth would sound: "I was going to try to kiss you, but I chickened out at the last second and pretended I was reaching back here and—this stuff isn't mine, by the way—"

So then I tried to, quick, think of a lie, but I couldn't think of anything that sounded better than the truth. I should've laughed and said something like, "No wonder Adam doesn't want his girlfriend to see this stuff of his." But all I could think to say was, "Hmm, Made in the USA."

So that was embarrassing.

I asked her, "Do you need a ride to work tomorrow?"

I'm pretty sure she took a quick glance behind my seat, and then said, "I don't think so. I'll call you if I do."

She never asked for my number, though, so that was definitely not an awesome sign.

I don't know. I figure there's got to be somebody somewhere who would've known some way to handle that whole situation in a way that would've ended with her tongue down my throat, and maybe my hand up her shirt, but I don't know what I could've or should've done.

I've been trying to work out some scenario in my head where I could get her and Adam together so I could casually mention to him, "Hey, you know, you've still got all that sex stuff in the back seat of my car," but I'm pretty sure he'd be all like, "What're you talking about? I don't have anything in your car," and that'd just make it worse.

* * *

And if that wasn't bad enough, I totally got lost trying to get out of her stupid trailer park. It was like I was stuck in this maze from hell. Either that place has ten different laundry facilities, or I drove past the same one ten times.

It sucked.

I probably drove past Tanha's trailer ten times, too.

She probably thinks I'm an idiot. Or a stalker. With a bunch of weird sex toys in my back seat. Driving back and forth for an hour with Radiohead blasting out of my car. I checked the place out on Google maps when I got home, and it's like a circle inside a circle inside a triangle with a bunch of diagonal roads going every which way. What the hell?

I still don't know how I ended up getting out of there. I would've kissed the driveway when I got home if I knew the nosey landlady wasn't watching.

Still, all that was pretty much the highlight of my day. Work today sucked. Sucked. From nine to twelve-thirty, it was pretty much all PowerPoints. I was so excited when Trainer Tim said we'd spend the afternoon out on the call floor, double-jacked with a regular TSR. I figured I'd get to hang out with Adam and Rob; finally chill out for a while. But then I got stuck with Gretchen, way far away from anybody cool. It sucked worse than suck itself. First of all, she's horrible. I don't think she had one call that lasted more than fifteen minutes.

She kept telling me, "I can't believe my calls are so short today," and crap like that, but I was amazed that some of them lasted as long as they did. The only thing saving her is that she talks so-o-o-o-o slo-o-o-ow. It takes her two minutes to get though a simple sentence. I don't know how many times her callers asked her, "Do you smoke weed?"

"Whyyyyyy doessssssss evvvverrrrryyyyybodyyyyyyy alwaaaaaaaaayssssss asssssssk meeeeeeee thaaaaaaat? I-I-I haaaavvvvvvve neveeeerrrrrrrr evennnnnnnn beeennnnnn drrrrruuunnnkk."

And then she'd be like, "I usually have one of the top ten AHTs every month," which is a total lie. I mean, even if she really didn't recognize me, and she really did think I was a new trainee, she still knows they post the results on the bulletin board each month. And her name's always hovering just above the If-you're-below-this-again-you're-going-to-get-fired line.

I mean, she's been at ATS almost as long as I have; I don't understand how somebody can work at a job—any job—for almost a year and still suck at it as much as she does. All she does is read the interpretation words right off the top of the cards. "And your sixth card is The Lovers: 'Love, beauty, perfection, harmony, trust, honor, beginning of a romance or friendship, deep feeling, freedom of emotion, testing of sincerity, marriage.' And your seventh card is the Three of Coins: 'Great skill in trade or work, mastery, perfection,'" blah, blah blah. Seriously.

I mean, even if all you did for almost a whole year was read off the cards like that, after that long, it seems like you'd at least have them memorized. But she read each one like it was the first time she'd ever seen it. She's the one who should be back in training, not me.

And she didn't do any of the stuff where you're supposed to adjust your reading to the caller's personality type. Pretty much every call, she was just trying to figure out how to work her dad into the conversation. He was always busy working and he never loved her the way she needed to be loved, blah blah blah. I was actually embarrassed for her until I remembered what a know-it-all beeotch she is.

Plus, she gave the most horrible advice in the whole entire history of horrible advice. No matter who called, she told them to break up with their boyfriend or their girlfriend or their husband or their wife—or at least start cheating on them. They could be calling to ask for their lucky numbers and Gretchen would say, "You don't need any lucky numbers; you need to find another man."

"My husband was paralyzed by a drunk driver."

"Sometimes significant events are a sign from God that you need to make a change. My dad was never around, blah, blah, blah."

That's pretty much what every call sounded like. I was just trying to scoot as far away from her as possible, in case God or Tunkasila or Whoever decided that she was finally due for a lightning strike. After a while I just tried to ignore her as much as possible and started writing in my notebook. Eventually she asked, "What are you writing?" and I should've known she expected me to say something like, "Oh, I'm just taking notes so I can remember all the amazing things I'm learning from listening to your calls."

But without thinking, I just said, "Sometimes I doodle when I'm bored."

I figured that was better than saying, "I'm writing down all the ways to describe you—ooh, I just thought of two more: a few bananas short of a bunch and a few mimosas short of a brunch." Even though I didn't say that, she still got all mad anyway.

"You know," she said, "the reason they have you new trainees double-jack with us is so you can learn by listening to our calls. It won't help if you spend the whole time doodling in your diary." She had this kind of scary, pissed-off, I'm-going-to-tell-on-you look on her face when she said it, too, so I spent the next infinity hours, it seemed like, just sitting there, listening to boring call after boring call. It was painful—I mean, my brain seriously hurt.

Finally, Liz came over to listen to one of her calls. I was thinking, at last, somebody will tell her that she sucks and then I'll get to sit next to somebody else.

And the call was awful, too. As soon as Gretchen did the greeting—which she does wrong, by the way, according to Smeagol's rules—the girl who called was all suicidal, like, "I don't want to live anymore. I'm going to kill myself tonight," and on and on like that. And Gretchen didn't even give the girl the suicide hotline number. That's day one training-type stuff. Everybody knows that. They always tell us, "Treat all suicidal comments as if they're serious, raise your hand for a supervisor immediately, and give the caller the suicide hotline number while you wait for a supervisor to double-jack into your phone."

Even if you don't remember that from training, it should be common sense. You don't say, "Well, let's see what your Tarot cards say," and then try to keep them on the phone as long as possible just to keep your AHT up.

After her call, Liz said, "Great job. Perfect call."

I was just like, *what the hell?* Seriously.

I didn't want to sound like a dick or anything so, in my nicest voice possible, I asked, "Isn't there a suicide hotline number or something that we can give to callers like that?"

"Yeah," Liz said. "But that girl never would've called it. All they do at those places is talk, anyway."

Gretchen said, "Yeah. I can never remember what the number is, anyway."

How can you not remember the number? It's 1-800-SUICIDE. How hard is that to remember? Seriously. And, even if you forget it, or if you're too stupid to know how to spell it, there's that whole list of numbers on that sheet right in front of your face.

Great call my ass. I mean, her call wasn't even in the same city as the ballpark of remotely barely good. And Liz says it was perfect? It's like I'm in bizarro world and I'm the only one who knows it. They should both be downstairs selling the Magic Peeler.

Plus, Gretchen talks crap about everybody. First, she pointed out Bea. "That lady in the blue dress? She tells everyone she can talk to their dead pets. It's such a ripoff."

Then she complained about Adam and Rob: "Those guys have contests to see who can make their callers do the most stupid things."

Then she complained about Frank: "He never even uses his cards like he's supposed to. He just gives every single caller the exact same reading," blah blah blah. She did that with pretty much everybody.

It got annoying after a while, especially when she was talking crap about Frank, because I've sat next to him a few times and he's cool as hell. And he gets great hold times, too. I don't know how he does it. He just closes his eyes and he's like, "Now your first card is the Ace of Cups. This is a very good card to have in your first position." He's actually pretty awesome. But Gretchen was all like, talking about how he was cheating the customer by not dealing any cards.

So yeah, that was work. I hope I don't get stuck double-jacked with her tomorrow. I seriously don't think I could handle one more day of that, let alone the whole rest of the week.

June 15

I've worked here for over a year and this is the second day in a row that somebody on the call floor acts like they've never seen me before. I mean, I know I always worked nights, but it's not like our shifts don't overlap. I don't know if I should be happy since nobody seems to know I'm redoing training, or bummed out that I'm apparently so forgettable.

Today it was Irene. Liz dropped me off to double jack with her. "Hi Irene," she says. "This is L.J. Is it okay if he joins you?"

Irene looked at me and said, "Why are you so blue?"

"Huh?"

"Your aura," she said, pointing around my body. "It's a dirty blue. And gray. And there and there—a couple spots of mustardy yellow. You don't need to be scared. Come here, dear. Sit down. Give me your left hand."

She started by tracing her finger in my palm. She had those cold, freckly, old-person hands with twice the necessary amount of skin, but it was the most action I've had since April, so I just kind of went with it. I kind of liked it, actually. I hope that doesn't make me some kind of granny-loving perv. I don't think it does.

She gave me pretty much the same spiel we give all our callers twenty times a day: "You've had your heart broken in the past. It'll happen again. Don't rush it, love doesn't follow a schedule." Stuff like that. Apparently since my head line and my life line are so far apart, I'm supposed to be super lucky. She also said something about the square on my mount of Saturn, but I forgot what that meant as soon as she started talking about my mount of Uranus.

Then she gave me the old standby: "Somebody loves you,

but you don't see her. It won't work, anyway. You're not ready."

"You can see all that in my hand?"

"No. I just know," she said. "Somebody hates you, too, and you don't notice them, either."

That was pretty much it. When she was done, she was like, "That's fifty dollars."

"For what?"

"For the reading. It costs fifty dollars."

"But I work here. I didn't come for a reading. I'm supposed to double-jack with you. See? My headphones? I'm supposed to plug these into your phone so I can listen to your calls."

"But you still got a reading. You owe me twenty dollars."

"I thought it was fifty."

"I have a special for ATS employees. Twenty dollars."

"I don't have twenty dollars."

"How much do you have?"

"Nothing. I'm broke. I don't have any money."

"Ten dollars."

"I don't have any money."

"Give me five dollars now and you can give me the rest tomorrow."

"If I give you all my money, I won't be able to get anything for lunch."

"Five dollars. If I don't charge you, everyone will want a free reading."

So I gave her my last five dollars. When I did, she was like, "Now, do you need any money for lunch?"

"No. I'm good."

"Now, dear," she said. "Don't you know it's impolite to say No to an old lady?" and she gave me my five bucks back.

Once we got that out of the way, we had a pretty decent conversation. She talked about her kids for a while and she showed me pictures of her grandson and a bunch of pictures of her granddaughter, who totally looks like a stripper—by the way. Even if you are a stripper, why would you give your grandma pictures of yourself dressed up like a stripper? Even if you spend all your money on whatever strippers spend all their money on, you can still take pictures of yourself at the mall trying on clothes you're never going to wear and then you can say, "Hi Grandma, here's a picture of me in church the other day."

We also talked about Mom and Dad for a while and how they'd be pissed if they knew I wasn't in college. Irene also said that the reason Smeagol got promoted from Trainer to P.M. was because he kept getting sexual harassment complaints, so they moved him up to the office where he wouldn't have access to so many girls. Apparently his wife used to be one of his trainees. I don't know why that made me feel better, but it did.

After this one call with some pregnant girl, Irene started talking about how stressful our job is, giving advice all day long, and how there's a right way and a wrong way to release that stress.

"What do you do?" I asked.

She looked all around before she whispered to me, "I steal things."

I thought she was joking, but she did one of those secretive head pointing things to get me to look down in her purse. She opened it a little with her foot and it was loaded with crap: an ATS coffee mug and a bunch of ATS ink pens and a brand new roll of toilet paper and the red and the blue dry-erase markers from the Announcements board. That was just the stuff I could see. For all I know, she had a couple phones and a computer in there, too.

She told me how she has this whole system worked out where she only steals stuff every eight days so people don't get suspicious. Monday one week, Tuesday the next, etc.

She smiled at whatever the look was on my face and then she said, "It's very therapeutic. And it keeps me sane."

Just as I was starting to sort of enjoy my first day of work in pretty much forever, Smeagol came up and he was like, "L.J., come with me."

I was trying to figure out what I could've possibly done wrong this time, so I was relieved when he said, "They're shorthanded on the first floor. They've been in queue all morning. We need you to go down there for a couple hours until they clear up all their calls."

"But I've never been trained on sales."

"They'll tell you everything you need to know down there."

"How do I log into the phones? I thought my code only worked up here."

"They'll give you a generic log-in when you get down there."

"When am I supposed to come back up?"

"They'll tell you when they're done with you down there."

"Am I supposed to clock out?"

"Stay clocked in and just go down there."

"So I guess I should just go down there then."

"You got it. Have you seen Derek?"

"No. But if I do, I can tell him to go down there."

Derek was totally pissed when he found out. He was like, "If we suck so bad that we need to repeat training, why the hell are they sending us down here?"

And then when we got down there, there was nobody to tell us how to do anything. There was just some hyper-stressed girl who plopped me down in a cubicle with a phone and a computer. She logged me in and said, "Here's your phone, here's your computer, here's your stylus for the com-

puter, just tap the monitor and read what's on the screen."
That was my training.

The phone beeped pretty much immediately. I was like,
"Thank you for calling your psychic advisor, this is Antonio,
may I have your first name and date of birth, please?"

click.

I had a few more calls like that before the guy next to me
was like, "Dude, just say, 'Thank you for calling,' give them
your name, then say, 'How may I help you?'"

The next caller was some lady wanting to buy the Time
Life Sounds of the Sixties music collection. Everything was
going fine; I got all the way through the sale and I got her
address and credit card information, and then I had to read
this screen explaining how she just unwittingly signed up for
every single CD in the whole entire Time Life collection—
she'll get a new one every month until she dies, basically. "Oh,
no, ma'am," I had to read off the screen, "all you need to do is
call and cancel as soon as you get that first one. So let's go
ahead and complete your order, okay?"

But she said she didn't want it because she'd forget to
cancel so then I read the screen about how, "all you need to
do is put a note on your calendar. So let's go ahead and send
this out to you today, okay?"

But she was like, "I don't have a calendar," which, as far
as I could tell, is something they don't have a pre-scripted
response for.

So I said, "My parents don't use a calendar either; they
tape notes to their telephone—"

"I don't have tape."

"You don't have any tape? In the whole house?"

"Nope."

"No Scotch tape?"

"No."

"Masking tape?"

"No."

"Duct tape?"

"I said I don't have any tape. So I'll have to cancel my order."

"What about bubblegum? Hot wax?"

"No. No."

"How do you write notes to yourself?"

"I just remember everything."

"Well, if you can remember that, you don't need to worry, so we can just go ahead and complete your order, okay?"

I didn't make the sale.

It wasn't too long before hyper-stressed girl comes over and she's like, "We need you to be faster. That last call took you nine minutes. Our target is two and a half. Get in, get out, get going. We've got a hundred calls in queue, that means we've got a hundred people waiting to buy our crap. They can't do that if you're having nine-minute conversations about Post-it notes with every caller. Get in, get out, get going. And close the sale."

My next call, or one of my next calls, was this psycho beeotch from hell who started freaking out on me as soon as I answered the phone. "How dare you take advantage of people? You should be ashamed! How do you live with yourself? How do you sleep at night?" and on and on and on.

Every time the phone beeps, this computer screen pops up with about twenty different possible products that they might be calling about. Apparently it's cheaper to use the same phone number for a bunch of different crap.

While this chick's yelling at me, I'm going through the list like a mofo, trying to figure out what she's so pissed about.

Ab Circle Pro? Better Sex Through Yoga? Century of Dimes Coin Collection? Eggstractor? Kangaroo Keeper?

Once I got to the No-Money-Down Real Estate, I figured that must've been it. It wasn't. It turned out it was some

Healthy Prayer thing I'd never heard of.

According to the script, the first thing I was supposed to say was, "What size of devotional investment would you like to make today?"

I never got the chance because she kept totally screaming about how God has a special place in hell for people like me, and then she was like, "You're an evil little loser. I hope you burn in hell," and on and on. Holy crap.

From everything she yelled at me, it sounded like the ad basically convinces sick people to send in their money so all their diseases will be cured. Something about how the money increases the volume of your prayers so that God can hear them better.

I wanted to tell her, "Hey, if it's half as bad as you say, I totally agree with you," but, the more she screamed at me, the more I wanted to defend this bogus church I never even heard of.

Whenever she'd give me a chance to speak—like, when she'd say, "What do you have to say for yourself?"—I'd say something like, "The Lord loves the greatest and the least of us," and that would piss her off even more.

She sounded like she was about to break a blood vessel in her brain or something. God, it gives me a headache just thinking about it.

That wasn't even the worst part of the day, though.

The worst part was dealing with all the first floor jerkwads acting all better than us because we work on the psychic line. I mean, first, they treated us like we're idiots because we didn't know what we were doing after getting no training. And then, when Derek and I took a smoke break, there were these people out there acting all like, "We're awesome because we sell stuff. Your psychic line is a scam. We run a legitimate business. You guys are worse than phone sex operators. At least with phone sex, the callers get their money's worth."

And then they got even more pissy when they found out we didn't ask for permission before we took our break.

I was like, "You need permission to take a break?" And then I was just joking when I asked, "Do you need permission to go to the restroom, too?"

Apparently they do.

"You guys on the third floor have it so easy. Our AHT has to be below three minutes or we get fired. You guys can talk as long as you want. All you do is chat on the phone all day. We have to sell stuff, and most of it's crap. And the crappiest stuff has at least three upsells of even more crap."

Derek was like, "I thought you said you work for a legit-imate business."

Of course that made them more pissed, so they just re-ferred to us as the two phone whores the rest of the day. Smeagol said they'd send us back upstairs after a couple hours, but they never did, so we were stuck down there the whole rest of our shift. It sucked and left me feeling all dirty inside.

Oh, and I also got a call for this New You Life Coaching thing where the caller calls up for a free life coaching session. As I'm reading the script, I start to think it sounds familiar and then I realize this is the same number I called about a month ago. When I called, I thought it seemed like the lady who answered was in a hurry. Now I know why. She was try-ing to keep the call under two and a half minutes.

There's a place in the script right before the upsells where you're basically supposed to hypnotize the caller over the phone. I could tell the lady I called was reading it, but I didn't know she was sitting in a call center cubicle.

I'm never buying another thing over the phone for the rest of my life.

* * *

After work, I asked Tanha if she needed another ride

81

home. She didn't, but Marpa heard me and he was like, "Are you offering rides? Because I need one."

I couldn't say No because I didn't want Tanha to think I had some kind of ulterior motive when I offered her a ride, even though, technically, I did. Karma Man had me drive him to the Gas 'n Shop out on Sheridan Avenue. The clerk there supposedly shorted him ten dollars last week—gave him change for a ten instead of a twenty. He didn't explain any of this until later. It would've been nice to know.

Apparently, the appropriate "karmic adjustment" for someone who gives you the wrong change is to fill up a 32-ounce plastic fountain cup with Sprite and walk around the store, "accidentally" sploshing it on everything you see. Then you take a box cutter and make tiny little slices in as many cartons of milk you can without looking suspicious. Slicing into a bag of flour or a bag of rice—or both—is also good. And it helps to clumsily drop a jelly donut out of the case on-to the floor and then, while you're pretending to look for it, step on it so you can squooge donut jelly and frosting all over the floor (this is also a perfect time to "spill" the rest of your Sprite—preferably onto the shelf, getting Sprite on as many bags of chips as possible). Next, pretend like you're trying to wipe the jelly up, but instead of napkins, use those wax paper donut grabber sheets so you can spread the jelly all the way across the aisle, insuring that anybody who walks past will help track jelly footprints throughout the store. Then you take a Hershey bar off the shelf and wedge it into the handle of the Slushie machine so you get Slushie pouring out all over the place.

And don't forget to hit the Start button on the coffee machine as you leave. Since the coffee pot's already full, the new coffee will overflow all over the counter and onto the floor.

Once we got out to the car, I was just like, "Dude, what

the hell?"

That's when he told me about the whole incorrect change thing, "and since starting pay at Gas 'n Shop is eight dollars an hour, I had to give him an hour and fifteen minutes worth of stuff to clean up. That way he won't suffer any karmic consequences."

I was like, "Wouldn't it hurt your own karma, doing all that?"

He looked at me all super serious and he said, "That's why they call it a sacrifice."

That made me laugh. I don't know why. He didn't think it was funny. I said, "Couldn't you help people by being nice to them instead? And then they'll do something nice for someone else, and that person will do something—"

"That's not the Marpa way. This is the best way I know to help people."

"That cashier should be thanking you," I said.

"Yeah, but they never do." He said it like he thought I was serious.

"Is this what you'll do for the rest of your life?" I asked. "'Help' people?"

"I have one more big project, then I'll retire. Until then, I try to help people where I can."

"What's your big project? What'd he do? Steal all your shoes?"

"He turned my fiancée into a porn star," he said. "Why is that funny?"

"It's not," I said. "Who is it?"

"I don't know."

"Then how will you know when you find him?"

"I made it this far, didn't I?"

Whatever that means.

When I dropped him off at his apartment, he offered me another ten bucks for gas. I didn't want to take it. I did—I'm not an idiot—but I didn't really want to.

In the meantime, I can never go to the Gas 'n Shop again, which sucks, because they have the best blue raspberry Slushies anywhere.

June 16

I met my new hero today. Seriously. I've got such a man crush on this dude, I'm about to get a stiffy just thinking about him.

At work, they sent us downstairs like they did yesterday, but today, they didn't even try to pretend like they wanted to train us. At least yesterday, Smeagol gave us the whole song and dance about how he really wanted us upstairs but, it turned out, they were shorthanded downstairs and they needed us to help out or the phone lines would explode or something from all the hundreds of callers on hold.

Not today. He didn't even bother.

Pretty much as soon as me and Derek clocked in, Smeagol was like, "They need you guys down on the second floor."

Derek was like, "The second floor? The DirecTV tech support line?"

That's the one.

The "training" was pretty much as nonexistent as yesterday on the first floor, which makes it worse, because the people calling tech support want you to help them fix something. If you suck on sales, the caller will just not buy anything and eventually hang up. None of these DirecTV callers would hang up because they didn't want to have to call back and wait on hold for another half hour.

I pretty much felt sorry for every single person who called me, even the rude ones from Massachusetts. Seriously, every time somebody was a total dick on the phone, I'd look at their address, and they were from Massachusetts. Every single time. But I still felt bad that I didn't have the slightest clue how to help them.

I mean, the absolute only thing I knew about DirecTV was that Peyton Manning does the commercials. And there's a satellite involved. That's it. I didn't even know it was spelled DirecTV until today. I've never had DirecTV, I've never been able to afford DirecTV, and I don't know why anyone would even want DirecTV when cable is so much cheaper and it never goes out on you. Plus, you have to buy some kind of receiver, apparently, and there's some kind of access card involved that maybe comes with the receiver but, for all I know, you have to buy that, too.

I'd just finished flubbing through another call and I was trying to figure out how to log it on my computer when Alex, the guy sitting next to me, starts tapping me on the shoulder.

I look over and he's telling the caller, "Okay, sir, now tell me when you've got that potato right on top of your receiver. It is? Good. Are you getting a picture? Now remember, you need that potato pointing north, so go ahead and rotate it real slowly. Slowly. That's right." Then, Alex hit this button on his computer that says, "Resend Authorizations," and the guy on the phone was so excited that I could hear him yelling through Alex's headset.

Alex was like, "There's no need to thank me, sir. I'm just doing my job. Remember, if this happens again, just follow those same steps, okay? It might save you some money for a service call."

After the guy hung up, Alex said to me, "I love button mashers. As soon as someone says, 'Okay, I just mashed the green button,' I know it'll be a fun call."

Coolest dude ever.

Sitting next to him made the day go by a lot faster. He tried to help me on some of my calls, too, but I was still pretty much worthless. I basically just had everybody do a thirty-second reset. Snowy screen? Thirty-second reset. "Searching for Satellite" message? Thirty-second reset. I did it so often that now I've got the whole script etched into my brain:

Would you please turn off your receiver, at the receiver, and then unplug the power cord from the power source? Let me know when you have done that.

What we are doing is resetting your receiver. This allows it to reset itself to the manufacturer's specifications. This reset can be done anytime there seems to be a problem with your receiver. If the problem still exists after completing this process, the receiver will need to be reset for five minutes. If the five-minute reset does not solve the problem, the manufacturer will need to be called.

Please plug your receiver back in to the power source and turn it back on for me. Let me know when you have done that.

Did that correct the problem?

When it didn't correct the problem, which was pretty much every single time, I just told them to do a five-minute reset and then call back if that didn't work. That's pretty much all I've been doing all morning.

* * *

Now we're outside in the designated smoking area and Derek is still standing on top of one of the picnic tables complaining because we didn't get our free pizza.

Every three months, the psychic line has this contest—the team with the highest AHT for those previous three months gets pizza. It's not that big of a deal; each person on the team only gets two pieces and it's always crappy Avalanche pizza and they always order the absolute worst toppings, like artichoke and jalapenos, or brussel sprouts and squirrel and sawdust. It's totally gross.

Still, it's pizza. And it's free. So when our team won again, Derek and I were pretty psyched to score some food.

But when we went into the break room, Liz wouldn't let

us have any pizza. "You're not on the list," she said. She said it kind of bitchy, too, like we were trying to scam the system for two pieces of broccoli and pickle pizza (seriously, those were the toppings; it was either that or all black olives, which I hate).

Derek was like, "But it's our team. Those other eight people wouldn't even have pizza if it wasn't for us."

Liz said, "I guess it's not your team anymore, is it?"

I mean, don't get me wrong, I was pretty pissed off too, especially when we saw the QAs taking the extra pizza out to their cars, but it's not like I was surprised. This is ATS, after all. You pretty much have to expect stuff like this. And it's only two pieces of cheap crappy Avalanche pizza anyway.

When I told him that, that's when he just totally snapped.

"That's my point!" he said. "Why do we have to expect to be screwed like little bitches at our jobs?"

And then he was like, "'TSR Appreciation Day'? That's a lie. They don't appreciate us. And they sure as hell don't respect us. They say the pizza is supposed to be a morale booster. Is your morale boosted? Mine's not. Screw this place," and on and on like that.

I'm not sure exactly when he got on top of the picnic table, but now he's talking about how we're just like the serfs of the Middle Ages.

America is turning into feudal Europe and we don't even notice because they've got us so distracted with sports and sex and video games. They're building their castles and gated communities with their armed guards and their panic rooms while they're treating us like little moving machine parts that they'll just keep throwing away when we don't work like we're supposed to until they can finally replace us all with robots, and that's when they'll kill us off with their made up wars and anthrax and some new disease that only they will have the antidote for and then they won't have to worry about the rest of us insects using up all their natural resources and they'll be able to go to Disneyland and Yellowstone and Las Vegas and not have to worry about the crowds or the traffic or waiting in line.

He finally stopped when the door made that clonking shutting noise.

We all turned and Smeagol was standing there with his arms folded in front of him. "Don't let me stop you," he said.

"My break's over. I've got to clock back in," Derek said, and he went inside.

Everybody else went inside, too. I don't need to worry about clocking in because I never clocked out, so I'm going chill out here and enjoy my cigarette.

Crazy day at the telephone psychic factory.

June 17

Here I sit, feeling great, getting paid to defecate. For the first time in my entire life, I'm making money while backing the big brown Cadillac out of the garage and, I must say, it's one of the greatest things I've ever experienced in my life.

I know that, officially, it might not count as getting paid to ride the porcelain pony because it's not like Smeagol came up to me and said, "As your Program Manager, I command you to go visit Mr. Hanky immediately." And it's not like anybody knows that right now I'm hanging out in the completely graffiti-free Supervisors' restroom with its ocean spray scent and its shiny tile floor and its cuddly-soft toilet paper, but I didn't clock out so, technically, I think it still has to count.

If I stay in here until my lunch break, it'll work out to almost twenty-five dollars they'd be paying me. To take the Browns to the Super Bowl. To drop a yeti into the whirlpool of doom.

Seriously, how awesome is that?

It's kind of like getting paid to have sex with a hot chick you wanted to have sex with anyway. And since that'll pretty much definitely never happen, I'll have to settle for this. And that's okay, because I'm getting paid to release the chocolate hostages. To pinch a loaf. To cut some cable. To feed a Ho-ho to the porcelain pig. To deposit a hundred grand into the porcelain bank. To deal a deuce to the albino lady. To unleash the chocolate snake from its fiery lair of darkness.

As soon as I clocked in this morning, Smeagol told Derek and me to go downstairs. After Smeagol went off to do his Smeagoling, Derek was like, "Screw that. I'm going up to the roof."

Apparently, he spent all afternoon yesterday up there,

too, while I was downstairs giving everybody the DirecTV Premiere Package for free.

I told him I'd join him as soon as I finished in here, but I'm in no hurry. I want to take my time doing my civic doody, making a chocolate offering to the porcelain god, giving birth to a politician, preparing some samples for Charlie's Chocolate Factory, giving my corn hole a chocolate milk mustache, adding the square root of four to zero.

What has two thumbs and gets paid to poo? This guy. That's right.

*   *   *

For some reason, everybody always thinks I'm doing funny stuff on purpose when I'm not. I don't know if it's something about my personality or what. Like, in high school when we had our physicals for sports and we were in that assembly line of urine checking, I seriously thought I was helping out—saving Coach Carlson a step—when I unscrewed the lid to my urine sample before I put it on the table. I saw the way he'd just struggled to unscrew Justin Thompson's, so I thought, *I'll do what I can to help.* I didn't know he would pick it up by the lid. And when he did, and he got my pee all over himself and Coach McDougal and all over all the papers on the table and he yelled, "Who the hell unscrewed the lid on their fucking piss?"

Everybody else was all like, "Luke, that was awesome! I can't believe you did that! You're hilarious!"

I just stood there like, *Holy crap, I'm glad I'm not going out for football.*

I was about the fourth person in line today at the vending machine, waiting to buy my CornNuts. The line wasn't moving at all. I wasn't paying attention to who was in front but it's like, if you don't know what you want, let somebody else go first, you know? So I was just kind of looking around, trying to distract myself from thinking about the CornNuts that were so close but so far away, and I noticed the girl at this table had a Napoleon Dynamite button on her purse. I pointed at the button and said, "Tina, you fat lard, come get some dinner," because that's like the funniest line in the movie.

The girl smiled because she knew what I was talking about, but the next thing I know, Liz comes around from the front of the line with a package of powdered donuts in her hand and she's like, "Who said that? Who said that? You all heard it. You're all witnesses to sexual harassment. Who said that? Was it you? Was it you?"

The guy in front of me was like, "I didn't hear anything." Then he turned to me and asked, "Did you hear anything?"

I shrugged.

Liz was like, "Fuck you. And fuck you. And fuck you. Fuck all of you."

Then she left, and now everybody in the break room thinks I'm the funniest guy in the world.

June 18

God, can a chick feel when her toe is brushing back and forth, back and forth, back and forth across your knee? That's what I want to know.

I mean, I was just sitting here, doodling up some new motivational slogans while Tim went through another round of PowerPoints. So far I had:

ATS Archie says, "SUCCESS begins with SUC"

ATS Archie says, "There's no I in Eat Me!"

ATS Archie says, "There's no I in Blow Me!"

ATS Archie says, "There's no I in Eye!"

Nothing particularly awesome, I know, but that's what I was doing. And then I felt this bump against my leg—not hard or anything, just like she accidentally kicked me while she was trying to get comfortable—and I figured it wasn't really her fault because I had my knee kind of just barely over on her side of the divider wall thing between our cubicles. So, no big deal, right? I figured I'd get around to moving my leg after I came up with another awesome slogan or two. No hurry. But then she kept her foot sort of up against my leg. And at first I thought, *Oh, she must think my leg is the cubicle wall thing*, but then she started doing the toe brushing back and forth thing real gently and it's like, she wouldn't do that against the cubicle wall thing, would she?

*   *   *

Before all this, about fifteen or thirty minutes or an hour ago, I wrote her this poem and passed it to her:

An eagle soars,

A woodpecker pecks.

How 'bout we chat

while we have . . .

93

lunch?

A while later, she wrote back: "You're funny." That's all she wrote. And she wrote it on the same note I gave her. So I figured I didn't really have a prayer, since she wasn't even impressed enough to keep the note, let alone take it home and put it under her pillow to read every night before she goes to sleep.

But now she's doing this toe thing, so I don't know what to think.

* * *

I mean, she has to know it's my knee, doesn't she? And if she knows it's my knee, what does that mean? Is she just teasing me, trying to see if she can give me a big chubb while Tim reads his PowerPoints? She can. She did. She is. Or is this her way of saying, "Lunch sounds good—so does anything that rhymes with 'pecks.'" Or maybe she's saying "I know you've had a crush on me since that first time we met; I've been waiting for you; why won't you ask me out?" I don't know. How am I supposed to know?

Maybe she's got some boredom-induced catatonia thing going on and she doesn't even realize she's doing it. That's why I'm not moving my leg one millionth of one millimeter, just in case, even if it means my pelvis will end up permanently twisted at a right angle to the whole rest of my body. People will stop me on the street when I'm like thirty and ask, "Hey, old man, how come your body faces sideways when you walk?" and I'll be like, "Well, stranger from the future, it was almost ten years ago, but I remember it like it was happening right now: We were in training at work, listening to a Power-Point about every single abbreviation we might ever encounter at work:

TA—Technical Advisor
TAD—Telephone Answering Device
TECH—Technician

TRN—Train or Training
TSP—Technical Support Professional
TSR—Telephone Sales Representative
TT—Talked To
TTHU—Talked To, Hung Up

and this totally hot chick was in the cubicle next to me. I was sitting kind of all pretzeled up, facing forward but with my leg back against the divider thing between us, which I think was somehow comfortable at first, and then her toe started brushing up against my business casual pants and it gave me kind of a warm and fuzzy, goose-bumpy feeling all over—plus a bulge the size of Mount Kilimanjaro in my pants—so there was no way I was ever going to even think about moving the slightest, most tiny fragmentary part of my body until she stopped, even if I had to stay like that until five o'clock."

I could totally imagine having that conversation in eight years.

* * *

W/—With
W/O—Without
WCB—Will Call Back
WI—Willful Incompetence
WKST—Workstation
WNCB—Will Not Call Back
WRK—Work

* * *

Back and forth and back the toe goes, when it stops, nobody knows. Hopefully never. I keep wondering if I should do something. What are you supposed to do when a totally hot chick is caressing your leg with her toe? It's not like I can reach down and start massaging her foot—that'd be too much. I need something more accidental or whatever. Like, if she decided she didn't like me, she could always say, "Oh, was my toe touching your leg? I didn't even know." I need something like that, because I could never say, "Oh, was I massaging your foot? I didn't even realize; no wonder I smelled baby oil." In two days, everybody in the whole entire building would hear about what a foot-fetishy freak I am. I need something where there's no danger of that happening. Something subtle.

Maybe I should say something. But what are you supposed to say when a totally hot chick is caressing your leg with her toe? "I love the way your toe feels on my leg"? Arrrgggghhhh! I want to do something! Should I do anything? I feel like I need to do something!

* * *

XFER—Transfer

* * *

God, why is she doing this? Does she even know she's doing it? And, if she does, is she doing it because she likes me or because she just wants to tease me? And, if she likes me, what do I do now? There's got to be some movie-star-perfect thing to do or say that would somehow convince her to tangle me all up in that super-long dark hair of hers. What is it, though? That's the thing.

* * *

ZABO—Zero Attendance Bonus
ZAHT—Zero Average Hold Time
ZCBO—Zero Call Bonus
ZPEBO—Zero Performance Bonus
ZPRBO—Zero Productivity Bonus
ZPDDD—Zippity-Pippity Damned Doo-Dah

* * *

I was thinking that maybe I could kind of move my leg. Just a little, like I was just doing it naturally, and then my leg could accidentally bump up against her foot and so then I could gently touch my hand on her thigh and say, "Sorry" (as in, *Sorry I bumped up against your foot; I didn't know it was there*), and then right away I'd say "Sorry," again, only this second one would be a gentlemanly *Sorry, I didn't mean to be so forward as to touch your thigh just now; it was merely my chivalrous reflex—concerned, as I was, about the welfare of your foot—because I'm a chivalrous-ass mofo.*

And then she'd think, *Wow, what a gentleman. If he ever wanted to kiss me/see my little boobies/lick the alphabet on my Venus Flytrap, I'd let him for sure.*

Yeah. That'd be awesome.

* * *

Too late. She's done.

What's the appropriate amount of time I have to wait to move my leg back? I can't move it right away, because then she'd know I only left it there because her toe was—either on purpose or accidentally—touching me. But I'd like to move it back as soon as possible, because it's uncomfortable as hell. And now that her toe's not touching me, I can tell just how uncomfortable it really is.

* * *

Okay, so I guess I'm going to be a pilot. I just called up this place in Columbus to ask him some general questions about flying lessons—apparently the proper term is "private pilot course"—and right away the guy was like, "Are you at least sixteen years of age?"

"Yes."

"Can you read, write and speak English fluently?"

"Yes."

"Can you pass a third-class medical examination?"

"I don't know," I said. "What's that?"

"Did you play any sports in high school?"

"Yeah. Golf. Cross country."

"The third-class exam is basically the same as you had in high school."

"Okay, yeah. I could pass that."

"All right. When do you want to get started?"

Before I knew it, I was signed up for their Accelerated Private Pilot Course. First, I'll do the ground school, whatever that is, from eight a.m. to six p.m. the next two Saturdays and Sundays, and then I take some test, and then I start flying. And the best part is that ATS has to pay for it since I've worked there for over a year (I double-checked my employee handbook while I was talking to the guy on the phone).

I keep thinking I should be more excited, but I don't think it's really sunk in yet. I didn't expect to be starting tomorrow morning. I just called the place because I was kind of curious about it because, after work, a bunch of people from our training class were hanging out in the parking lot and this one dude was all bragging about how he was in the Aviation program at OU and Tanha was like, "That's so cool. You'll have to give me a ride when you get your license."

He was like, "Definitely."

I was just like, I don't know. I mean, I was kind of hoping I'd get a chance to talk to her or hang out or do something—at least find out if that toe thing was real or just my imagination—but they all made plans to play around on the rock climbing wall at the Ping Center.

I had to pretend like I had something else to do because I didn't want to announce to everyone that I can't get into Ping because I'm not allowed anywhere on campus while I'm suspended from OU. I'm not sure I was even really invited, anyway. When I did the ATS training the first time, a lot of us hung out together—I still kind of hang out with Derek—but this time it's different. Maybe it's because I've spent most of this week either downstairs or, like today, getting totally baked up on the roof. I don't know.

All I know is, I'm starting my pilot training tomorrow and ATS has to pay for it. Hell yeah.

Maybe next time they won't be so stingy with the pizza. I doubt it, though.

June 19

If college would've been anything like basic pilot school or flight training or whatever it's called, I might've actually applied myself.

Class here feels so much more like you're actually learning something, without all the bullcrap and busy work. I mean, first of all, it became pretty obvious after about fifteen minutes that I'll learn more in two weekends here than I learned in over three years of college.

* * *

Disconcerting revelation of the day: I'm the worst student in our private pilot class. That's never happened to me before. The worst part is that I don't think it's even very close, that's how bad I am. I mean, first of all, I'm pretty sure I'm the only person who didn't read the textbook before class. But it gets worse. Oh, yes.

I didn't understand—and I still don't—how it is that a plane's engine doesn't work harder in cold air than it does in warm air. Cold air is more dense, I get that, and more-dense air would hold a plane up easier, I get that, too. I also get that, with each propeller rotation in cold air, a greater volume of air will be displaced.

What confuses me is that there are other forces at work on the plane: first, the resistance that the propeller encounters as it spins through the air and, also, the friction or wind resistance of the plane itself as it travels through the air. Like, for example, the propeller—and therefore the engine—would have to work a lot harder traveling through water than through air, and the plane itself would have a lot more trouble flying through water than air. So I still don't get it.

But when I was asking about it in class today, I could

hear people behind me doing that shut-the-hell-up groan and that's when I realized, *Oh, God, I'm the annoying douche in class who asks the stupid questions!*

Right before that, too, I had just finished thinking how awesome the class was because we didn't have anybody asking a bunch of stupid dumbass questions. So that sucked.

I was totally psyched about the class this morning, but now I'm just totally intimidated. I mean, just the instruments alone make me feel like my brain will explode. There's the compass, which I understand, and the airspeed indicator and the vertical speed indicator; I'm good with those, too. And the altimeter tells you your altitude, but there's a difference between true altitude and absolute altitude, and I can't remember which one is which. And I don't know how the turn coordinator is any different from the attitude indicator, because they seem exactly the same to me, but I assume they must be different somehow.

I don't know how I'll remember everything. But it's like, I have to. If I don't pass the class, ATS won't pay for it. Plus, I've kind of been looking forward to having a pilot's license, not just so I could give Tanha a ride and she'd be so excited and grateful that she'd jump my bones at five thousand feet, but also so I'd have something to tell Mom and Dad just in case they find out I'm not at OU.

I was daydreaming pretty much all last night about Mom and Dad sitting me down on the couch while they stood above me—Mom on Dad's left, then on his right, then on his left—all prepared to give me one of their "We're disappointed in you" talks, and I'd look at them, all confident for a change, and I'd say, "Hey, don't worry about it. I've got my pilot's license; I'm working for United Airlines." I mean, I spent some time imagining all the possible variations of the whole Tanha thing every now and then, too, but mostly it was the Mom and Dad one.

The trouble is, I found out today that there are about a million problems with the whole fantasy I'd conjured up. First, it turns out that you need more than a private pilot license to fly jets—which, I mean, I pretty much knew all along, but I didn't realize how close to nearly impossible it'd be for it to happen for me. You'd basically need about a million dollars to pay for all the hours of flight time you'd need, or else you'd have to join the Air Force, and I don't see either of those ever happening.

Second, the book had a picture of the instrument panel of a big jet and, holy crap, if I can't tell a turn coordinator from an attitude indicator, there's no way in hell I'd ever be able to handle all the gauges on a 747. Third, even if I could fly jets, the average pilot doesn't make much more money than we make at ATS. I'm pretty sure there were more, but I can't think of them right now.

At least I can hold on to the Tanha fantasy a while longer. Even though there apparently are a bunch of laws against making sweet love while piloting a small aircraft, that won't stop me from trying. At the very least, there's always a blow job.

June 20

Controlled vs. uncontrolled airport
Civilian land airport: alternating white and green
Civilian water airport: alternating white and yellow
Military: green and two white

* * *

VASI (Visual Approach Slope Indicator): red over red, you're dead; red over white, you're all right.

* * *

Controlled vs. uncontrolled airspace

* * *

VFR transponder code 1200

* * *

Alfa, Bravo, Charlie, Delta, Echo, Foxtrot, Golf, Hotel, Juliett, Kilo, Lima, Mike, November, Oscar, Papa, Quebec, Romeo, Sierra, Tango, Uniform, Victor, X-ray, Yankee, Zulu.

* * *

Nine = niner
One-eight-niner-niner
Nothing could be finer than to be in Tanha's 'giner in the morning.

June 21

Liz: "Do you have any questions?"

Viking Boy: "Yeah. Is this workspace in compliance with the regulations of the Occupational Safety and Health Act?"

Liz: "I don't know and I don't care. Anything else?"

Viking Boy: "Is the universe finite or infinite? Or finite *and* infinite? Or neither finite nor infinite?"

Liz: "Are you retarded or something?"

Viking Boy: "That depends upon how you define 're-tarded.'"

* * *

Memorandum

To: Third-Floor TSRs

From: Thomas Snyder

Date: June 8

Re: COTS and Opportunity Sales

I've received information today that I wanted to share with you as soon as possible. Many of you are aware of our COTS (Computer Operated Transfer System) and how it works. Recently there has been an addition to the COTS in the form of Opportunity Sales. When a client finishes using the COTS, we have put into place an automated script that is twenty seconds long. The script simply informs the caller that if they want to learn about promotional offers or purchase products they should stay on the line for a Specialty Consultant.

Twenty seconds from a machine—not a human being—and the COTS gets over a sixteen percent transfer rate. Sixteen percent!! I find it incredible that a twenty-second blurb from an automated script can generate four times the transfer rate than our call center. The COTS does not "sell" a customer. The COTS does exactly what we have been asking each of you to do—just make the caller aware. We don't want you to hard sell a customer. Just make them aware that ATS has this particular avenue available.

So many times I have heard TSRs talk about the ATS values, and how ATS cares about our customers. How is it that we are allowing an automated script to be more effective than we are when assisting a caller? Are we really addressing a customer's concern on every call? Are we doing our customers a disservice by not letting them know about all of their available options? The COTS percentages prove that callers want to have this information . . . now let's give our callers the human touch that only ATS has the ability to deliver!!

Thanks!!

Thomas Snyder

ATS

* * *

We finally finished training and we're now in OJT, so we were on the phones all day. I hope that means I don't have to go downstairs and sell any more Tiddy Bears or Bacon Genies.

During a lull, I overheard Brainless Amy (actually, I don't think I overheard, so much, because I think she meant for me, specifically, to hear): "I can't believe these people who talk about themselves or their family to callers. I would never want any of these callers to know anything about me, but some people are, like, every call, saying, 'my brother did this,' or 'my mom did that.' That's just insane."

So I know she was talking about me, because I do that on almost every call. "Your dad is gay? *My* dad is gay! Your dad hates gay people? *My* dad hates gay people! You've never had a dad? *I've* never had a dad!" It's the easiest way to keep callers on the line.

If she listens to all my calls, she must think I have one *messed up* family.

Before Brainless Amy went off about me, my last caller was like, "I'm worried about my brother going to prison tomorrow because I heard they treat child molesters real bad in prison."

I was just kind of like, "Uh, yeah. I know my brother had it tough when he went to prison."

"What happened?"

I was trying real quick to think what I remembered from prison TV shows and movies and all I could think to say was, "Well, one time, he said they made him eat fifty eggs in an hour." As soon as it came out of my mouth, I was just thinking, *That's the best you can come up with?*

The lady on the phone was like, "Wasn't that in a movie or something?"

"I think so," I said. "I figured that's where they got the idea."

Then I said, "My brother said he couldn't eat for three days," because details make the lie believable.

Then I said, "He's okay now, though," because you need to give them some good news so they don't get all depressed and hang up.

I can just imagine how freaked out Brainless Amy will be when she gets home tonight: *He hates his dad, he doesn't have a dad, his brother's in prison, he doesn't have a brother, he has eight brothers and they're all in prison . . . how will I ever sleep tonight?*

If she had a brain, it'd probably explode.

* * *

Tanha just came up to me and asked if I was busy after work.

I said, "I don't think so. Why?"

"Do you want to maybe get a beer or something?"

"Yeah. Sure."

* * *

I kissed Tanha! I kissed Tanha! Holy crap, this has been the most awesome day ever.

Apparently, Tanha was all stressed from her first full day on the phones. As soon as we got in my car, she was like, "What do you say to an eighteen-year-old girl who wants to know if she should get pregnant on purpose to get her boyfriend back?"

So I went all Tao of Steve on her. I was like, "Tell her, 'The cards say you will definitely lose him if you get pregnant.'"

She said she tried that and that the caller said some other psychic told her that the Two of Cups in her sixth position meant she was supposed to get pregnant and all that. So then I went through all the stuff she could say to that and she was totally impressed.

Still, she wanted a beer, so we went to Lucky's because we figured we could talk there. But then her ex-boyfriend came in with her old roommate and, when they started making out at the pool table, Tanha ordered some shots and another pitcher and dragged me out back to that patio they have there.

She was still holding my hand when we sat down, so I tried to move in for the forehead magnet maneuver. When she turned toward me, she let out a dainty little surprised, "Oh!" and let go of my hand to brush a little leaf or something off my face with her sleeve.

So I was just like, Okay, she let go of my hand, but she did it to brush something off my face, and isn't it a sign of familiarity or something when a girl touches your face?

But she touched me with her sleeve instead of her bare

hand.

But it was a soft sweater sleeve, so maybe that's supposed to be more affectionate.

But she never put her hand back in mine, so that was a drag.

But she did tap my knee, and that had to mean something.

But she tapped it rather than rubbed or squeezed or caressed it, so maybe it was more like a this-is-to-indicate-that-we'll-never-be-more-than-friends tap.

I didn't know what to think.

Eventually I decided that I'd lost my chance to do the forehead magnet maneuver and, without the forehead magnet maneuver, I didn't know how I'd be able to ask her, "What would you do if I kissed you?" because I can't imagine how I could ever ask, "What would you do if I kissed you" if our foreheads weren't pressed together.

And, if I didn't ask, "What would you do if I kissed you?" I didn't know how I'd ever be able to actually kiss her.

I mean, I feel like I can talk to girls okay. And once I get to the forehead magnet thing, I feel like I've got a pretty good shot at keeping it going. But it's getting from the talking to the forehead magnet thing where I suck. I don't have any game between the talking and the forehead magnet, which probably explains why I've had fewer women than I have fingers on my right hand (even when I count my right hand as one of the women).

I tried moving in again, but it didn't look like she was ready for me to kiss her.

But, just as I was pulling back, then it did look like maybe she wanted me to kiss her after all, so I went in again. But then I realized that she didn't have that *please kiss me* look on her face and I got scared and pulled back again. We did that a couple more times, while pretending like we weren't really doing that, even though we probably both knew we were.

The whole time, I was trying to think up any kind of lame reason that'd give me an excuse to kiss her. The best I could come up with was, "Ooh, my lips are cold."

It's probably best that I didn't try that.

Finally she was like, "I have to pee."

The whole time she was inside, I was just thinking that, you know, it shouldn't be that hard. I mean, I've kissed plenty of girls before. I've had sex (not a whole big ginormous amount of sex, but I have had sex—I even had a one night stand with a total stranger dressed as Catwoman once, so it's not like I don't know what I'm doing). I should be able to just kiss a girl when I have the chance.

But no, not me. I suck.

I don't know what happened when she was inside, but when she came back out to the patio, the first thing she did after she sat down was give me this big juicy kiss. I'm sure it was probably some kind of revenge kiss or something, but I didn't care. Then we kissed again. I don't know if I kissed her the second time or if she kissed me or if we kissed each other but we kissed again, and then we kissed again and again and then we had a five-minuter and then we talked about I don't even know what and then we had a ten-minuter and talked and kissed and talked and kissed.

And then she turned her head real fast and puked in that bush they have in the corner.

I was ready to keep kissing her after that, but she was like, "No, I'm gross. I'd be too embarrassed."

I didn't want to push it because I figured I'd sound desperate.

Tanha Tanha Tanha.

I hope she liked it as much as I did.

When I took her home, I asked her (sort of out of the blue but not weird or anything), "Did you have fun tonight?"

She said, "Yeah," but I don't know if she was talking about the talking, or the drinking, or the kissing or what.

I wonder if she's thinking about me even remotely as much as I'm thinking about her.

Probably not.

The more I think about it, the more paranoid I get. I don't know.

When I dropped her off at her place, I wanted to walk her to her door—like a gentleman and all—and, maybe I was hoping she'd take me inside and we'd continue the kissing thing in her bed or at least on her couch.

But she lives in that trailer park where her front door is like five feet from where my car was. I can almost see the look of disappointment on Dad's face, but it's like, to walk her to her door, I would've had to shut my car off really quick and basically sprint after her, and that didn't really seem like the cool guy thing to do.

I did wait and I watched that she got inside okay, though, so Dad can be happy about that.

What sucked was, like a total idiot, I asked her, "Should I get your phone number, or will I see you at work?" which was totally the wrong way to phrase that. I should've said, "Let me get your phone number, okay?" or something like that, because that's more assertive and it ends with a positive, affirmative, agreeable course of action without suggesting an equally-acceptable alternative. (I guess I learned something in ATS training, after all.)

But since I did suggest an alternative, Tanha answered, "You'll see me at work."

I don't know if that's supposed to be a bad sign.

Maybe I'm thinking too much into it.

I need to focus my thoughts on something else.

June 22

When I wasn't looking, Tanha put a note in my cubicle: "Thinking of you and our last night together—your secret admirer." It was a lot more fun to read than a memo from Mr. Snyder.

* * *

After work, I went with Tanha to the mall because she needed me to try on some clothes because I'm apparently the same size as her brother. It didn't take long, since there's only one marginally decent clothing store in the whole mall, so then she was like, "Let's just walk around the mall for a while."

So we walked around, just kind of talking about everything, but then again talking about nothing. Eventually we had one of those lulls in the conversation and I started spacing off when we passed the gyro place.

Tanha was like, "What're you thinking about?"

Apparently, with all the money he makes underpaying us and overcharging our callers, Mr. Snyder built his own rock climbing wall somewhere on his huge estate (because, clearly, the rock wall at Ping isn't good enough for rich people) and, last weekend, his son was visiting from Yale or Harvard or whatever expensive school he goes to, and he fell off the wall and broke a bunch of bones and now he's in O'bleness Hospital in a full body cast or something. Today at work, Liz fixed up this big collection bucket with a note on it: "Chip in to buy Tommy Snyder a get well present!"

The note had this super-long list of crap that would make Tommy feel better, with the price of each item written next to it, so we'd know how much to give, I guess.

Most of the stuff was video games and movies and crap

like that, but she also had a bunch of super-expensive stuff like an iPad and a new DVD player, and only one cheap thing: "gyro with curly fries—$3.95 each."

I mean, first of all, who still refers to themselves as "Tommy" after they get out of the fifth grade? And second, why should we chip in for Tommy Snyder's get well present when Mr. Snyder's too cheap to give Derek and me two slices of pizza? (Yeah, I know it's been almost a week, but I'm still bitter.)

Obviously, I wasn't the only one who thought that, either, because the bucket was completely empty by the time it got to me. Liz came by to pick it up and she asked me, "Where's all the money?"

I shrugged. "Maybe nobody had anything to give."

She said, "I put ten five-dollar bills in here before I passed it around," and then she looked at me like I was the one who took it.

"It was empty when I got it."

"*Really?*"

I'd pretty much been fantasizing ever since about being in a hospital bed with a bunch of broken bones, having people I don't even know bringing me gyros and curly fries.

For once, I wouldn't have to worry about getting to work on time, or getting in trouble once I got there. If Mom and Dad ever started yelling at me like, "What were you thinking, climbing up that wall?" all I'd have to do is make that grimace face and try to reach toward one of my broken bones and they'd shut up right away.

When Tanha asked me what I was thinking about, I was like, "I was thinking about Mr. Snyder's son in the hospital," which was sort of true, I guess.

Tanha thought I was Mr. Sensitive, though, and she made this "Ahh" kind of noise and sort of leaned into my shoulder.

We were right in front of that jewelry store when she did it, and this salesman was like, "It's time you bought the young lady a ring," and all that kind of car salesman-y stuff.

Tanha played along and put her arm in mine and she said, "Yeah, honey, when are you buying me a ring? Don't you want to be with me forever?"

I know she was just joking, but I kind of liked it, to tell the truth.

So I played along, too. The sales guy was being kind of a douche, so we figured we'd waste his time for a while. She tried on all these expensive rings and she had me putting them on her and taking them off. She's got kind of long, slender, soft sexy fingers. It was fun pretending we were dating and that I was making three grand a month at the Pepsi distributor. But then the sales guy started asking if I knew this guy or that guy or this other guy who also worked there so we left as soon we could.

I was kind of hoping we could somehow continue where we left off last night, with the kissing and stuff, but how are you supposed to breech/breach/broach/whatever that topic? I mean, you can't just say, "Hey, you wanna get drunk and make out again?"

Still, I tried. Before she drove off, I asked, "Do you want to do something?"

"Like what?"

"I don't know. We could go to the bar or—"

"No-o-o," she laughed. "No bars for me."

Then she gave my hand the tap-tap and thanked me for helping her with the clothes and she drove off."

So now I'm home alone and she's off doing whatever it is she's doing.

I don't know. It seemed like I had a shot there for a while.

But it's like my shot is always this vapory cloud of smoke

and I don't know how to catch it or whatever. I mean, all this stuff online says to find things that she's interested in, but how are you supposed to figure out what she's interested in? Without stalking her, anyway.

That's what I want to know.

* * *

And now I can't stop thinking about gyros.

* * *

I forgot that today was karmic enforcement day. I was walking out of the mall with my two gyros and curly fries and a large Dr. Pepper when I saw this raggedy guy trying to get in his car. I was about to ask him if he needed any help when I recognized him.

"Marpa?" I said. "What're you doing?"

"Don't ask." He acted all douchey-serious, like he was on some top-secret spy mission. "You don't want to be here, man. Trust me."

He was squooching this Loctite stuff in all the door keyholes. I was like, "Why are you dressed up like an old bum?"

"Security cameras."

"In Athens? I don't think so. That ginormous hole in front of Tractor Supply has been there since my freshman year; I'm pretty sure they're too cheap for parking lot cameras."

"You need to leave. Now."

Okay.

He had already walked off behind the movie theater by the time I got my car started and my seatbelt fastened. I kind of wanted to wait and see whose car it was, but I was worried it might look suspicious if I waited until then to drive off.

I also wanted to eat my gyros while watching *NCIS*.

June 23

Today I learned that, when somebody says they don't like fire, or anything that has anything to do with fire, you don't hand them a lighted Roman candle and say, "No, here, hold this; you'll be fine."

Derek had a trunk full of fireworks he picked up in Indiana last night after work and, on break, we thought it'd be cool to go up on the roof and help Tanha get over her fear of fireworks. I should've known the Roman candle would be a bad idea when she was too freaked out to light one of those little snakes that Derek bought for his daughter.

The first thing Tanha did was closed her eyes, which wouldn't have been so bad if she hadn't aimed it almost straight down.

When Derek and I were both like, "Whoa!" she turned a little bit and shot the first one right into the air conditioner or whatever that big boxy metal thing is. The next couple ricocheted around the roof. Those flaming balls are fast. And they bounce a lot more than I ever expected, too.

Tanha started screaming, "I don't want this! I don't want this! Take it! Take it!" waving it around like a magic wand.

We're trying to get behind her and grab it so she doesn't shoot us in the face, but that thing's hot as hell if you grab it too high. Finally I got behind her and put my hand over hers and we shot the rest of them into the cornfield across the fence.

"See? This isn't so bad," I said.

After the last one, Tanha was like, "What do I do with this empty Roman candle stick?"

Derek said, "Just throw it out into the cornfield."

Right as she cocked her arm back to throw it, one last

flaming ball shot out behind us.

Derek was like, "That was awesome!"

I didn't see it, but he said it bounced off the satellite dish and right down into the parking lot. When we looked over the edge to see where it went, right in the back seat of Smeagol's convertible was this little black smoking hole.

I was ready to start freaking out, but Derek was like, "That's the best thing I've seen all year! Nice shot!"

Tanha punched me kind of hard in the shoulder. "I told you I don't like burning stuff! Now do you believe me?"

Yes. Yes I did.

We spent the rest of our lunch in the break room watching Judge Mathis.

Smeagol's car didn't explode or anything like I was afraid it would, and his back seat didn't burst into flames, but I'm guessing he's got a pretty huge hole back there. I was scared to go in for a closer look—I didn't want to look suspicious or anything—but I'm guessing it isn't any smaller now than it was.

*　*　*

The phones went down at about two o'clock, which is always awesome—getting paid to not take calls—but it usually only lasts for about five minutes, tops, so nobody was getting too excited at first. After about fifteen minutes, people started milling around and the floor supervisors started sending groups of people who didn't know any better on their breaks.

Tip of the day: Never go on a break when the phones are down. Wait until they come back up—actually, wait for another half hour after that, because they might go down again right away. That way, you get paid fifteen more minutes while you're not on the phone.

Once they let us start milling around a little bit, I went back to hang out with the fun people.

The first thing Rob said when I got back there was, "L.J. Your turn: what's your ideal last day of work?"

"No call, no show."

Adam was all like, "That's lame," but then his was to be one of those guys who have to be escorted out while they're screaming and cussing and stuff.

"*That's* lame," I said. "Somebody does that every two months."

"That's what I told him," Rob said. "Remember when Larry Jacobsen got fired? He was like, 'That's bullshit! QA's full of shit! That's fucking bullshit! You suck!'"

Adam said, "Those guys are always sitting up front by the door—they only get one or two good *Fuck you*s in before they're outside. I'll be sitting way back in this corner so every single person on the whole floor will hear me all the way out the door. Plus, mine is the only way to get fired where you'll never work here again. Think about that."

I can see that. Still, I like mine better. For once, I'd know what it'd be like to be rich and not have a job to worry about and not have any place I had to be or anything I had to do.

Adam was like, "Quitting your job won't make you rich."

"Yeah, but I'd know what it'd feel like, even if it was only for a couple days."

Tanha said, "That makes sense," and Adam kind of shut up for a while after that.

Pretty soon, we were talking about close encounters or whatever with ghosts. It seemed like everybody had a story but me. I wish I did. I'd love to know for sure that stuff like that exists—not that I want it to exist, necessarily—I'd just want to know for sure one way or the other. As it is now, I just have to take somebody's word for it if I want to believe it, and Tanha was the only one with a story that I could almost believe.

She said, when she was little, her neighbor died in a car wreck. And she was out in the yard playing when it happened and she said she was having a conversation with the guy and all the adults were like, "Who are you talking to?" and she told them she was talking to George or whatever the guy's name was and they were all like, "No, honey, George is in Seattle" or wherever. And then a couple hours later, they found out he was in a car wreck.

Then Adam said, "Wouldn't it be crazy if there really were dead people watching us all the time? That would freak me out."

Tanha said, "Why? Are you worried they'd see you masturbate?"

It was like you could see exactly what Adam was thinking. First, it took him a few seconds for it to sink in, then he had this totally embarrassed look on his face. So of course we made fun of him for that.

We just talked about random stuff for the next five or ten minutes. Then, I don't know exactly what we were talking about—our favorite movies or something, I think—and just out of the blue, Adam blurts out, "What is it about porn that always makes me have to take a shit? Especially the close-up stuff where they zoom in real tight on the goat's knuckles—makes me go every time."

First of all, who admits something like that in public, ever? And, second, we weren't talking about anything even remotely related to either porn or poo, so I have no idea how he could've made that connection.

We all just kind of looked at him like, *Dude, what the hell is wrong with you?*

Finally, he started to sense our discomfort or disgust or whatever and he was like, "Uh, I can eat a whole pie. A big, round, nine-inch apple pie. I ate a whole one once in one sitting."

We just kind of sat there like, *Okay.*

After that, every time there was a break in the conversation, somebody would say, "I can eat a whole pizza," or, "One time, I ate a whole wooly mammoth."

Finally, Adam got all pissed he said, super loud, "Can *you* eat a whole pie?" like we all suck because we can't eat a whole pie. "I can eat a whole pie, so shut the hell up. You're all a bunch of asshole douchebags."

He was basically screaming when he said it. But what did he expect? At least we didn't mention his whole porn and poo fetish again.

Somebody up at the podium must have heard all his inappropriate language on the call floor, because we spent the next hour doing one stupid contest after another to keep us busy.

At four o'clock, they made all the three-to-eleven people take their lunch break and they sent all of us trainees home—woo-hoo! I was hoping Tanha might want to hang out or something, but she said she had to buy her books and stuff since summer classes start next Monday.

Now I've got the perfect opportunity to finally read my Jeppesen *Private Pilot* textbook.

Maury starts in five minutes, though.

Decisions, decisions.

June 24

Memorandum

To: All ATS employees

From: Thomas Snyder

Date: June 23

Re: Unwelcome union incursion

Recently, it has come to our attention that rumors have been circulating regarding union activity on ATS premises. We want to clear up any misconceptions and make you aware of your rights as an employee of ATS.

One common myth you might hear from a union representative is that membership in a union will increase your bargaining power with ATS. In fact, the opposite is true. The CWA wants to take away your voice. The CWA does *not* care about your best interests. . . . Don't be fooled by the CWA's empty promises! . . . Respect and dignity come from communication and cooperation among all of us, not from a union contract! It is always better for employees and managers to continue to engage in direct, one-on-one communication, rather than through a third-party representative who doesn't know you and who doesn't care about your individual needs.

You might also notice that there is little mention of the dues structure with the CWA and, in fact, any union. Do you *really* want to share *your* paycheck . . . with a *union*? . . . Right now, without representation, your hard-earned money goes into *your* pocket for you and your family . . . The CWA is here so it can *take away* part of *your paycheck* every single month . . .

That is what *union dues* are all about—you give and the CWA takes! Not only that, but there is no limit on what unions can charge in dues every month . . . they can charge as much as they want to take your voice away!

It is important that you *don't settle for the* CWA's *fairy tales* . . . Union organizers will say anything to get your vote . . . The CWA cannot guarantee that you won't lose what you already have (including your job) in their contract negotiations, . . . *tell the union that your job is too important for fairy tales.* The unions don't tell you that they could force you to not only lose your superior benefit package, but also be subject to the many other arbitrary obligations of union membership.

If you are asked to sign a union card or petition, say No. Tell them that you are against the CWA and against paying union dues and against letting this Union gamble with your future.

While we would never attempt to control the activity of any employee when they are not at work nor on company property, we would like to remind all employees that any activity—whether in support of a union or otherwise—is strictly prohibited while on company property or "on the clock" and such activity will result in immediate termination. In an effort to encourage fairness for all of our employees, a fifty-dollar reward will be given to an associate each time he or she identifies a coworker not adhering to this policy. Feel free to speak with us or any of your supervisors if you have any questions or concerns. We will do our best to answer any questions you may have.

Thank you!!

Thomas Snyder, ATS

*   *   *

Okay, so I'm sort of freaking out. Kind of close to really freaking out. Outside in the parking lot right now are Smeagol and Security Guard Gary and some other guy, and they're all leaning over Smeagol's convertible, poking around the hole in Smeagol's back seat.

Security Guard Gary's trying to go all CSI on the scene; it looks like he's trying to figure out the exact angle of entry. Smeagol is either really pissed or he's squinting from the sun. Or both. Probably both.

I'm pretty sure, before our shift is over, that there'll be a new flier on the bulletin board: "Reward: eighteen thousand dollars for information on the person or persons responsible for the hole in the back seat of Daniel Leech's convertible."

I'm trying to remember if anybody was around yesterday when Derek kept going on and on about how awesome it was when the fireball shot into Smeagol's back seat. Did he tell anybody else? Probably. He was pretty excited about witnessing the whole deal.

And I'm pretty sure that whoever he told would be pretty happy to get an eighteen thousand-dollar reward.

Hell, I'd turn myself in for eighteen thousand dollars.

God, I don't want to go to jail. I don't know how I'd explain that one to Mom and Dad. "Hey, Mom, you know how you thought I was still in college? Well, surprise, surprise!" I don't even want to think about how that conversation would go.

Actually, I already know how my part would go: I'd be saying "Yes, yes, yes" to whatever they say. It'll suck, that's for sure.

But I'm still pretty sure it'd be better than jail.

Crap.

June 25

Good news with regard to my latest vandalism!

I was paranoid and guilty and scared as hell and everything else you could possibly be after sort of helping burn a ginormous hole in the back seat of Smeagol's convertible and I went in to work today all prepared to come clean with Smeagol. I wasn't going to mention Derek or Tanha. I was just going to say I bought a Roman candle and it slipped out of my hand and one of the balls somehow miraculously bounced into his back seat.

I'd been practicing the speech pretty much all night since I couldn't sleep anyway.

I got here early and went to his office, but he gave me kind of a douchey don't-bother-me look. I didn't know at first that he was talking on the phone because he was using one of those tiny little ear things. I hate those things. Anyway, I waited around outside his door and pretended to read last month's AHT stats.

After a while, I realized he was talking to either his insurance guy or his car repair guy about his back seat. He said, "It's pretty big for a cigarette burn, isn't it?"

Then he said, "I do. My wife doesn't."

Then he said, "I don't know. I saw it yesterday morning. We had it detailed two weeks ago, so any time after that, I guess."

Then he said, "Don't you think I would notice if I did that?"

Then he said, "We drove it to Columbus last Saturday."

Then he said, "How long?"

Then he said, "Okay. Thanks."

Then he said, "L.J. You still out there?"

When I peeked my head around the corner, he said, "Make it quick. I've got to get my car to Columbus before six."

"Is everything okay?" I asked.

"Yeah. Apparently some idiot tossed their cigarette out their car window just as I drove by."

"What a drag," I said.

"What do you want? I've got places to go, things to do."

"I, uh, was just wondering if last month's stats are up."

"Are you blind? They're right in front of your face."

Then, I don't know if he meant for me to hear it or not, but he said, "Bunch of fucking idiots working here."

So I said, all happy, "Sorry about your car," and came out here for a couple smokes before three o'clock.

What a dick. I can't believe I almost told him I messed up his car.

* * *

Viking Boy's question of the day: "You know the expression, 'Butter my butt and call me a biscuit'? Do you think anybody's actually done that?"

* * *

TGI Fridays Cheddar & Bacon Potato Skins taste like ass. I usually hate that expression, because, after all, what does *ass* really taste like? But now I know.

And I'm pretty sure that there's nobody in the whole entire world who could eat these things and not say to themselves, "Wow, now I know what ass tastes like. I never thought I ever would in my whole entire life, but I really do. Thank you, TGI Fridays Cheddar & Bacon Potato Skins."

I was down on the first floor, all ready to buy the last bag of CornNuts in the whole entire building, and I was standing right in front of the vending machine with four quarters in my hand, when Marpa came up behind me and he was like, "L.J.! Just the guy I wanted to see! What're you doing down here?"

I said, "I came down to get some CornNuts."

"Yeah. CornNuts. Awesome." And he totally stepped right in front of me and put a dollar in the machine and pressed B5 and for a brief little second I was like, *Wow! Cool! He's buying me CornNuts!*

But then he opened the bag and started eating them right in front of me.

I was just like, *What the hell?* I mean, who does that? I said, "I thought you were a breatharian or whatever and you only eat air?"

He said, "That doesn't mean I'm unable to eat food if I feel like it. My teeth still work." He said it like it was a totally stupid question, too, which pissed me off even more.

I mean, if he was big into CornNuts and just had to have some right then, I could understand that—needing CornNuts so bad that you can't let anything get in the way—I know the feeling. I'd still be pissed, but at least I could understand.

But he just took one handful and he was like, "Blech. How do you eat these things? They're awful," and then he threw the rest in the garbage.

I was beyond pissed. I was just like, "Dude!"

Then he was like, "Hey, I'm having a party at my place Sunday night. You've got to come."

"Will you have food there?"

"Yeah," he said. "Food, beer, tequila, other stuff. Bring everybody—telephone psychics only, though. Especially if they worked here eleven months ago. I should've thought of this party a long time ago. Before Tuesday, anyway."

While he was talking, I just kept thinking, *I'm going to your party and I'm going to eat all your food, you CornNuts stealing bastard.* I mean, what kind of ass muncher steals somebody else's CornNuts? From right out in front of me? Especially after I'd just told him that I specifically went downstairs for the sole purpose of buying those CornNuts.

The worst part was, they were Ranch-flavored, which I'd been craving all day. So, yeah, I told him I'd go to his party. I'll make sure Adam goes too, since Adam can eat a whole pie.

In the meantime, I have to eat these TGI Fridays Ass Chips.

June 26

There's no way in hell I'll remember all these clouds.

I kick ass doing the navigation and all that, because those are like story problems in math and, for some reason, I always thought story problems were easy. Like, if your plane leaves Columbus at 3:00 and the wind is from two-seventy at fifteen knots, and the true airspeed is eighty-five, I could figure the true course and the arrival time and everything, no problem. That's stuff I can do.

But if somebody asks me what type of weather accompanies altostratus clouds, I couldn't answer that to save my life.

I mean, I can read a METAR and I know what all the abbreviations mean, but I totally don't understand anything about a warm front or a cold front. I know that cumulonimbus clouds are bad, but I don't know if it's the cumulo part or the nimbus part—or both—that makes them bad. And I think there are other clouds that are bad, too, but I have no idea what they are. Basically, if I ever get my pilot's license, the only time I'll ever be able to fly is when the sky is perfectly clear.

June 27

I now officially have my ground license. It's awesome. I feel like I actually accomplished something. I haven't felt like this for a long time. I was kind of an okay golfer, but I never won any tournaments. I won a yellow 4-H ribbon for some chocolate chip cookies I baked in fourth grade. That's about it.

My ground license is way cooler. Now all I have to do is set up an appointment for my physical and I can start flying. I'm kind of nervous, actually, but excited.

* * *

Dear Twinkies,

I just figured it out: the cream inside of you is like an orgasm wrapped inside the dream of me having an orgasm. Seriously. If you could replace the cake part of yourself with more cream filling—like a Twinkie that was Twinkie filling inside Twinkie filling—that'd be the greatest thing ever. Thank you for your consideration.

Sincerely,

L.J. Davenport

P.S. Even though I'm really super high right now, I'm almost completely positive that I'd feel the same way if I wasn't.

* * *

Are you a woman who feels trapped in a relationship with another woman while secretly loving another man? If so, call us at 1 (866) 99-Maury.

* * *

Why do I always laugh when Maury says, "You are *not* the father"? Even with the volume off, it's still funny. And it doesn't matter if it's the guy who runs backstage or the girl, I still have to laugh.

This time it was the guy. "Oh, boo-hoo, Maury. When she said, 'Would you like to go on *Maury* so I can tell you a horrible secret,' I didn't know it'd be bad, boo hoo."

That always cracks me up.

Now Maury's got his arm around the not-father, trying to act all like some cross between Dr. Phil and Snoop Dogg: "Yo, homes, I can izzle with your gizzle, but you gots to pizzle the bazizzle, you know what I'm sazizzling?" What a douchebag.

And now the not-father is shaking his head and Maury's still talking: "Yo, my homie. What's the pazizzle with the fazizzling shizzlenit?"

"Yo, Maury. When she said she knew Jacob is my son because we've got the same huge *beep*, I was believing it because, you know, I've got a monster in my pants. But now I know she's had sex with another guy with a big monster, and I don't think I can handle that."

"Gizzle bizzle fizzle wokajommyizzle-pazizzle."

"Maury, I may be nodding to everything you say, but that's because I'm thinking in my head: 'You're a dumbass. Yeah, you're a dumbass.'"

* * *

The sit-down part where they just sit there and yell at each other is getting old, though. As you watch, you see what a douchebag the guy always is and you start to think maybe it'd serve him right if he actually was the father, and you start to sort of hope for that.

But then Maury says, "You are *not* the father."

And the girl, who'd just gotten done saying, "I'm 187 percent sure that he's the father," runs to the back, flailing her arms and trying to cover her face at the same time, and you think, No, this was definitely better.

Still, I think they should just cut out the whole sit-down part and just get right to the results. Bring the people in assembly-line style and do about fifty paternity tests per show.

Maury would be like, "In the case of seven-month-old Cassandra, Jonathan, you are *not* the father.

"In the case of one-year-old Stanley, Carl, you are *not* the father.

"In the case of eleven-month-old Vanessa, Timothy, you are *not* the father."

Don't even mess with the midgets or the super-fat kids or the abusive wives or husbands; just do all paternity tests, all the time.

That'd be awesome.

* * *

And for God's sake, if you know your girlfriend doesn't trust you, and you get invited on *Maury*, and you're in Maury's Green Room (which you know, if you've ever seen a *Maury* episode, has about twenty million hidden cameras), and some super-hot, super-slutty, "I'm-going-on-*Maury*-to-break-up-with-my-boyfriend-because-I-need-sex-too-often" chick starts hitting on you, and you know she's twenty times too hot for you even on your best day, then you should probably think twice before dry humping her on Maury's couch. That's all I'm saying. (They just showed the preview for the next *Maury*.)

* * *

"You think this shit is funny, motherfucker?"

Oh, crap.

Ignore him, ignore him, ignore him. I'm writing, writing, writing. Busy, busy, busy. I didn't even hear you, Chainsaw, because I'm so focused on writing this paper that's not due for this class I don't have. Well, technically, I did hear you, but I figured you were talking to someone else, even though I'm the only one here, except for Tanha, who's passed out on the couch.

Rob and Adam were making fun of me for bringing my

notebook to a party; they wouldn't be making fun of me now, if they were still here.

* * *

I want to know what the hell Marpa's doing. He has to hear all the yelling. How could he not? Wouldn't a normal person come out and try to diffuse the situation? Be like, "Hey, Chainsaw, chill out. These are my guests," something like that.

I mean, yeah, we were sort of teasing Marpa earlier when we played Truth or Dare. But what are you supposed to do when somebody admits they once destroyed their whole apartment building and blamed it on a gas leak?

Actually, I think he was more bummed out when we found the pictures of him from last year, all dressed up in a suit and tie. You have to expect us to make fun of that, though, when you go around telling everyone you've always been this hardcore hippie who's never worn shoes, especially when there's contradictory video evidence on your computer. That doesn't mean you go hide somewhere for the rest of the night. Especially when you've got a psycho roommate named Chainsaw who is stomping around like he wants to kill someone.

The last time I saw Marpa, he was passing his cell phone around to everybody, saying, "Here, someone wants to talk to you."

And then the chatty chick on the phone started talking pretty much nonstop. "Antonio! I'd recognize your voice anywhere! It's me! Samantha! Remember? What're you doing in Florida? How do you know Peter?" blah, blah, blah.

I think all I got to say was something like, "Do I know you? You know Antonio's not my real name, right?" Then Marpa grabbed the phone out of my hand and went back to wherever he is now.

Come out, come out, wherever you are. You've had plenty of time to jack off or take a dump or whatever it is you're doing.

What is he doing?

Probably hiding. I guess I'd be hiding, too, if everybody I invited to a party ate all my psycho roommate's food.

*　*　*

If I was smart, I would've left when Rob and Adam did, but I didn't want to leave Tanha here. Plus, I was wa-a-a-ay too wasted. I would've had to crawl out to my car.

I had a better chance flying home. But I wouldn't have been able to stop. I would've flown all down Highway 32 and before I'd know it I would've been passing Cincinnati and St. Louis and Denver and that Lake Powell Mike's always talking about and Las Vegas and California and then I'd come out of it about half-way to Japan and I'd look down and see all that water and then I'd start thinking how refreshing it must feel and then thinking how sore my arms were and then I'd realize I was flying when I didn't know how to fly and I'd crash in the ocean and get chewed up by a big killer whale on crack that just busted out of Sea World or somewhere.

All I could really do was melt into this sticky beanbag and wait to come down.

*　*　*

So I'm basically all alone, stuck in this beanbag chair while Marpa's crazy, axe-murderer-looking roommate—who just wants a goddamned bite to eat after another goddamned double shift at motherfucking Applebee's—again goes through his list of food that's mysteriously missing from his and Marpa's kitchen.

"Four fucking slices of motherfucking pickle and pimento fucking loaf, all the motherfucking Blueberry fucking Pop Tarts, a brand-fucking-new bag of motherfucking Cheetos, three fucking cans of Cherry motherfucking Vanilla fucking Dr. cocksucking Pepper, and all the ice cream bars. All the

motherfucking, cocksucking, sonofabitching ice cream motherfucking bars. And the motherfucking leftovers from Long
John Silver's? Muh-ther-fucker. There were three fucking
hushpuppies in here."

I'm trying to act busy as hell and completely oblivious,
hoping that if I keep writing he'll assume that I'm assuming
that I've got nothing to do with whatever it is he's yelling
about.

I'm going for that vibe that says, *Hey, dude, I heard the
word "food" and so of course I knew that whatever it is you're talking about had nothing to do with me because I haven't been anywhere near your kitchen tonight. Kitchen? You and Marpa have a
kitchen? See? I didn't even know. That's how oblivious I am. I
don't know any more than Tanha, who's passed out here on the
couch. I'm minding my own business, trying to give you your privacy as you talk to whoever it is you're talking to about whatever
it is you're talking about.*

I'll keep pretending I don't notice him until I think of
something better to say than, "Maybe you have mice"—which
seems believable when you look around this crappy place.
And it's a lot better than telling him the truth: "If I knew it
was your food, I wouldn't have told Rob and Adam to come
here and help me eat everything to make up for my
CornNuts."

I hope I'm pulling it off, because I'm pretty sure this
dude is completely psycho. Like Nick-Nolte-mug shot psycho.
Like Charlie Sheen-on-a-coke-binge psycho.

Right now, he's pacing faster and faster back and forth in
a little figure-eight—fridge to stove, fridge to stove, fridge to
stove—while he tears at his Nick-Nolte-mug shot hair and
mumbles "blueberry Pop Tarts" and "motherfucking Cheetos"
between louder and louder growling noises.

I'm just writing writing writing.

Busy busy busy.

Oblivious oblivious oblivious.

Huh? What? Huh?

I just hope he doesn't look in the trash.

This dude seemed so normal a half hour ago when he got home. Well, I mean, he seemed more normal then than he seems now.

He was like, "Hey, I'm Chainsaw, Reverend Marpa's roommate. You want a bong hit?"

I took one, even though I totally didn't need it, and everything was cool for a while. We had a nice little conversation. He was like, "Pretty lame party, huh?"

"Yeah, I don't know. I got here late. There were more people here earlier."

Chainsaw picked up a piece of paper off the coffee table. "'Together we can beat the Man! Fight for fairness at ATS! The union needs your support!' What's this?"

I said. "This guy Derek was here earlier. He wants all of us to join a union."

So we were having a pretty normal conversation for a while. Then he said, "I hear you've been helping the Reverend with some of his karmic corrections."

"Yeah. I guess. Sort of."

"I haven't got to help him with one yet, but I'd be great at it," he said.

Then he leaned over to me and, in his gravelly cigarette voice, he told me about this time he stalked some dude he knew for a whole year—"I knew everything about him, son. I knew his bank PIN numbers, I knew where he went to lunch on Wednesdays, I had a key to his apartment, I set up hidden cameras in his bedroom and kitchen."

He went on and on. I was hoping for some punch line like "Since he was so homophobic, I had him convinced he was gay" or "Now, whenever he sees a Chevy ad on TV, he cries like a little girl," something like that.

Instead, Chainsaw told me how he turned the heat way up on the guy's fish tank, and then he took the guy's dog "for a permanent walk, if you know what I mean," and all this other stuff.

Then he looked right at me and he said, "Then one day he came home early and I hid in his closet and *bam!* right in the face."

He did the *bam* so loud, it made me jump out of this beanbag a little.

I just looked at him like, *What the hell?*

He winked at me again and he said, "You know what I'm talking about."

No, I don't know what you're talking about, Chainsaw. Seriously, *What the hell?* Why would he think that I would know what he's talking about? That's what I want to know. What kind of psychotic freak tells a story like that to some-body he just met? How does he know I won't go to the police as soon as I get out of here? That's what scares me. I don't know if it's a true story or if he just made it up, but he looked completely serious when he told me. I didn't know what to say, so I just kind of did a fake chuckle and I was like, "Yeah, that's pretty crazy."

"The Reverend says that maybe I can help him when he finds the guy that broke up him and his fiancée. Give him some pointers, at least. What do you think?"

"It sounds like you'd be good at it."

"I'd be fucking great at it," he said. "The Reverend says he doesn't want me to have the karmic burden of helping him with something big like that. But he says I could be his con-sultant. I can help him fuck that guy up."

That's why right now I'm pretending that I don't know anything about any food that anybody might have eaten in anybody's kitchen and that's why I'm pretending I don't hear him yelling "Motherfucker" this and "Motherfucker" that.

Here a fucker, there a fucker, everywhere a motherfucker—angry Chainsaw had some food, but now it's all gone.

I'm pretty sure he's woken up everybody in the neighborhood, plus the whole entire county and probably pretty good chunks of Ohio, Pennsylvania, West Virginia and Kentucky.

If he does whatever "*bam!*" is to some random guy in Reno he never met, I don't want to know what he does to somebody who ate all his motherfucking Blueberry fucking Pop Tarts.

"Motherfucker, motherfucker, motherfucker."

Busy busy busy. *Don't mind me*, my obliviousness clearly says, *I'm just an innocent guest who is totally oblivious to what I can only assume must be a friendly conversation between you and Marpa about whatever it is two roommates have friendly conversations about.*

"Ate all my Goddamned pickles."

That wasn't me. I hate pickles. I always have. I like pickle loaf, but that's because I always thought that the little green specks in pickle loaf were olives. Until, like, two months ago. I don't know why, because I know the difference between olives and pickles, and I know it's called pickle loaf and not olive loaf, but I just always used to think that those were little green specks of olives. Which is weird, because I don't like olives either. And now, even though I know they're pickles, I still like it. And I like relish, which I've always known was pickles. But I still hate pickles, so I know it wasn't me who ate his pickles. I don't think.

"What kind of sick motherfucking fuck eats all the motherfucking marshmallows out of another man's Lucky fucking Charms? Without the marshmallows, it's just a fucking box of Alphabits without the fucking alphabet."

Okay, that was me. But I'm still pretty sure I didn't eat the pickles.

Now he's digging in the trash. Crap. Party's over.

"Goddamned motherfucking cocksucking son of a motherfucking bitch. The cream out of my motherfucking Twinkies? The goddamned cream out of my motherfucking Twinkies?"

Crap crap crap crap crap.

June 28

God, this has to be the greatest morning ever in the whole entire history of mornings throughout the whole entire history of the universe. Seriously. First of all, I've got Tanha crashed out in my bed, lying on and under and in my sheets, hopefully drooling on my pillow. Which, alone, should put this in the top five of all-time great mornings—top two, probably—even if she does still have most of her clothes on. But then I also just took the absolute best-in-every-way-possible dump in my entire life. Plus, I've got this whole glad-to-still-be-alive giddy feeling going on. All of which makes this the best morning ever.

It's like those old beer ads they have on You-tube: "It don't get any better than this." Instead of a bunch of guys sitting around a campfire or whatever, they should have an ad with me, waiting for the incense smoke to clear out of the bathroom before I try to crawl back into bed as if I only just left for a quick sleepwalking pee.

"Hmm?" I'll say sleepily when I crawl back into bed. "No, my breath always smells this minty fresh in the morning," and then I'll flop my arm back on top of her like I thought I was dreaming about polar bears or something.

Which is why I have to wait for the smoke to clear. If there's incense smoke, then obviously I've been up long enough to burn incense, and if I've been up long enough to burn incense, then obviously I'm not as incoherently groggy as I'll be pretending to be and, if I'm not as incoherently groggy as I'll be pretending to be, then how the hell will I be able to explain why my hand will be planted on top of her little boobie?

I still can't believe Tanha is in my bed. I wish I knew

what combination of charm and good luck and offerings to whatever supreme being it took to make that happen. I keep hoping it isn't a dream. I'm actually kind of worried that I'll wake up to either a raccoon or my landlady licking peanut butter off my nuts.

I mean, I remember Chainsaw freaking out about his food, and then Tanha and I sneaked out of there the first chance we got, and then we came here and, I don't even know how, but somehow we started kissing and then she was on top of me for a while and all that hair was draped over and around my face and it was the coolest thing ever. It totally reminded me of making a blanket fort in the dining room. Only this was like eighteen million times better than playing G.I. Joes with Jeff Waters.

After I don't know how long, she was like, "Whoa, I'm dizzy."

"Do you want to lie down?"

"Yeah."

So maybe this isn't a dream after all.

Then it was like, we were spooning in my bed and my hand was in her crotch and she was wearing these little tiny sexy bikini underwear (it was too dark to see, but they felt like they were white) and then she said, "What're you doing?" Only she didn't say it mad or anything. I don't know how she said it, but she didn't say it mad.

So I said, "Teasing you."

"Well, stop teasing me." She didn't say that mad, either, I don't think.

I'd already caressed her little teeny-tiny boobies until her nipples were hard, and she never grabbed my hand or tried to stop me, so I didn't know if she wanted me to stop the teasing thing because she was on the verge of becoming uncontrollably horny, or if I was just annoying her. But I stopped.

And then, when I asked if she wanted to snuggle, she

said Yes like she was glad I asked. So that's a good sign.

I almost screwed up, though. We were all snuggled together and it felt really super nice and, like a total dumbass, I sighed all happy like and said, "This is nice," and she kind of laughed like I was a total idiot.

The only thing that saved me was I put my hand in her hair right away and I was like "And you have such beautiful hair," and she laughed because we were making fun of Adam earlier when he was hitting on her and telling her how beautiful her hair was.

I can smell her on my shirt. Kind of a combination of maraschino cherries and the color blue is the best way I can describe it. And I can't stop thinking about her voice and the way it goes into me and fills me and soothes me like warm cocoa. And her big wet silky soft pillow lips. It's like, you can hear those lips getting in the way while she talks, like her sexy little whatever accent trips over her lips when the words come out. And the way she sort of bites her bottom lip when she's thinking real hard. I'm kind of getting a stiffy just thinking about it, to tell the truth.

She makes me feel all warm and fuzzy inside—I don't know how else to explain it. I mean, before, I think I mostly just wanted her body. But now, it's like I just want *her*. All of her.

When I look in her eyes, it's like when I heard Radiohead's "Idioteque" for the first time. I was just like, *Damn! What just happened? That was amazing.* And then you want to experience that again and again and again. What are they saying? What's going on in there? What is it that makes me feel the way I feel right now?

I still want to jump her bones, though, too.

I could totally see myself eventually falling in love with her. I mean, even though we were just *sleeping* sleeping together, as opposed to *boom-chucka-boom* sleeping together, it was still the greatest thing ever. I swear to God, I don't know how anything could ever possibly be better. Unless it was Tanha and me with the boom-chucka-boom thing. That's the only thing that could even come close. I'm kind of glad we didn't do all that, though; I'd hate to not respect her now.

I think it's time to crawl back into bed.

This is going to be the most awesome day ever.

* * *

I just got home from having lunch with Tanha at that Mexican place out on East State Street. It was nice. We ate out in the shade on their patio and she took off her sunglasses—it was great the way she did it, slowly turning her glance from my face to her lap, then demurely taking them off (lightly squeezing both sides with four fingers and slowly pulling them off, whereas I grab the corner with my thumb and forefinger and kind of twist mine off) and it seemed like she did it because she couldn't see my eyes and she wanted to make sure I could see hers. And so I took mine off.

I think I did everything right and said everything right except once I asked if it seemed like we knew each other more than we should be able to for knowing each other for so short a time and she kind of shrugged her shoulders and said "Yeah, it seems like that."

I was kind of caressing my fingertips on the top of her hand when I said it and she didn't answer until I looked up to her eyes. It seemed to tell me that she thought I was getting too close too fast. So now I've got to proceed with that in mind.

The good thing is, though, when we got to her place, she was like, "Do you think I could smoke some pot with you sometime?"

"I thought you couldn't because you have that impulse control disorder thing."

"I know," she said. "But it looked like you were having so

much fun last night doing that puzzle on the Lucky Charms box."

So I've got that to look forward to—getting her stoned, her losing control—it should be fun. I just need somebody to score me some weed. I wish I still had my Grab Bag. That'd totally blow her mind.

Time for work.

* * *

Holy crap, I don't want to be here. I wish I could go back in time about nine hours and crawl back into bed with Tanha. That would be nice. It'd beat the hell out of being at work.

Every call I've had so far has been a general reading. Every single one.

They're not so bad every now and then, but when it's general reading after general reading after general reading, it's a total drag. Pretty soon, you're just praying for a call from a sexually confused teenager or a lady who found a strange woman's panties in her husband's car and she needs a psychic to find out if he's cheating on her.

General readings suck because the caller never gives you anything to work with. They answer all your leading questions with "Yes" or "No" or "Maybe" or, sometimes, "I don't know; sort of, I guess."

You basically have to just sit there, like, "oh, I see some disappointment you've had to work through; is that why you're careful about sharing your true thoughts and feelings? . . . I see someone who used to be close to you, but they're no longer around . . . and somebody else—somebody important—but they're not as close as they should be . . . you like to help people, but your current situation doesn't allow you to do as much as you'd like."

Which is pretty much what we do all the time, anyway, but with normal calls, at least they eventually say something like, "Yeah, my grandma died last year," or "Yeah, my job sucks," and you've got somewhere to go to get them talking.

When they don't give you anything, you're pretty much doing all the talking yourself for the whole twenty minutes. And you have to be interesting enough or whatever to keep them on the line. Six calls in a row like that and you've basically been talking nonstop for two whole hours. It sucks.

Plus, Liz is acting way more crazy tonight than normal, which is sort of partly our fault, I guess. But at the same time it's like, what did she expect? I mean, if you have a stupid "Name the new Banners" contest when the phones are down, you have to figure that at least some of us will write some messed up stuff on our entries. And we're not stupid; we're not putting our own names on the cards.

And how was I supposed to know that she would let all of us vote for the winners? I don't know, maybe she mentioned that, but I didn't know those would actually win. So it doesn't seem like she should be taking it all out on me.

I mean, my slogan didn't even win. Mine was something stupid like, ATS Archie says, "Positive Encouragement Never Includes Sarcasm."Adam wrote the "Constantly Use a Nurturing Tone" one and I think Jeff or somebody did the "Together We Are Terrific," and those are the two that won, so I don't see why it's all my fault.

She's given me three Step One PINs already. The only reason they weren't Step Twos is because she didn't want to have to explain them to Smeagol.

Still, it was worth it to see her make that big show of putting up her new banners and congratulating Gretchen and Katrina. "If the rest of you would apply yourselves, you could win something, too."

All Gretchen and Katrina had to do was say, "Those aren't the banner slogans we wrote; we don't deserve these crappy prizes," but instead, they both were like, "Oh, yeah, that's mine," all happy to take some gift certificate that everybody knew they didn't deserve.

The best part was when Liz brought Smeagol out for more pictures. Part of her never-ending ass-kissing quest to be the Queen of ATS. We couldn't hear what he said, but it must've been something like, "Take those down now, you stupid, big-assed bitch," because she basically ripped them off the wall and slammed them into the trash can—we heard that—and then she went crying out into the parking lot.

She's been on my ass ever since.

Actually, now that I think about it, she gave me the PIN for Inefficiency before any of the banner stuff even happened. And that one was total bullcrap, by the way. All I did was took my Tuition Reimbursement Request form up to the podium, and she came up to me like, "You know you're supposed to be logged into your phone within four minutes of clocking in."

I was like, "I've still got a few minutes. It's not even three o'clock yet."

"It goes by when you clock in, not what time it is. You should know that after going through training—twice."

I just kind of ignored her after that and took my time, chit-chatting with the big-boobed girl at the podium, because, even though Liz was technically right, it's a stupid rule and everybody knows it's a stupid rule—Tim even told us in training that it's a stupid rule—which is why nobody ever gets a PIN for it as long as they're logged in four minutes after their shift starts. Except for me, now.

Then Liz got all nosey about the form I was filling out. She was like, "You know they'll deny that, right?"

"Why?"

"No reason."

The podium girl told me, "If they don't approve it, you can fill out a Request Review form."

I asked, "What if they deny it the second time?"

"Oh," she said. "It's a nice day outside. You need to think positive."

I positively wish my break lasted longer than fifteen minutes. I wanted to wait to take my break until I saw Tanha get up for hers—do one of those, "Oh, what a coincidence that we happen to be taking our break at the same time!" things—and then I'd be like, "Hey, do you want to get together tonight?"

But after two hours of general readings, and a new PIN from Liz for Unapproved beverage container, I was just like, Screw it, I need a break now.

* * *

Irene just came up to me and said, "Just because you *can* do something, it doesn't mean you should. It's not always easy to know the right thing to do. When it's clear what the right thing is, that's a gift from God. Don't waste it. You have some choices coming up. You're a smart boy. Be good."

Then she left.

That was weird.

* * *

Dear Vending machine vagina,

What the hell, dude? Seriously. What possible reason could you have for replacing the CornNuts in every single vending machine in the whole entire building with TGI Fridays Cheddar and Bacon Potato Skins? You know they taste like ass, right? And don't act like you replaced the CornNuts with those crappy strawberry Danishes; all you did was moved the Danishes from B4 to B5 and then put the Ass Chips in B4.

And what's up with those strawberry Danishes, by the way? Could you not find a brand cheaper than Awrey's? I'm guessing you couldn't. My question is, why did you have to pick the cheapest, crappiest Danishes in the entire world for our vending machine? I mean, I'm sure the Hostess ones cost more, thus cutting your profit margin, but how much money are you making when nobody buys the Awrey's ones? I'm still ashamed and disgusted with myself for eating one three months ago. First of all, they don't have hardly any icing. And then they position their label in such a way that you don't know until it's too late that there's not enough strawberry spooge to even cover one of your nipples. I guarantee that nobody will ever buy one of those more than once.

And I wouldn't buy the TGI Fridays Ass Chips if I had another choice. But the Cheetos and Doritos are a total rip off since they started filling their little bags less than half full. "Settling of contents," my ass; they're just trying to screw us.

So because of you, vending machine vagina, I'm stuck with the choice of starving to death or eating these ass-tastic bags of crap.

How do you sleep at night?

Sincerely,

L.J. Davenport

*   *   *

Dear TGI Fridays Cheddar and Bacon Potato Skins inventor or flavor tester or whatever you are,

I want to thank you, from the bottom of my heart, for creating TGI Fridays Cheddar and Bacon Potato Skins. Your chips have saved me the hassle and disgrace of having to tongue-punch somebody's fart box just to know what ass tastes like. Now I know.

I gave you another chance. I thought, maybe my last experience with your chips wasn't indicative of their real flavor, maybe it was just a bad bag, so I figured I'd try them again (and it's not like I had a whole lot of choice, since the vending machine vagina replaced all the CornNuts with your dumbass potato skins). It has been confirmed, though: your Cheddar and Bacon Potato skins definitely do taste like ass.

I'm curious, though. How did you come up with this unique flavor. Let me guess (I'm a psychic, after all): Were you sitting in your kitchen with your handful of spices on your right side and some wrinkly old guy's hairy ass on your left, thinking, *Okay, maybe a little more cumin. And some paprika*—sniff, sniffffff—*and maybe if we add some of this stuff here, maybe that'll capture the full-bodied essence of ass.*

Seriously, how did you get your job? You suck.

Sincerely,

L.J. Davenport

* * *

Before work, I stopped by the Cool Spot to get my CornNuts and Sobe green tea for the night. I had two bottles of green tea and two bags of CornNuts—$6.78 total, with tax—and both my credit card and my debit card were declined.

I mean, I know I'm not the best at balancing my checkbook and all that, considering I don't actually balance my checkbook, ever. But I don't know how I can have no money in either my checking account or on my credit card. Still, I was thinking positive, like, *Okay, no big deal, I'll just pick up some extra shifts at work.* I mean, rent's due on Thursday, but we get paid on Friday, so I figure I can ignore the landlady for one day, tell her I'm late for work and I'll get it to her after work. That sort of thing.

So before I finished my break, I logged into Vantive, but it says I can't pick up any extra shifts because I'm still in OJT probation, which doesn't make sense because yesterday was supposed to be my last day of OJT.

So I figure, okay, this is just a mistake; I'll talk to Smeagol to see when they'll update the system.

But then Smeagol tells me that I'm still in OJT because I didn't complete the fifteen consecutive days of training.

"Yes I did," I said. "I was here every day."

"You missed three days during the second week of training."

It took me a while to figure out what the hell he was talking about until I finally realized that he was referring to those three days that he sent Derek and me downstairs to take tech support and sales calls while everybody else was upstairs double-jacked with someone.

"But you were the one who sent us downstairs."

"Regardless of the reason," he said, "it's still company policy. You need fifteen consecutive days of training."

I was too shocked or whatever to be pissed. I'm pissed now that I've had time to think about it, but then I was just like, *what the hell?* Plus, he got me all confused when he acted all like he was doing me a favor for not making me repeat training or OJT again. All I have to do is not miss work for the next eight days.

Until then, I can't add any shifts—oh, and also, I'll get paid as a trainee instead of a regular TSR during those eight days.

Crap, man.

I swear, it's like they're just trying to piss you off enough to quit.

Derek was like, "See? This is why we need a union."

June 29

The next time somebody from anywhere near southeastern Ohio says to me, "Hey, L.J., we're having a party. You should come," I'll . . . actually, I don't know what I'll do, but I won't go to their party.

I don't care how many times they tell me, "Oh, we've got so-o-o-o much weed," or, "Oh, we'll get so-o-o-o drunk," or, "Oh, there'll be all these women who are s-o-o-o drunk and stoned."

Or, "Oh, we're going to party in the woods."

"Hell, no," I'll say. "Hell, no." I mean, when I picture myself in *Deliverance*, I like to imagine that I'm Burt Reynolds, or at least Jon Voight. Not Ned Beatty. Never Ned Beatty. I don't ever again want to hear "Dueling Banjos" strumming through my head, knowing that I'm the most likely candidate to be squealing like a pig before the sun goes down.

The big-boobed podium girl at work, Regina, heard me telling Rob that I needed a bag of weed as soon as possible. She was like, "My roommate and I are having a party tomorrow. You should come. We can get you a bag then."

"All right."

Then today, she called and told me to bring my hiking boots because we were going to party in the woods. I was kind of psyched because, even though I've been in Athens for three years, I didn't really know any good hiking trails. I thought it'd be great to finally hike with some people who were super familiar with the woods around here.

When I got to their house, hardly anybody was there. It was just me and Regina and this wookie-looking beast chick whose name I forgot right away and the QA from work whose name I thought was Ben, but apparently it's not. When I told him I thought his name was Ben, he was like, "I thought *your* name was Larry Jacobsen." He was kind of being a little bitch about it, too.

But other than that, we were having fun; I was talking to Regina about work and I was talking to Chewbacca and Not-Ben about guns, to show them I'm a manly, outdoorsy man, too.

Then somehow they started talking about how you want to have your extra ammo clips on your left hand so you can—*quick*—reload. Your handcuffs, too (and your baton). Flashlight. Nothing but your piece on your gun side, buddy. At one point, I was able to add, "There's not much recoil in a nine-millimeter, so all you're really doing is increasing the report with a ported one."

So they assumed—or at least pretended to assume—that I knew what I was talking about, and I pretended to know what they were talking about, but the conversation was way over my head long before that. About the only thing I did know was that nobody would mess with *us* in the woods.

Then Chewbacca started talking about Iraq and all the weapons they had there, and she's using all these abbreviations and acronyms or whatever that I never heard of and then she got all sentimental for a minute, talking about how she missed it and how there's no better high than being in combat, having people shooting at you, shooting back. I was just sitting there thinking, I have nothing to add to this conversation.

Finally we were ready to leave after Chewbacca finished explaining how to lead a running target when you're gunning down hostiles. I found out then that nobody else was coming to their "party." For some shady reason, we couldn't take their minivan, even though it apparently runs just fine, so Chewbacca said to me, "You won't be able to fit in our car unless you squeeze in, and I wouldn't want to squeeze in if I were you, so you can follow us."

I was like, "Okay."

And then we're almost all ready and Chewbacca said, "I'll ride with L.J."

I didn't think anything of it; I was just glad to know I wouldn't get lost driving to the trail.

It was Chewbacca and me in my car and Not-Ben and Regina in their car. Everything seemed cool. But before we drove even a block, Chewbacca got all serious and said, "We need to talk."

I was like, "Okaay."

And then she said, "I think it's great that Regina has you to talk to—"

"Yeah, she seems pretty cool."

She went on, "Well, Regina hasn't had that in a while and it's good for her."

Okay.

She went on and on and then she said, "The thing is, we don't even *know* you."

I was like Okaaaaaaay, wondering where this was going.

Then she babbled some more and said, "I don't want you at our house when I'm not there."

Okay. It wasn't like I'd ever planned to, anyway.

But then she said, like I'd already done something which I hadn't even thought about doing, "Come *on*. We're married. We've got a house and a dog and an aquarium full of gold-fish."

I didn't see that coming. It took me a few seconds to figure out that she meant Regina was married to *her*, which is okay I guess, but I just wasn't expecting it.

Then she said, "If you've already done something, just be a man and tell me now."

I don't know if she was waiting for me to say something

or what, but she just sat there and didn't say anything and I didn't know what to say, so I just stupidly said for the third time in five blocks, "Yeah, she totally reminds me of my sister."

She didn't say anything after that, and I didn't know what to say, and I didn't know the etiquette or whatever on turning the volume back up on the stereo, so we just sat there silently the whole rest of the drive.

Finally we got to the trailhead. I felt guilty because everybody was carrying way more than me. Chewbacca had a big military looking backpack, Regina had a big daypack full of food and water and whatever else, and Not-Ben had this stuffed-full worn leather backpack. All I had was my little book bag with a bottle of water and my notebook—everything I figured I'd need while we hung out comfortably somewhere at the edge of the woods.

Then we started on the trail. And we walked . . .

and walked . . .

and walked. . . .

And . . . walked. Into these deep woods. We hadn't been on anything even remotely resembling a trail for at least thirty minutes, and we were way past beyond being anywhere near the vicinity of anything that could reasonably be referred to as "the edge of the woods." It sucked.

I ran out of water.

Then I said, partly to find out how much longer we'd be walking and partly to break the ice, "This isn't the part where you take the new guy and dump his body out in the woods, is it?"

I've said the exact same thing on at least three similar occasions. The group would always laugh at what a ridiculously preposterous idea it was, and then we'd talk more now that they realized I was the type of guy who joked at the mere thought of death. But, instead of laughing and chatting like everyone else always has, these people just got completely silent.

That's when I realized that—*oh, crap!*—I didn't know these people, either. They seemed nice and normal, but so did Ted Bundy and Jeffrey Dahmer, didn't they? I started remembering all the things we'd been talking about earlier—guns and hunting and how it's fun to watch pumpkins just *explode* from a shotgun blast.

Did Not-Ben have a weird glint in his eye when he was talking about field dressing a deer?

And how many times did he mention that he can't wait for a new *Texas Chainsaw Massacre* movie?

And I remembered that *Not-Ben* was pouring a couple handfuls of .22 bullets into a little nylon pouch before we left the house, and I knew that, even though a .22 doesn't have much stopping power, fifty of them in my ass would be enough to make me part of the Appalachian ecosystem. Even if he didn't have a .22 in that big backpack of his—or a .44; he'd asked earlier if I'd ever shot a .44 magnum because that was a "kick ass fucking gun"—he had a huge knife on his belt.

So now, "Dueling Banjos" was *pounding* in my head and I kept getting these images of Ned Beatty that I just didn't want to think about, and we kept going deeper and deeper into the woods, and then *Not-Ben* would keep straggling way back behind us somewhere and I didn't know if he was loading his gun or building some kind of . . . something, and nobody was talking and I didn't know where I was and none of my friends knew where *I* was and my phone was in the car and, even though these seemed like okay people, if they were going to take me out into the woods to kill me, this'd be exactly how they'd do it.

I tried to reassure myself, *We wouldn't have had that talk in the car if they were going to do that, would we?*

Maybe. Who knows how the mind of a psychotic murderer works?

So I started looking all over the ground for anything to defend myself with. I figured Not-Ben was the one I'd have to take out first, since I could outrun Regina and since Chewbacca had the biggest backpack. I got the impression that Chewbacca was a good wife/husband/partner (even if she did turn out to be a homicidal pig-raping, devil-worshipping psychopath) and that she'd protect Regina first, even if it meant missing out on the opportunity to sacrifice my body to whatever god of the Appalachians they worshipped.

So I had that going for me.

But I still didn't have anything to defend myself with. And, even if I did, I couldn't start taking them out one by one, when they least expected it, because there was still a chance that they *didn't* bring me up here to sacrifice me, or pig rape me, or make me a part of their hillbilly coven. But I needed to be prepared.

I kept asking myself, "What would Jet Li do?"

My car keys were in my book bag, but that would be bad if my bag fell off while running away. So I surreptitiously grabbed my keys and put them in my pocket. Then I saw this big sturdy stick and I picked it up and pretended it was my walking stick. I tried to pay attention to where the hell we were on this sort-of-trail. That didn't work, except sometimes I could see through the trees and tell if I was going North or South.

I kept asking innocent little questions like, "Which way is the river?" because I figured I could always float back home if I had to. And they'd answer questions like that, but we always just kept on going deeper and deeper into the woods.

Finally, after over two and a half hours, we stopped on this clearing. Regina said she had to pee and Chewbacca was like, "We'll go down into that ravine to give you some privacy." I figured that was it; I'd be naked and tied to a tree in less than five minutes, squealing like a pig. I'll get killed before I even get a chance to fly a plane and impress Tanha. About the last thing I really wanted to do was go down into a deep ravine in the middle of nowhere with two people I didn't know, but I couldn't think of any way out of it.

I wanted to stay on top with Regina where I figured I'd be safe, but I knew I couldn't do that after the talk I had with Chewbacca in the car. It's not like I could say, "Yeah, I used to always watch my sister pee."

I kept reminding myself that I hadn't had any weird dreams lately that warned me of anything, and the survival experts always say to trust your gut because you can usually sense approaching danger. So that was good.

But then again, I was nervous as hell as I stood on top of that clearing, and I was about to go down into some remote ravine with a wookie woman who didn't seem to like me much and her friend who had a big knife and bullets and maybe a gun . . . so maybe it wasn't so good.

I'd been trying for the last hour to slyly ask Not-Ben what he had in his bag, but he always pretended he didn't hear, and it wasn't one of those things you wanted to keep asking, because maybe he'd snap and be like, "You want to know what's in my bag, motherfucker?" and then he'd pull out his .22 with his extra clips and that would be the end of it.

But I didn't know what else to do, other than running aimlessly through the woods like a lost little schoolgirl. So I took a deep breath, held tight to my stick and, as I walked down the hill, rehearsed in my head my plan of attack: swing my stick into Not-Ben's crotch, swing it across Not-Ben's face, poke it into Chewbacca's stomach, poke it into Chewbacca's eye or uppercut her in the chin, grab Not-Ben's bag and run like hell while digging for his gun.

As we hiked down, I saw that at least there were no crude pentagrams made out of fallen logs, and there weren't any tiki torches set up. No coven of hillbilly witches. So that was good; there'd be only two to fight off.

They gave me the pipe first, but there was no *way* I was getting baked—even if they didn't kill me, I still had a buttload of walking to do to get out of these stupid woods—so I pretended to take a hit, and another when it came back around, and then I faked a hacking cough or two and watched for any sudden movements. There weren't any. Until Regina yelled something and Chewbacca yelled back, "What?" and she didn't answer.

Chewbacca and Not-Ben ran super-fast up that super-steep hill. I was trying to keep up to show I cared as much about Regina's safety as they did. But I was too slow. Then it occurred to me that maybe I shouldn't show that I cared as much about Regina's safety as they did.

So I slowed down.

Then it occurred to me that maybe her yelling was the signal to start the sacrifice and/or the strap-on pig rape.

So I stopped.

Then I turned around. And then I sprinted faster than I ever thought I could possibly sprint over sticks and logs and moss-covered rocks and through thorny vines and prickly bushes and one spindly little tree-ish thing that gashed the crap out of my face.

I ran like that, in God-knows-what-direction, for at least five minutes. It would've been longer but I was holding my stick kind of too-horizontal when I tried to run between two trees. That hurt like hell. I don't know if it knocked the wind out of me when I clotheslined myself or if it knocked the wind out of me when I fell backwards on my ass, but that hurt, too. But I had a chance then to hear between my gasps that there was nobody behind me, so at least I didn't have to worry about getting Ned Beatty-ed by a bunch of crazy war-vet witches with strap-ons.

But I didn't catch a buzz, either. And I didn't know where the hell I was or how far I was from my car. And I'm pretty sure I broke my ass-bone, and the whole front of my body looks like I got attacked by a weed whacker.

When I finally got home, it was after 7:00. I missed the Reds game. I don't even care. They lost again anyway. I'm just happy I'm still alive and that my alimentary canal is still intact. I must've hiked at least fifteen miles. It sucked.

I just wanted to buy a bag, maybe find a quiet spot to take Tanha on a date. It didn't happen.

At least the night can only get better, so I have that to look forward to.

*   *   *

Crap, I just realized that I forgot to call the doctor to schedule my flight physical.

June 30

I finally remembered to call the doctor's office to schedule my flight physical and the nurse lady or receptionist or whoever was like, "When can you come in?"

"I'd like to do it today, if I could. How long does it take? What all do they do?"

She said they do something, something, something and something, but the only word I heard was, "urinalysis." Then she said, "Since you're free today, we can get you in at four o'clock."

"Oh, I just remembered I can't do it today. I have to take my grandma for a walk."

"How about tomorrow?"

"I have to work. I might be able to do it next Tuesday."

"Four o'clock?"

"Okay."

Yeah, that didn't sound suspicious at all. I was going to say I had to take my dog for a walk, but then I figured that would be a stupid excuse, so I said "grandma" instead, but then I didn't have anything to follow it with. I might as well have just told the lady that, if I took a drug test today, I'd light it up like a Christmas tree.

So I have a week to figure out how to pass a drug test. And I probably have to really pass, because she probably put a big red sticky note next to my name that says, "Double check his pee."

*   *   *

I just got off the phone with this lady at this little printing place where I applied for a job. It was just like, doing graphics and stuff in Photoshop, which I'd be awesome at.

I thought we had sort of a decent phone interview, but

157

when I told the guy my name, he got real quiet all of a sudden. Then I could hear him put his hand over the phone and I could hear him talking to someone in the background.

After a while, this angry old lady gets on the phone and she's all like, "Now you listen here, this is a family business with a good reputation and we don't want your kind around. You can call the ACLU and you can sue us or do whatever you want. This business has been in our family for over fifty years, but we'll close it all down before we hire a child molester to work for us." *Click.*

I was just like, *What the hell was that?*

I mean, I'm not really bummed that I didn't get the job. I can't really afford to quit ATS until they pay my flight school tuition. Plus, if I get a new job, it might somehow mess up whatever I might have going with Tanha, but the whole child molester thing kind of freaked me out. I don't know what that was about.

July 1

I got in to work early today, hoping I could finally catch Tanha and say, "Hey, are we still getting together tonight after work?" I never saw her. But Rob and Adam were there and the first thing Rob says to me is, "I heard you met Artie Conrad." And then they both laughed.

"Who?"

"Artie. Regina's partner."

"Her name's Artie?"

"It's actually Arati," Rob said. "She looks more like an Artie, though, don't you think?"

Or a Chewbacca. I didn't say that, though. I was like, "Yeah, I met her. We went on this long-ass hike from hell."

They kept laughing like they were in on some joke, and then they started going through all these stories about all these people she's beaten up and how she busted Rob's windshield (I missed something in that story) and broke the door handle on his car and how she blew up somebody's bathroom making meth and a bunch of other stuff like that.

When I told them about the conversation we had in the car, they thought it was just the funniest thing in the world.

Then I had to tell them all about the hike and how I got clotheslined by a stick (I told them I was chasing after a rabbit, too; I didn't want it to get around that I was running away) and then they spent the next five minutes arguing about whether or not Chewbacca's still making meth.

Rob was like, "I've been to their place, man, and she's not making meth anywhere inside there."

Adam said, "I'll bet you money that she's doing it somewhere. She's got that sulfur smell oozing from her pores."

"I'm telling you, man, she's got absolutely no place to do

it."

"You said yourself she still spends all her spare time cleaning those old Indian arrowheads."

"You don't need to be on meth to do that."

They kept going back and forth like that.

I just figured, no big deal, right? It's not like I'm going on another hike with them and I'll sure as hell never go over to their house when Chewbacca's not there and I'll avoid the hell out of Regina and the podium when I'm at work.

But then I check my email when I get home after work and there's this crazy-ass email from Regina, saying . . . I don't remember exactly what it said, but there was something about the rage and jealousy her roommate feels for me (she kept referring to Chewbacca as her "roommate," instead of wife or partner or lover or whatever), and then some other crap which finally made it obvious to me that the whole expedition into the woods—supposedly to get me a bag of weed—was her way of using me to make Chewbacca jealous.

And then she had some other stuff in the email, like asking if I wanted to go over to her place when her Chewbacca goes to California and crap.

What the hell?

I talked to Derek about it after he read the email (he came over after work to pick up some cash for a bag; I figured this'd give him something to talk about besides how he's for sure starting a union at work). He asked why I wasn't even going to write Regina back or call her, and so I told him about Heather.

I knew Heather from when I was dating Ashley. After Ashley and I broke up, I never saw Heather until one night when I was working at the country club. This was about a month after high school graduation. Heather pulls up, and she's all surprised that I'm still working there and she just happened to come in because she needed to use the phone and I just happened to be working that night, and oh wow what a coincidence.

We chatted a bit after she was done with her call and she told me that she and her psycho boyfriend had broken up and I was thinking *Alright*, because this was a *smoking*-hot chick. *Smoking*-hot.

I don't remember if I gave her my phone number—I probably did—and then she left and I didn't think any more about it because it was one of those summers where a lot was going on: golf every day—practice and giving lessons and gripping clubs and playing tournaments—plus, we were hitting a *lot* of concerts and partying pretty much all the time, plus, Brian was working for his uncle and he got this huge box with a thousand doses of Valium and something else, I can't remember what.

I just remember that one night, we didn't have anything going on, so I dosed up on the Valium early—I'm pretty sure we were doing a lot of Whip-its that summer, too—and I was out when the phone rang. It was Heather. She was all like, "Do you want to go out tonight? I'll pay for the beer, and the gas, blah blah blah" . . . I don't remember what all, but I remember she said she'd pay for the gas and the beer. I mean, what're you *supposed* to say to that?

So I'm at her place about an hour later—I can't remember what we had floating around that summer to wake me up, but it worked—and we're driving back to my house (she lived in Fairfield, a block away from Ashley) and there's this car just totally on my ass and I say, "There's a car just totally on my ass," and she turns around and she says, all freaking, "Oh God! it's Gene!"

I said, "I thought you guys broke up."

"We did," she said.

I said, "It doesn't matter, anyway. He doesn't know you're with me."

"Yes he does."

"How?"

"I told him."

I was just like, *What the hell?*

After a while, he got off our ass, but there was no way I was taking her to my place, no matter *how* much I wanted to explore those big, beautiful breasts in the privacy of my own bedroom (Mom and Dad were at some convention somewhere, so I had the house to myself). So I took her to the country club. It was closed. I had a key. It was perfect.

So we were on the couch, getting hot and heavy, then she'd go down to the restroom and come back and be completely out of the mood and so I'd do my magic and we'd get going hot and heavy again and then she'd go down to the restroom and be completely out of the mood again. We went through that cycle one or two more times and then I was ready to call it a night.

I took her home without getting any skin-on-skin contact (not skin that mattered, anyway) and didn't think much more about it.

A couple days later, I'm at work. We used to have this little pouch of towel money—whenever somebody needed a towel, they'd give us a quarter and we'd give them a towel—and we used to dig into the towel money when we wanted some CornNuts or something from the candy machine.

So I'm sitting there, digging in the towel money, drooling at the thought of these CornNuts I'm about to be eating, and this car drives real slow by the big front window, and then I see the driver pointing at me.

So I'm thinking, *Oh, crap! somebody just busted me digging into the towel money and they're going to tell Doug.*

But then I heard the car squeal its tires (which nobody ever did there) as it turned around at the end of the parking lot, and then as he drove back around real slow again, that's when I realized it was Gene the psycho boyfriend.

Or no, before that—I think it was before that—I'm home and I'm all in one of those super-happy, we're-going-to-do-acid-tonight moods when my phone rings and I answer it all happy and the guy asks how I am and I remember I said, all happy, "I'm doing *great*," because this girl, Amie Henderson, had just that summer given me a lecture because I used to always just say, "Oh, I'm okay" when people asked how I was, and she said I reminded her of Eeyore.

So I'm excitedly happy, like I'd just gotten laid or something, and eventually I realize the guy on the other end doesn't share my zest for life.

Finally he says, all serious, "Do you know who this is?"

I said I didn't and he said "This is Gene,"

I didn't realize who Gene was at first until he said that he wanted to get together and talk about why I'm screwing around with his girlfriend, blah blah blah.

I mean, what're you *supposed* to say to that?

It was a couple days later when he showed up at the country club. And then he told a friend of mine from Fairfield that he was going to beat me over the head with a tire iron until they had to dig me out of a ditch with a spoon.

Then he showed up at the country club again, only this time, he waited for me down at the bottom of our long driveway so he could . . . whatever.

I had Kurt Mozelli give me a ride home that night, and I found out from my friend that Gene had waited for me till three in the morning. Then he just started showing up at the club—he'd never come in, he'd just yell and cuss at me from the parking lot: "come out here so I can kick your ass, motherfucker"—that sort of thing. It was embarrassing.

He came one time while we were putting on one of our golf tournaments—all these upstanding golf parents looking at me while this freak's screaming and cussing at me. It sucked. Plus, I'd been trying all summer to get something going with Amie, and I had to explain that I couldn't pick her up because my car was at the country club and then she asked why, and this was before I really lied to women so much, so I told her.

She was like, "Why were you messing around with this girl if you want to go out with me?" There were no way I could fix that. As I think about it now, I should've been the one wanting to kick Gene's dumb ass.

I assumed he'd just eventually cool off, but that didn't seem to be happening, so finally I broke down and called Ashley and I was just like, "What the hell?"

She'd already heard all about it and she started bitching me out, "You should've known better than to go out with her, blah blah blah; you knew they were going out, blah blah; she just does this every few months to piss him off, then he beats the crap out of the guy, and then they're fine again." She says all this like I should've known it. "You *knew* they were going out. You *knew* he'd beat the crap out of you, blah blah blah."

I tried to explain that I barely even knew that Heather girl, and that I'd only met her psycho boyfriend once, but she was completely unsympathetic.

I didn't know what to do, so I just started golfing more and more and more—all the time, actually—with Casey, this big, bulky bodybuilder who had only golfed seriously for about two years. It sucked to golf with him because he was slow as hell. He took about twenty practice swings before each shot, plus, I don't think he hit one fairway that whole summer.

Still, it was better than trying to golf in a body cast.

All I could do was just hope for summer to hurry up and get over with so I could get away to college far, far away. That's one of the main reasons I went to OU instead of Miami.

So Derek wants to know why I don't want to talk to Regina after she used me to make her psycho roommate/wife/husband/partner jealous. Says it like I somehow owe her something or like it's the polite thing to do. Screw that. I'm avoiding the hell out of her. I don't care if I never talk to her ever again.

*　　*　　*

At least one good thing happened today. Tanha left me another secret admirer note on my windshield after work: "I've been thinking about you all day. I didn't know if you'd come in to work tonight. I'm glad that you did. I haven't been able to stop smiling since I first saw you walk back to the break room. Thank you for making my day. Until next time. . . ."

So that was nice.

July 2

Memorandum
  To: All ATS employees
  From: Thomas Snyder
  Date: July 2
  Re: The risk of losing our union free advantage

Recent comments we have heard have compelled us to outline for you just a few of the things you would lose if we no longer had the benefit of a union free workplace. Here are a few things you should know about a unionized business environment:

The relationship between employees and supervisors would become less collegial.

All supervisor/employee communication would be controlled by the union.

Employee suggestions for changes and improvements to the workplace environment are usually resisted by a union.

Employees would no longer be promoted or rewarded based upon their performance.

There could be an interruption of ATS service or production because of a possible work stoppage.

We would no longer be able to attract the best workers who refuse to be employed in a union workplace.

ATS operational costs could increase by up to 25%.

Often, the best employees are either forced out or choose to leave after a union arrives.

The worst workers would be protected by the union and best workers would not be rewarded in the same way that they are now. *Look at your fellow employees on the call floor who are most in favor of a union. Are they your role models? Your leaders? The TSRs you look up to? Nine out of ten times I bet the answer is NO!*

Unions, by their very nature, must foster distrust between employees and employers in order to justify their existence.

Unions take credit for any benefits or wages received by employees, even though everyone knows that the employee is always paid by their employer, not a union.

A union would not allow us to react quickly to changes in an ever-evolving teleservices business climate.

ATS employees will no longer work toward a common goal and, instead, become helpless victims in a unionized business.

It is difficult to correct inefficient or ineffective work practices in a unionized business.

Polls show that even employees believe that non-union businesses have a noticeable advantage or unionized businesses.

Unions consistently discredit management and present management as the enemy.

Unions often hire outside agencies to harass employers.

Unionized workers will be required to follow the guidelines of their contract, even when they morally and ethically disagree with those guidelines.

A unionized workforce is contractually obligated to fulfill the requirements of a new, binding contract that must be adhered to by not only the employer but also each employee. Even if you personally disagree with that contract, you are still obligated to fulfill it.

You cannot turn back. Changes cannot be made to the contract without a new, delayed, vote by the union. Before you fill out a union petition or persuade a union to invade ATS, consider the consequences.

Please consider your future and the future of your friends and coworkers of ATS before thinking about joining a union. Think of the damage a union can cause.

Thank you!!
Thomas Snyder
ATS

* * *

Bust a nut, bust a nut. Grab a bag of CornNuts and bust a nut. They're lightly toasted and loud as helllllllll. Enjoy yourself. We won't tell.

* * *

Do people seriously not know how loud CornNuts are? I mean, Regina came into the break room just now and sat down across from me, and now she's talking to me, but all I hear is *Crunch, crunch, crunch, crunch.* Eating CornNuts is like having headphones inside your head and they're cranked up to eleven, with "Crunch, crunch, crunch" playing on repeat.

One time I was partying at Woody's apartment and, after everyone went to bed, I stayed up practicing hockey on their Xbox because I was tired of getting my ass kicked. About an hour later, Woody's girlfriend comes out of his bedroom and she was like, "What've you been eating? We can hear you through the walls." The next day, everyone was making fun of my "feeding frenzy," so it seems like Regina would have to know I can't hear a word she's saying. But she keeps talking. Her lips are moving, anyway.

I figured if I just pretended to be busy writing, she'd eventually just leave, but that doesn't seem to be happening.

Maybe I should tell her that I can't hear her, but then

she'd just repeat whatever it was, and I'd have to not eat my CornNuts while she's repeating it and I've only got fifteen minutes for my break, and I want to smoke a cigarette and take a leak before I go back out on the call floor, and I've been trying to politely avoid her, anyway, since the whole car ride with Chewbacca, so I'll just smile and nod every now and then and pretend like I'm listening while I'm writing something totally unrelated to whatever the hell she's saying.

* * *

Viking Boy's question of the day: "When a naked woman bends over, does it look from behind like a carousel or a Buddhist temple?"

* * *

This is the second night this week that Tanha has blown me off (and not in the good way). I was afraid to write about how psyched I was that we were getting together tonight because I was afraid I might jinx it somehow or something, but that doesn't seem to matter now.

Anyway, I just checked my email to see if she wrote me anything like, "Hey, I'm running late, but I'll be there at two—is it all right if I sleep at your place?" No such luck.

But I did have another email from Regina. At least this one was short. All it said was, "Here's the website I told you about tonight" (I assume she meant when she was talking and I was eating CornNuts).

So I click on the link and go through all the "you must be 18 years old" stuff, which should've been my first warning, and then, Bam!

I don't know what I was expecting, but I definitely wasn't expecting a gazillion naked pictures of Regina all over the place.

Don't get me wrong, I like porn as much as the next guy (unless that next guy is Adam), and I'm all for women sending me naked pictures of themselves. In theory. But this is like, from zero to porn in 4.2 seconds. I think that would kind of scare me even if there wasn't a big, hairy Chewbacca situation going on.

Plus, maybe I'm old fashioned, but I prefer the porn where the girl's all shy like, "Are you sure no one will see these pictures?" or sometimes where she's like, "Tee-hee, I can't believe I'm doing this."

I can also get into the porn where she's kind of like, "Oh, I forgot you had a camera. I'm just relaxing like I normally do; I hope you don't mind that I'm naked. I just don't like to wear clothes when I'm at home reading the newspaper, or drinking my tea, or doing yoga."

That's the kind of porn I like.

Personally, I've never been too interested in the porn where the girl's like, "Look at all the things I can cram up my butt."

Apparently, Regina is into it—making it, anyway.

She ended her email with, "Let me know if you have any questions."

I have a bunch of questions. Like, first of all, "Doesn't that hurt?" and, "Did you start small and work your way up to the Sobe tea bottle, or just one day think to yourself, 'I wonder if this would fit'?" and, "When you do number two, is it like super-ginormous around?"

It's the last one that I'm most curious about, but I can't think of one single situation where I could ask somebody that.

Adam's always saying that, when I get older, I'll have a better appreciation for weird porn, but I don't know. I can't imagine a day where I'll ever be like, "I want a woman who can fit an assortment of kitchen appliances up her fart box." If I ever become an international drug smuggler, maybe. But I'm pretty sure I still wouldn't find it sexy.

I also want to ask, "Aren't you worried about getting CornNuts dust in your happy places?" and, "Do you know that Sobe Green Tea looks just like pee when you pour it on yourself like that?" God, I hope she doesn't.

Does it get worse? Why, yes. Yes, it does.

I'm scrolling through all these pictures where she's contorted in different ways and dressed up in different slutty outfits, when I get down to these later ones where there's this girl with short straight black hair wearing a Catwoman outfit.

I'm not exactly sure, but I think my thoughts went something like this:

Hey, that kind of looks like the Catwoman I had sex with in April behind Konneker Hall.

Then: *I was pretty schwasted, but it looks like her.*

Then: *No, wait, it is her! See the snake tattoo around her bellybutton?*

Then: *Does that mean Regina knows my Catwoman? That'd be awesome!*

Then: *Here's some of Catwoman without her mask.*

Then: *Hey, didn't Regina have a tattoo around her bellybutton, too?*

Then: *Oh crap! Scroll up! Scroll up! Scroll up!*

Then: *Now back down! Back down! Back down!*

Then: *Look at the eyes. Look at the pictures where she doesn't have the mask. Now imagine her with straight black hair. Now imagine Catwoman with blonde hair.*

Then: *What about that piercing?*

Then: *Oh, crap.*

Then: *Now I know why I've never gotten any attendance points when I've clocked in late.*

So, yeah. The Catwoman I had sex with in April and Regina are apparently the same person. I don't know. It was like, she was wearing a mask, and I was wasted as hell, and it's not like I ever paid a whole lot of attention to Regina in the first place, so I guess it's possible.

I still didn't want to believe it until I Photoshopped Regina's wavy blonde hair over Catwoman's short straight black hair. (Actually, I still don't want to believe it now, but I can't really deny it anymore.)

That's right. Chewbacca's wife or partner or whoever, who I promised I would stay away from, has already taken a ride on Sir Lancelot. And now she's sending me nasty naked pictures.

Right now, I'm like this combination of confused or amazed or whatever that I didn't realize this sooner, plus scared as hell that Chewbacca will want to kill me, plus freaking out wondering what I'm going to do, plus all topped off with a little bit of horny.

I need to figure out how to handle all this.

I think I'll start by rubbing one out.

July 3

According to Frank, you used to be able to walk in to any decent concert and there'd be people walking against the crowd talking kind of like they were talking to themselves, trying to remember what to pick up at the grocery store, except if you listened real close, you could hear them saying, "Mushrooms. . . . Mushrooms. . . . Mushrooms. . . ." or "Kind buds. . . . Kind buds. . . . Kind buds. . . ." or, at the real good shows, "Doses. . . . Doses. . . . Doses . . ."

Then as you're passing you'd say, "Hey!" like it was some old friend of yours that you didn't expect to see there, and then you'd go over behind a tree and act like you're talking about old times but you're really saying, "What you got?"

And he or she would say, "I got some killer kind buds, dude—all red hairs and crystals, no seeds or stems—a hundred bucks a quarter, fifty for an eighth."

If it's a private enough place and the dude's cool, he'd let you choose between four of five different bags (several little buds are usually better than one big bud because the one big bud always has that giant stem in the middle) and then you'd pull out your money without making it look like you're pulling out money and then you'd ask if he knows where to get some decent doses and he'd say, "The only person I know for sure is a tall guy who wears a red hat with a yellow Woody Woodpecker on it," and you're like, "All right."

I wish we still had those days. It beats the hell out of sitting alone in Rob's crappy car outside some dark trailer park somewhere in the middle of the Wayne National Forest while Rob—who still watches *Pulp Fiction* at least once a week—hangs out for . . . how long has it been? a half hour? with your eighty bucks and your pipe.

So you wait.

And hum the *Jeopardy* theme—Hu-hum hu-hum hum-hu-hum, hu-hu-hu-hum huh-hu-hu-hu-hu-huh, hu-hum hu-hum hum-hu-hum, humm! hu-hu-huh hu-hu-humm. Humm-Humm—wondering where Chewbacca is. Wondering when she'll come after you.

*   *   *

Cast

(not in order of appearance)

CHEWBACCA: Age indeterminate. Bears an uncanny resemblance to the similarly-named wookie of *Star Wars* fame. May or nay not be a psychopathic freak (Rob and Adam both say she is, and they would know). May or may not want to kill our hero, L.J. (it's not like I plan to ask her to find out for sure). May or may not think her wife/ girlfriend/ partner/ kinda-sorta-like-a-sister-according-to-Regina is cheating on her (apparently she is). May or may not be hiding in that overturned refrigerator across the road.

L.J.: Our hero. Starts to think maybe he should quit taking Ritalin recreationally, because it makes him paranoid as hell (or *does* it? Maybe he's just intensely perceptive). Getting chowed on by a big buttload of mosquitoes because the automatic window on Rob's piece of crap car won't roll all the way up.

ROB: Absolute worst person to go to for weed because he's always overcharging you by at least twenty bucks and then he says, "Those are 'friend' prices," like he's Eric Stoltz in *Pulp Fiction*, and you just want to smack him, but you don't because, well, he'd smack you back, plus, you know the only reason you called him in the first place is because everybody else is out of weed and you didn't plan ahead, and you figured this was easier than driving to Cincinnati even though now you're not so sure because eventually he'll come back here to the car with a tiny quarter full of stems and seeds and say,

"Yeah, it was eighty," and then he'll pause and say, "And those are 'friend' prices," and all you'll be able to do is say, "Thanks, man," like you mean it and you won't even bother this time saying, "It looks pretty light," because you know he'd pull out his cheap little scale and it'll weigh right at a quarter ounce because it's in a Ziploc bag, and they probably steamed the buds before they weighed it, too, to make it even heavier, so you'll just offer to get him stoned like you're supposed to do, even though it'll be totally obvious that he and his buddies inside have already been smoking your weed for the last half hour.

(A note for you kids out there: never buy weed in a Ziploc bag—if you can help it, anyway; just trust me on this one. First of all, if they're too lame to get the regular sandwich bags like a normal drug dealer, then they're *definitely* too lame to know what real weed—*good* weed—is supposed to look like or smell like or feel like or, most importantly, cost. Plus, since they're so lame, they'll usually figure in the weight of the bag when weighing out your weed so, with a Ziploc, you're barely getting six grams of weed plus a one-something-gram bag.)

*   *   *

SCENE ONE

Two thirty-seven a.m. Fullish moon. Bright enough to see shadows moving. Quiet enough to hear . . . whatever that crunchy noise is. Inside Rob's—what kind of crappy car is this? a LeBaron? a Malibu?—a brown-haired man of medium build and probably average height sits in the driver's seat, alone, writing furiously in his notebook. Writing about the little loaded one-hitter he'd just found in Rob's glove box when he was looking for something to defend himself with from either Chewbacca or the angry hillbillies who may or may not be hiding behind that overturned refrigerator across the unpaved street. But right now he looks more focused than scared. And he's got some severe cotton mouth. He takes a big drink of too-warm water from a bottle in the back seat and lets out a loud "Ahhhh." He reaches for his pouch of tobacco to roll himself a cigarette, but throws it on the seat. He's trying to quit. He continues to write in his notebook. A voice in his head narrates as he writes:

I wish he'd hurry the hell up. Over a half hour? Come on. I'd rather not be here any longer than I have to be. I mean, when I was online today I listened to this 911 call from Denver or somewhere and you could hear this crazy jealous ex-boyfriend shooting all these people because they gave his ex-girlfriend a ride home. And I could totally see Chewbacca doing something like that. The people on the tape were freaking out, like, "Oh my God! Oh my God! Oh my God!" That could totally be me. What's to stop that from being me? That's what sucks.

So hurry up, Rob. Hurry up!

* * *

Mission accomplished.

God, it took forever. Rob came out to the car and he was like, "You have to come in. Sid wants to meet you. He doesn't like selling weed to anybody he doesn't know."

I mean, I'm no drug dealer, but if I was selling weed, I wouldn't want strange people just coming into my house so they could identify me. And then, the first thing he does, after I get a drink of water, is shows me his spare bedroom with all his "babies." And it's a room with, like, thirty big-ass pot plants.

I was just thinking, *Why are you showing me this?*

And then he was like, "The first thing all the grow-your-own books say is 'Don't tell anybody you're growing weed.'"

Yeah, that's probably good advice.

Then he saw my notebook and he just started freaking out. "What's that? What're you writing? If you're a cop, just arrest me now—actually, do you mind if I take another bong hit first?"

Then he got even more paranoid when I didn't want to smoke.

I was like, "I've got to take a drug test on Tuesday."

"For the police academy?"

So I had to explain that it was for my private pilot's license, which I didn't want to admit in front of Rob, because I know he'll blab it all over work tomorrow. But I couldn't think of a good lie, and this dude was acting paranoid enough already, so I just told him.

He was like, "Hair test or piss?"

"It's a pee test, I think."

"Here's what you do: get a quart of vodka and some lemon juice and drink the whole thing the night before your test."

"That doesn't work," Rob said. "You need to get a box of the clear gelatin and mix it with half the water you're supposed to, and then drink it twelve hours before your test."

While we were there, two other groups of guys showed up, and they all had their own suggestions.

"Drink Certo mixed with cranberry juice and three tablespoons of vinegar the night before your test."

"Goldenseal, dude. That's all you need."

"They test for Goldenseal now, man. All you need to do is take four aspirin five hours before your test. Drink it with a teaspoon of bleach in a buttload of water."

"All that'll do is dilute your piss and make you sick."

"It changes the pH to match what a clean sample would look like."

Then it turned into this whole bleach, anti-bleach debate. Finally, another guy showed up right before we left and Sid was like, "Hey, Bert, they still drug test you at work, right? What do you do to pass those?"

"Go up to that head shop in Lancaster and buy a bottle of Vales. Then follow the directions."

By the way, Sid the horrible dealer took each of those

new guys back to look at his babies, too. If he's not in prison in six months, I'll be surprised.

And of course we couldn't just leave after that. Oh, no. When he found out I work at ATS, that's all he wanted to talk about. He hates the place even more than Derek.

He started naming all these names, asking if I knew them, and I didn't know any of them except for Smeagol and Trainer Tim. It sounds like he totally hates Smeagol, the way he was talking about him and calling him all sorts of names, but he never did say exactly why.

When I asked Sid why he didn't work at ATS anymore, he went into this big long story about how he got electrocuted from his headset or something and, since ATS didn't want to pay his insurance, according to Sid, they gave him a drug test and when he failed it, they said that was why he got injured and so they didn't have to pay his hospital bill.

I started spacing off after a while, just kind of listening while he was talking about ATS and Smeagol and smoking, as far as I could tell, and Sid said, "Every once in a while I'll see him try to take a sniff of my cigarette smoke, but other times it just makes him sneeze." Then he said, "Do you think he's addicted?"

And I thought he was still talking about Smeagol and I figured if Smeagol sits and sniffs the smoke off your cigarette, then yes, he's addicted, so I said, "Definitely."

Then Sid said something like, "He's still a pretty healthy dog," while he's looking at the dog and then I realized he was talking about the dog all along, but I have no idea when the subject changed.

And then, Sid was loading a bowl and he was looking down and the dog was right in front where he was looking and Sid said, "Did you get a buzz?" and so I figured he was talking to the dog, so I didn't say anything, but then he kept asking, "Did you get a buzz? Did you get a buzz?" and then he looked up at me like I'm an idiot because I thought he was talking to the dog.

I don't know what that had to do with anything. Maybe I'm still kind of baked.

Anyway, three hours and four or five or seven bong hits later, I've finally got a bag of weed for Tanha.

I'll probably for sure fail my drug test, but at least I can get her baked and hopefully naked.

July 4

God, I'm so sick of all these stupid memos about having a union. "Let's celebrate Independence Day by vowing to be independent from a restrictive union."

I never really cared one way or the other before, but every time I see a new memo about this crap, I want a union more and more just so these stupid memos will stop.

I miss the good ol' days when the memos were all complainy about what a crappy job we're doing.

And then, you come into the break room, our memo-free zone, but instead we've got to stare at all these stupid-ass ginormous fliers on the employee message board:

Reasons Not to Join a Union

FACT: Our money is OUR MONEY! We do not have to pay dues to keep our jobs. If we take a leave of absence for any reason, when we come back we do not owe back dues.

FACT: You still owe dues if you are on vacation or sick leave.

FACT: An $11.00 an hour thirty-hour employee will pay approx. $1,279.67 union dues over a three-year period. That could've been in *your* pocket! (Do you have extra money to give away?)

FACT: The president of the CWA makes more in one year than most of us will make in our lifetimes. (and how is his salary paid? from your union dues)

FACT: There are very few teleservices companies in southeastern Ohio and if ATS closed, very few of us experienced TSRs would be able to find a job doing what we do best. Is that a risk you want to take?

FACT: The CWA thinks you are weak, vulnerable

and need them to speak for you. I have heard how the CWA speaks to us. They encourage the belief that ATS employees are weak and subservient and you need them to take care of you.

FICTION: ATS employees are victims and need another corporate bureaucracy to care for us.

This is America—Freedom of Choice.

Don't pay a union—Stand up for yourself!!!

Don't trust a union with *your* money and control over *your* own job! You have a choice and you have a voice.

SAY NO TO THE UNION!

DO NOT SIGN A CWA PETITION!

This flyer was created and distributed without assistance of any kind from the management of Appalachian TeleServices. E-mail questions or comments to: atsfloorsupliz@gmail.com.

The employee message board is supposed to be for stuff like carpooling and daycare, not crap like this. Which is why I mess with these fliers every chance I get.

There's a whole process involved since they have security cameras all through the break room. Most of them are probably pointed at the vending machines and the TV, but I'm guessing that at least one of them covers this whole area around the message board. So I have to start by taking the flier down from the board like I want to get a closer look at it, just in case they're watching through the security cameras. Then I sit here like I'm really reading it. Then I set it aside on the table like I've forgotten about it and am now concentrating on my CornNuts and whatever's on TV.

Here's where I have to get creative. I can't do the same thing every time, in case they are watching, because then they'll know it's me and then I don't know what would happen, but it would definitely be worse than if they didn't know it was me. So, like, with the "Union Lies" flier last week, I had to "accidentally" spill my tea on it and then, when I got some paper towels to wipe it up, I "accidentally" wadded up and tore the crap out of the flier in the process.

The next one, I stared at the TV while I blew sideways through a straw to blow it off the table. Once it's on the floor under the table, I can pretty much stomp and rip and mangle the crap out of it. I think I'll do the same thing with this one, only I'll act like I'm pinning it back up on the board when, woops, it'll fall out of my hand onto the floor. Then I can do the whole clumsy, *Where did it go?* thing before I put it back up on the board with a big shoe print on it. Yeah.

I'm celebrating Independence Day by releasing my anger on these annoying as hell fliers.

* * *

This chick on the phone—Melinda, age twenty-three—is right now reading me my Tarot cards so I can just sit here and chill out a little.

She said she's talked to me a bunch of times before and she acted all pissy at first when I told her I didn't remember.

I'm thinking, Do you know how many people I talk to every week? Take three calls per hour—at the very minimum—times seven hours a day, times five days a week, equals a shit-ton of people. I don't even remember the guy I talked to five minutes ago. I wouldn't know his name was Joe if it wasn't written on my call log sheet. But I can't tell her that, of course, so instead when she was going on and on about how wonderful our last call was, I was just like, "Yeah. How've you been?"

I'm definitely not supposed to tell her that I don't believe in all this crap. So when she tells me I have the Falling Tower in my sixth position and the Two of Cups in my eighth position, I say, "Hmm, interesting."

"It looks like you have a lover, but you've been ignoring

her. Or, no, a secret admirer, maybe? Somebody you don't know. Have you gotten any secret admirer notes yet?"

I admit that I have, but we both know that's just a lucky guess. The "secret admirer" line is what you fall back on after you've just incorrectly guessed that they have a boyfriend or girlfriend.

*   *   *

Holy crap! Okay. I've been trying to play it cool for the last hour and a half, but I've been dying to take a break so I could write this down: I touched boobies! At work! While I was clocked in! It was awesome!

I probably shouldn't be so psyched about it considering the circumstances, but still, I don't know. Maybe I should. I mean, I got to touch boobies.

That super-quiet chick, Taylor, is sitting next to me tonight. When she came back from her break, she was sort of freaking out and shaking and trying not to cry and everything.

We were like, "What's wrong?"

She said, "I just got felt up by the boss in the break room."

So of course when Adam hears this, he's completely interested and totally ignoring his caller. He's like, "Which boss? Who was it?"

"Mr. Leech."

"The Production Manager, Daniel Leech? Smeagol? He felt you up in the break room?"

She nodded.

Then Victoria was like, "He's a perv. The only reason he comes out on the call floor is to look down all the girls' blouses."

Adam kept bugging her for details. Typical Adam questions. What did he do exactly? How long did he do it? Are you sure it wasn't an accident? Did you like it?

When he asked if she could demonstrate, she grabbed

both my hands and mashed them right into her boobs and held them there for, like, three or four seconds and she said, "Does that look like an accident to you?"

I was trying to be all cool like, *I'm just helping a coworker with a demonstration*, but, holy crap, man, she was mashing my hands right into her boobies. I tried not to smile. I'm pretty sure I did, though. Adam was looking at me all jealous, which made me want to smile even more. I mean, I know I wasn't supposed to enjoy it. I kept trying to tell myself that this is merely a reenactment of the trauma this poor young woman experienced. But on the inside, the only thing going through my mind was *Boobies! Boobies! Real live boobies!*

We were all like, "You've got to report him. You've got to report him."

"Who am I supposed to tell?"

"Tell HR. Call them tomorrow."

"I need this job."

"They can't fire you for that."

This was only like the fourth pair of boobies I've ever really touched, if you don't count church camp in seventh grade. Maybe more. Whatever number it is, it never gets old. And I got to touch them at work so, technically, I got paid today to touch boobies. I thought it was awesome to drop a dookie at work. This was way better.

Way way better.

I feel like maybe I should feel bad or something, though, but I'm not sure if I do.

* * *

If Adam wasn't jealous of me before, he definitely is now.

* * *

It's been like five hours now and I'm trying to watch *Maury*, but still all I can think about are Taylor's boobs. Maybe if I was more sexually experienced, I wouldn't be obsessing about them so much. Especially since the whole thing didn't mean anything to her.

Mom's always saying, "Never look a gift horse in the mouth."

I was thinking for a second that somehow applied to this situation, but I can't remember how now. Brown cow.

I'm going to bed to twist one off and hopefully fall asleep and dream about puppies or something.

July 5

My day, in poetry:

Nine a.m.: The Spider in My Clogged Toilet

As easily as Christ
he scurries across the water,
determined to escape this sanctuary.

Using all his strength,
he skates over the surface, then
crashes into the rim.

A gentle breath slides him back,
or forces him ahead,
as his only escape plan is tried in vain, again.

He grows blind to the futility of his efforts
and quickly gains momentum
before bouncing once more off the porcelain.

Finally bored with this meaningless display, I help him
to freedom.
As he stands, appreciating the miracle,
I squish him against the lid.

*   *   *

12:30 p.m.: As the Bikinied Girl Enters the Laundromat
on a Monday Afternoon in July

Suddenly,
as if there were an explosion,

six eyes look up from the Reds game
when she opens the door.

Moths gape, able to swallow whole salmon,
while pupils dilate, trying to focus on the finely hone
legs
and the bikini sewn
to her firm derriere.

They stare with painfully crossed eyes.
Necks crane over upside-down sports sections, or
around
the Pepsi machine
as she tosses her panties into washer 13.

They watch the extra-large Abercrombie T-shirt
flirt with her naked breasts
and the honey-blonde hair
that bounces upon her shoulders.

A sock strays from her hamper
and falls to the floor,
unnoticed.
The fat woman with red shorts and cottage-cheese
thighs
retrieves it, then turns,
hoping to intercept a passionate glance for herself.

The men move closer.
The bartender buys a Pepsi.
The psychic checks his load, still filling,
and the jock asks for change.

But she, oblivious, finishes loading washer 11

as a red Porsche parks beside the beat up Camry.
A cross between Vincent Chase and Vin Diesel steps
out,
strolls in, and inhales.

She adjusts her hair.

With a pair of jeans
on the spin cycle,
he escorts her from the scene
and the red Porsche disappears toward Dairy Queen.

Back inside,
three chins sink into lethargic palms
as we all silently imagine how lucky Vin Diesel must be.
Our eyes slowly return to the tube
and Joey Votto's third strike.

* * *

2:50 p.m.: Break Room Before Work

Regeena, RegIna,
stay away with that vagina.
If you give me head, I will be dead
unless I move to China.

Regina, RegIna,
I don't want your vagina.
I made a mistake
for goodness sake
you're giving me angina.

* * *

Five p.m.: On the Call Floor

Some days I hate this stupid job.

I hate it hate it gobs and gobs.
Some days I hate working on the phones.
I hate it hate it in my bones.
Some days I hate the people who call.
I hate them hate them one and all.
I've grown to hate our pervert boss.
We should castrate him with dental floss.
And I don't know why Liz hates me so.
Two PINs already and six hours to go.
I may not have the balls to quit,
but I can drop a deuce and get paid for it.

* * *

Midnight: My First Real Date with Tanha

Because she stood me up three times before,
I think I want to see her even more.
I hope she doesn't make me wait much more,
but thirty minutes late—is this number four?

Before tonight, her excuses were good:
". . . too drunk to move;" "Today I gave blood."
Maybe she'll call tonight: "My beagle chewed
my favorite dress, and I just can't go nude."

I don't know why I should feel such pain.
"She's not so great," I lie to me again.
But while I've tried for a week to remain
unfazed, her kiss still lingers in my brain.

* * *

Two a.m.: Tonight at the Bar

Perfect curves; the loin spots
her from in the brush.
That gazelle is beautiful;

simply fabulous.

With hungry eyes, he admires
each hindquarter's shake
while carefully he schemes
what approach to take.

Finally upon his prey,
he looks up, and lo!
She is no gazelle, but a
water buffalo!

July 6

I passed my physical!

I'd never been so nervous about a test the whole time I was in college. It was pretty basic, though: "Can you see this? Can you feel this? Can you hear this?"

Yes. Yes. Yes.

The hard part was they made you wait until the very end to give them a urine sample. I had to pee like a mighty mofo. I bought a bottle of the Vale's, and you're supposed to drink the whole bottle of that an hour or two before your test, then fill the bottle back up with water and drink that. So that part sucked. But it was worth it. I am now officially authorized to begin my flight training.

* * *

I was in a totally good mood about the whole passing the physical thing, and I wanted to do something or talk to somebody at least to share my good news, but I didn't want to call Tanha because, I don't know . . . she's kind of been blowing me off lately and I didn't want to seem desperate or anything and the whole flying thing was supposed to be a surprise and I didn't want to ruin it yet.

So I called Marpa instead. I was like, "Hey, man! It's Tuesday! Karmic Enforcement Day!"

At first it was like he didn't even know what I was talking about. I was like, "I thought that was your thing. Don't you have some project to do or somebody's life to mess with?"

He was acting all hush-hush, like he's some CIA secret agent. "I'm working on something big right now," he said. "You'll be the first to know, I promise."

"You're not doing anything today?"

"Not exactly."

So that was a drag.

I could hear Radiohead's "High and Dry" in the background, so I figured he wouldn't be much fun, anyway.

Then I broke down and called Tanha. I was still all happy and psyched about passing my physical, so I was in this super-elated mood when I called. Pretty soon, I noticed she sounded kind of bummed. Plus, she was listening to Radiohead, too. I was just like, is everybody in the world playing Radiohead right now?

Don't get me wrong, Radiohead's the greatest band of all time, for sure, but she was listening to "Fake Plastic Trees," which is kind of melt-into-your-couch Radiohead, and I was more in the mood for some jump-up-and-dance Radiohead like "Bodysnatchers" or "Weird Fishes." Not that *In Rainbows* is my favorite Radiohead album, by far, but I mean, I just passed my drug test! I wanted to celebrate or do something or something.

"Is everything okay?" I asked.

Then she told me about how the cable guy dropped a doghouse or something on a bunch of baby raccoons. I don't know why, but it just made me laugh the way she told it. I don't know if it's because the raccoons here are always knocking over my garbage and basically being loud and annoying as hell practically every single night, or what, but I couldn't stop laughing.

She didn't think it was funny.

All I could think to say was, "Yeah, it's baby raccoon season." I have no idea how I know that; she didn't seem impressed that I did.

Needless to say, it wasn't an awesome conversation.

After I said, "Okay, I guess I'll talk to you later," she was like, "Did you tell Reverend Marpa that you and I slept together?"

"What?"

"Did you tell Reverend Marpa that you and I slept together?" She didn't sound mad. More like disappointed at what a dumbass I must be.

I still don't know a good way I could've answered that. Because if I said, "Yes," then she would've thought that I'm either some uncontrollable bigmouth who she wouldn't be able to trust to keep my mouth shut if we ever do have sex, or else I was so giddy after kissing her that I needed to tell someone, in which case she would've thought I was an emotional pussy who she wouldn't want to deal with.

"Yes" didn't seem like the right answer.

Telling her "No" didn't seem much better, because then it'd be my word against Marpa's, and I could totally picture the whole conversation in my head. She would ask, "Why would Marpa make that up?" and, "How did he just happen to make up all those exact details?"

Still, with "No," I figured I had an unlimited number of possible ways to explain what happened—maybe Marpa was just guessing; maybe you heard him wrong; maybe he read my mind.

Whereas with "Yes," there's only one choice: Yes. I did it. Busted. And I wouldn't know how to spin it to make me look good. With "No," I had all these ways to make me look like a great guy. Like, "No, I couldn't have told Marpa anything about you, because I was rescuing puppies from . . . wherever," or, "I don't know when he would've seen me. I was mentoring all day at the local after-school program."

Before I had a chance to say anything, she said, "I guess I have my answer."

"I don't know," I said. "It might've come up in a conversation."

"What kind of conversation were you having?"

"I don't know. I might've mentioned that you crashed out here that night after his party." That was sort of pretty close to the truth.

She didn't say anything. She just let out one of those I-just-lost-all-respect-for-you-now-that-I-realize-you're-stupid-enough-to-ruin-your-chance-to-experience-something-as-amazing-as-me sighs.

I was like, "I never told him we had sex or anything. I swear."

Finally she said, "Okay," and then, "I've got to go," and that was pretty much our conversation.

So that sucked. One day, I see her in the break room getting excited when she hits Stop on the microwave right as it beeps down to zero—which is my thing; I know she got that from me—and the next day, it seems like, she doesn't even want to talk to me.

I don't know what I'm supposed to do now. I feel like I should be mad at somebody, but I don't know if I should be mad at the cable guy, or the raccoons, or Marpa, or myself.

Probably myself.

At least I start flying tomorrow. After I get my forty hours in, I'll be able to nonchalantly say to her, "You like to fly? I didn't know that. I've got a pilot's license. I can take you up sometime, if you'd like," and then she'd totally want to bob on my knob just out of gratitude.

* * *

I've been getting these emails from Regina since we went hiking in the woods. Pretty much every day for the last week, she'd send me at least one or two and I'd usually just delete them without ever opening them and then just pretend I never got them.

But then I see this one tonight after work with a subject line that says, "break room fantasy," so I opened that one and it started out like, "I'm sitting in my bedroom wishing I had to work tonight because then I would be closer to you."

So right there I should've known there's something seriously wrong with her. I mean because, how crazy would somebody have to be to actually want to be at work? If they worked at ATS, anyway. No matter how much I like Tanha, for example, there's never been a moment where I ever thought to myself, *You know, I'd happily give up a day off to see Tanha.*

The email:

> I'm sitting in my bedroom wishing I had to work tonight because then I could be closer to you. Right about now, I imagine you are taking your first break, two small bags of Ranch CornNuts in front of you, slightly to the right, a bottle of Sobe Green Tea to the left, and *Pawn Stars* on television. The first thing you will do when you open your tea is read the inside of the cap, then arch your eyebrows as if to say, "Hmmm, interesting," even when you don't think anybody can see you.

> In my bedroom I can imagine being closer to you than I would ever actually dare in the break room. In my bedroom I can imagine sneaking up behind you right now, putting my hands over your eyes and saying, "Guess who!" as you fumble to place your CornNuts on the table so you can feel my hands. Would you be able to identify me? Would you recognize my fingernails? What if I sneaked under the table? Would you know me then? Would you want to?

> In my bedroom I can imagine what would happen next. On top of the table. Your CornNuts would drop, plink plink plink, on the seat of the metal chair and your bottle of tea would spill on the floor. "I'll buy you a new one," I would promise.

> "Don't worry about it," you will say, breathlessly, as the table rocks violently back and forth, thud thud thudding against the wall.

I know this can only happen in my bedroom, in my mind. Yet I still long to be with you at work. Closer, yet further away.

L8r—

R.

(By the way, I hate the L8r for "later." I don't know why.) So anyway, I'm thinking, I don't know. I mean, I definitely want to avoid her, especially after that talk Chewbacca and I had in my car on the way to our hike, but it still seemed like no big deal.

The next ones she sent were just kind of blah-blah, and blah-blah. In one, she described (in excruciating detail) some dream she had about going to Wal-Mart and I was there in the pet section giving a snake charming demonstration, crap like that.

Another one had this quiz where I could answer the questions and tell her how I felt about her:

    a) You're cool and I'd like to hang out with you.

    b) You're warm and caring and I'd like to talk with you.

    c) You're hot and I want to rub baby oil all over you.

    d) You're kind of annoying; that's why I avoid you and never answer your emails.

    e) All of the above.

Okay, so they still seemed fairly normal—completely normal if you don't consider the Chewbacca situation—I was kind of flattered or whatever. But still I figured, you know, No big deal. I'll just keep making sure we don't end up alone anywhere, make sure I don't do anything to give her the wrong impression, stuff like that. Eventually, she'll get interested in someone else. I'll just wait for the problem to go away, I guess.

But then tonight, I was getting in my car to come home from work, and there was this note on my windshield and it was from Regina and it's totally psycho. Just a bunch of stuff like,

> You need to tell me what's going on so I'll know what you want from me. Why won't you talk to me? We can't keep avoiding each other forever. What have I done to deserve this? I thought maybe I came on too strong there for a while, so I backed off and gave you some space, but you still have done nothing to bridge the gap between us. And now you act like whatever I do is wrong. Maybe we've miscommunicated. Maybe you sent me an email that I didn't get.
>
> Or are you avoiding me now because you're scared I'll be mad at you for avoiding me before? I'm not mad. What kind of bitch do you think I am? And you don't need to worry about my ex, I would never tell her anything about us. That's none of her business, and she knows it. She respects my privacy now and she's promised to let me live my life. As for our marriage, it was never recognized in Ohio, anyway, so there's no need for she or I to do anything in that regard.

Those are the highlights. It was six pages, front and back.

I read it and I was just like *Wtf?* I mean, seriously, *Wtf?* I mean, she's obviously crazy, but I don't know how I'm supposed deal with that or what to do about that. She's always talking about how we're soul mates because we like the same bands, but I keep telling her over and over that I hate Dashboard and Conor Oberst and all emo music in general and it's like she won't even believe me.

I don't have a clue what I'm supposed to do.

I mean, I've been trying to be gentle and let her down easy without ever giving her the impression that I would ever want to be more than friends, but it's like I have to keep being less and less subtle and more and more rude and I'm not sure what it'll take unless I totally just scream at her in front of everybody at work or something.

I don't want to be mean or anything but, *damn*. I don't have a clue what to do. Scooby dooby doo.

Right now, I'm going to smoke a bowl and try to forget about it.

*   *   *

I just turned *Maury* on and he's got the people who are afraid of weird crap like mustard and balloons and stuff. The first lady was afraid of potato chips. That has to be fake, doesn't it? Seriously. How can anybody be afraid of potato chips? If you don't like them, just stomp on them until they're not potato chips anymore.

It's episodes like this that make me question all the *Maury* stuff. Like, are all the paternity tests fake? That would be a drag. I mean, the episodes with the fat kids and the midgets are real (even the fat kids, though, could be just normal kids wearing fat suits, but you can't really fake being a midget). But when I see some otherwise normal-looking lady screaming off backstage because somebody's carrying a platter full of potato chips, it's so completely bogus that I can't even watch.

I mean, even if you are that terrified of something like potato chips, why would you come on the show when you know he's going to screw with you like that? It's got to be bogus.

Worst day off ever.

July 7

Flying sucks giant donkey dick. Seriously.

First of all, before we even got started, I was weaving back and forth on the runway like a drunk Shriner heading home for a late dinner (not sure what that means). I was weaving back and forth because, when the plane's on the ground, you steer with the rudder, which you control with your feet. To go left, I think, you push with your left foot—or maybe it's the right foot—whichever one it was, it was the exact opposite of whatever my brain kept thinking it should be. And I don't even have the rudder figured out before he's got me either pulling out or pushing in on this knob (the throttle—I know that) to give it more gas until we get up to however-many knots and he was saying something about something and my radio was cutting in and out the whole flight but I don't know if I would've known what he was saying anyway because I was so focused on trying to stay on the cement part of the 500-I-think-foot-wide runway (though it didn't seem that wide at the time) and I hear him say something about getting up to a certain airspeed and I glance too quick at the airspeed indicator to know how fast we're going and when I look out I realize we're off the ground and we may have been for a while.

And somewhere in there he said something into the radio like, "Ohio State University traffic, this is Cessna 0230 Uniform, we are departing traffic to the southwest" and then he told me, "Okay, do you remember when they talked about left-turning tendency in an airplane? Remember, it's even greater at takeoff because you have a slower airspeed and a higher angle of attack. So you want to compensate for that by giving it some right aileron." Then he said, "No, that's left.

Here, I'll take it for a minute."

"You have the controls." The whole flight, that's the only thing I could remember to say properly, and I was a stickler for that. I didn't remember what the airspeed indicator was supposed to say and I couldn't remember what the attitude indicator is even for, but I remembered the correct procedure for passing over the controls. The pilot who is getting the controls says, "I have the controls," and then the person handing them over says, "You have the controls," and the person getting them confirms again, "I have the controls." In our plane, it was more like, "Here, I've got it."

"You have the controls."

"Uh, yeah. I've got it."

"You've got the controls."

And then there'd be a huge exhale into the mic. That part I always heard.

I realize now that when he said, "Give it some right aileron," he wanted me to turn toward the right. For some reason, I kept turning left—but never more than fifteen degrees; more than that made me think I was going to slide right out my door.

Pitch, trim and power, I think is what he said controls altitude. Or determines altitude. Or maybe it's trim and power that determine pitch. I was so tense the whole entire thirty or forty minutes we were up there that I don't remember much of anything except bits of what I heard through my headphones.

"Okay, see how now we're at 3,500 when we wanted to hold steady at three thousand?—that's one of the main things we try to teach our new pilots, is how to maintain straight and level, unaccelerated flight."

Then he said, "If you put your four fingers on the top of the dash here, the horizon should be at the top of your index finger."

Then he said, "Remember, if you have your trim properly adjusted, you should be able to maintain straight and level flight without using your elevators."

Then he said, "Remember, on this turn we want to angle about thirty degrees. Here, you're between five and ten."

Then he said, "Okay, see how your heading—this arrow—isn't in the orange bracket anymore? Let's see if we can just keep going south."

Then he said, "Okay, now remember how we said we didn't want to descend faster than 500 feet per minute? Your vertical speed indicator shows we're descending a little faster than that."

I thought it'd be awesome, but it sucked.

For the last month, I've been working it all out in my head how I'd casually mention—without bragging, of course—that, oh, yeah, I have a pilot's license and I'm not just a lame telephone psychic like all the rest of you losers.

Eventually Tanha would hear that I'm a pilot and she'd have some emergency and she'd need me to fly her . . . somewhere . . . for something, and then she'd be eternally grateful. And her expression of that gratitude would somehow involve her big, juicy lips and assorted parts of my body.

But today, every time I looked down, it was like, *The only thing separating me from a three thousand-foot fall to certain death in a cornfield is this flimsy 1960's-era safety belt that may or may not be properly buckled and this more-rickety-than-a-Yugo door that took three rattle-y slams to close.*

I mean, I'm sitting here, trying to rationalize why I'm never taking any more flying lessons—ATS will only pay the tuition, not the fees, which are the expensive part; and when you figure all the time spent reserving the plane, and inspecting the plane, and doing your flight plan, and on and on and on, it's quicker to just drive to Cincinnati, stuff like that.

I had some others, too, but the real reason is because it pretty much scared the holy crap out of me.

July 8

I guess I'm getting a new neighbor. I don't know; I'm not really a big fan of living next door to people I work with. I mean, first they'll want to hang out after work and you can't use the normal excuses like, "I have to go to such and such place" or, "I'm just going home to crash," because now they can just walk by your window and see your lights on.

Either that, or they'll want to carpool. Or else they'll want to come over and hang out whenever they're bored, which could be like every day, for all you know, but the only thing you'll have in common is work, and so that's all they'll want to talk about and, before you know it, the one sanctuary you had from work is now polluted by work.

Living next to people you work with sucks. But it's not like I had any choice.

Tanha called today and she asked if I wanted to hang out before work. Of course I said Yes.

When I got over to her place, she was all fussing with her hair—putting it in a ponytail, putting it up, letting it down. She asks me which I think looks better.

They're all hot, if you ask me. The ponytail's kind of sporty-sexy. With her hair up, she's got that sexy librarian thing going on. But when she let her hair down, it was just like, *Damn*, you know. I couldn't stop thinking about the night she spent over at my place and how her hair was all covering me while we kissed. "Down is good," I said. "Down is great."

"I'm worried it'll get all frizzy with this humidity."

"I don't know anything about that," I said. "It looks great no matter how you do it. It's just totally sexy when it's down like that."

She smiled that beautiful smile of hers and whispered, "*Sexy*," to herself. Then to me, she said, "Okay, I'll leave it down."

So of course I'm all psyched that she's trying to look sexy for me. I figured this was a perfect time to create some kind of situation where we could somehow find our foreheads magneted together so we could kiss, but nothing was working.

Not that I have a whole awesome repertoire of get-your-foreheads-magneted-together moves, but I'm pretty sure I was being smooth as hell.

She either didn't get it, or she got it and she was letting me down super-easy by doing an awesome job pretending she didn't get it.

Eventually, I got her kind of pinned up against the wall, but she kind of lightly tapped my chest and said, "We better get going."

So that was kind of a drag, but I figured maybe she wanted to hurry and do whatever it is she had planned for us before we went back to my place to smoke the weed I've been saving for her and then we'd really go crazy kissing and making out and who knows what after that.

She won't tell me where we're going, so I'm kind of excited because it seems like she's done some planning for this. She's driving out toward Albany, trying to read her directions, when she suddenly slams on the brakes right at the entrance to Lake Snowden.

I was just like, if I knew this is where we were going, I could've told you how to get here.

She's still reading her directions as she drives back into the campground part. I was about to say, "I don't think we can be here unless we're camping," right as she parked right next to Marpa's Jeep.

Marpa comes out from around a tree and he's all like, "You made it!"

I'm just sitting there like, *what the hell?*

Tanha said, "So you're really living out here now?"

And Marpa was all like, "Oh, boo-hoo, my roommate kicked me out of my apartment because those guys ate all his food and now I have to live in this crappy old tent."

I don't know, he might not have said it exactly like that.

I was just like, "Dude, you've got a Marmot tent and a nice-ass brand new propane grill. It's not like you're roughing it."

I mean, seriously, he had like the Donald Trump of campsites. He was trying to tell us, "Oh, I just happened to have this stuff in my Jeep for when I go camping," but who goes camping with all that crap?

I mean, he even had a mini-fridge! Who just happens to carry around a mini-fridge in their car, "just in case"?

And I know that tent costs $579 at Campmor (I checked online when I got home). I'm sorry, but nobody needs a huge-ass $579 tent, unless they're climbing Mount Everest or hiking to the Arctic Circle. His propane grill costs about one-fifty. I don't know about the mini-fridge.

He asked Tanha, "Do you guys want to go inside my tent and smoke a doobie?"

Who says "doobie" anymore, by the way?

She said, "Yeah!" all excited. Not "sure" or "I guess" but, "Yeah!"

Inside his tent, he had two Kelty sleeping bags and a Thermarest mattress pad—that's probably another five hundred just for those three things—plus a Black Diamond lantern.

I was just like, "Dude, how do you afford all this stuff?"

"Most of it I've had forever. I either got it used or people gave it to me before they threw it out."

That's total bullcrap. It was totally obvious that all his junk was brand new. Everything still smelled like it was just out of the package and you could still see the factory folded creases in the tent. His lantern didn't have a single scratch on it.

After a while, Tanha was like, "What do you do if there's a tornado?"

"I guess I'll just pray," Marpa said.

I said, "We passed a tornado shelter on the way in; it's two campsites away."

"I can't let you live here," Tanha said. "You can stay at my place until you find an apartment."

"That's okay," he said. "I wouldn't want to be in the way."

"Don't be crazy," Tanha said. "You can stay with me. Please."

That's when I said, "My landlady has an apartment next door to me. It opens in a week."

It just suddenly seemed like I'd never have any kind of shot at all with Tanha if he was living with her, the way she'd been getting all pretty before we left, and then the way she slammed on the brakes, and the way they kept finishing each other's sentences—yeah, they were doing that, too—kind of like at the end of the Austin Powers movies, only annoying instead of funny.

Oh, and speaking of movies, he was totally ripping off lines from movies and pretending like he just made them up, and she was totally believing it. She told me once that she never watches movies or TV. I thought she was just exaggerating like everybody does when they say that, but no. She must not have any pop culture knowledge whatsoever because Marpa used that one line from *Bull Durham* where Kevin Costner is like "I believe in" all that stuff he believes in, and Tanha was like, "You're amazing."

I was just like, "Seriously?"

He also used a line from *Avatar* and I'm pretty sure

Finding Nemo was in there somewhere, too.

And then, when he kept going on about pizza—"Why does it have to be 'buy one, get one free'? Why can't it be 'get one free and then decide if you want to buy one'?"—Tanha was all like, "*Yeah,*" like Marpa just solved some super unsolvable mathematical equation or something.

And speaking of tornadoes, she lives in a trailer. If the tornado thing is why she wants him to move in with her, it's a pretty crappy reason.

So, yeah, I'm getting a new neighbor.

I don't know if it'll help, though, because as we were leaving, Tanha told him, "I'm looking forward to this weekend."

"Yeah," he said. "Hopefully it won't rain again."

I don't know what that means and I couldn't think of the right way to ask.

God, I'm just totally bummed right now.

* * *

Regina just dropped off this note from whoever the official note writer is at ATS: "Your request for tuition reimbursement has been denied at this time due to:" and then it had the box checked next to "does not meet minimum continuous employment qualifications as outlined in section VIII.C of employee handbook."

According to Smeagol, section VIII.C of the employee handbook basically says that, when I went back to training, that somehow meant I became a brand new employee all over again.

So, basically, I'm out about a thousand bucks for the privilege of spending an hour in a rickety flying Yugo, about to have a heart attack.

Half the stuff they wouldn't have paid anyway, because the books and the flight calculator and the headset and the flight and the gas all count as fees, which, according to the fine print, they wouldn't pay even if I did somehow qualify.

But it pisses me off that they won't pay my tuition for the class.

I mean, if you want to offer tuition assistance, that's great. If you don't want to, that's fine, too. I never took this job because of your awesome Tuition Assistance Program. I never even knew there was a Tuition Assistance Program until Derek told me about it.

But don't *say* you offer tuition assistance and then make it impossible for anybody but some brownnoser like Jackie to get it. That's just a bunch of crap. If you don't want to give us money for college, then don't give us money for college. Just don't make up some ridiculous rule about how, when I went back to training, the whole year I already worked here got deleted from the system or whatever.

Don't tell us, "Hey! We want to give you money for college!" if you don't want to give us money for college. How tough is that?

* * *

Hopefully this is the last email I'll ever get from Regina.

She pissed me off enough the other day that I finally sent her my own angry email back which, hopefully, did the trick (but, like I told Derek, this is like the third time she's sent me an email that says, pretty much, "Oh, I get it, there was never anything between us and I just completely misinterpreted everything," so we'll see).

In this last one, all she wrote was:

> Okay. I got it. Loud and clear. Thanks for finally explaining things. It hurts, but at least now I know.
> be well—

(Come to think of it, I'm not exactly sure what this email means. What did I say in the last email that I didn't say before that made the last message "loud and clear?" God, I just want her to please go away so I don't have to deal with her any more. Please.)

July 9

Apparently Regina didn't get the message.

She called me today before work like absolutely nothing happened and somewhere in there she said something—I can't remember exactly how she put it, but somehow she made it sound like if I "broke up" with her, even though we were never dating in the first place, that she'd tell Chewbacca that we had sex.

When I was like, "Are you threatening me?" she acted all like I completely misunderstood her or something.

So now I don't know what to think. Is she crazy? Am I crazy? Wtf?

* * *

What're you supposed to do when the person who wants and desires you the way you want to be wanted and desired by the person you want and desire is some crazy psycho, while the person you want to want and desire you thinks you're just some crazy psycho who wants and desires her the way she wants to be wanted and desired by the person she wants and desires?

Yeah, I'm high.

* * *

I was sitting in the break room today, minding my own business, when Regina and a couple other girls sat down at my table. Pretty soon they started talking about Marpa. Marpa this and Marpa that. Marpa, Marpa, Marpa.

"I love his hair."

"He's so-o-o-o-o sexy."

"And he's so-o-o-o-o smart."

I figured that was my chance to get the conversation back to me, so I said, "I've never thought of myself as a smart man."

I got a 2120 on my SATs, and I'm pretty sure I'd accidentally let that fact slip into at least one or two conversations while they were around—Regina for sure—so I was kind of at least expecting Regina to turn to me, and maybe gently squeeze my arm, and say something like, "Oh, but you are. I can't believe you'd ever think that because you're the smartest man I've ever met," and then everybody'd start talking about what an amazing guy I am.

But instead, Regina was like, "I don't think you've ever thought of yourself as a 'man,' period."

I've been trying to ignore Regina as much as possible, but for some reason, I couldn't ignore the not-a-man thing. It occurs to me now that maybe that's because there was some truth to it.

I don't think of myself as a man—not a real man, anyway.

When I was in junior high and high school, I'd always assumed that, when I got to be twenty-two, I'd be one of those guys who drove a big, gas-guzzling, screw-the-environment pickup truck, tailgating the punks in their wimpy Toyota Camrys to get them to speed up before I'd pass them and splash mud on their windshield and then pull over—without using my turn signal—to help some pretty young woman replace her timing belt on the side of the road and say, "No need to thank me, ma'am; you can put yer shirt back on," before driving on to whatever manly job I had.

Or at least I'd be one of those cool drifter guys like Kwai Chang Caine, calmly drifting into new towns all across the world, trying to calmly teach the redneck locals about tolerance and, when talking didn't work, I'd kung-fu their asses and then drift off into the sunset with my tiny rucksack and my walking stick after saying to the grateful woman whose honor I'd just protected, "The Tao teaches that the softest of all things is water. Please replace the garment upon your shoulders before I learn otherwise."

And I expected to be hairier. It takes me three months to grow what might even remotely be considered a beard. I can go days at a time without shaving and nobody would notice. Ashley had more chest hair than me. Granted, she only had five or six peach-fuzzy ones compared to my three or four, but still . . . I expected to be hairier.

What I didn't expect was to be twenty-two years old and getting offended because somebody made me realize I don't think of myself as a man. It's not something I really want to admit, even to myself, but there it is. I mean, I see Keith, and *he's* a man. He's just so, "I'm in charge, here. Follow me and do this and this and that and buy this stock."

I'm not like that. I wish I could be. I think.

And Uncle Hank is a manly man. I used to watch him to see what he does that's different than me.

The main thing I notice is he's got about a million stories involving poo. And he'll tell them at the dinner table. His last one: they were in the jungle, in the middle of this firefight with the V.C. or gooks or whatever he calls them and their sergeant stood up and took off his pack while all these bullets were whizzing past and he said, "Sarg, get your ass down or yer gonna get shot," and the sergeant said, "I can't; I can't," "and he pulled his pants down real quick and bent over toward the V.C. and squirted this stream of shit twenty yards into the jungle."

Then he finished his story with, "It was those damned malaria pills. After you had to take those, you weren't right for days." I'm pretty sure that I'll never have a story like that to share with anybody ever.

And last year he gave Dad an antique hog scraper—and he could explain to Dad exactly how it worked: "I've never seen one like this with two handles before. The ones I've used had one handle and were bell-shaped and sharp all around and you'd go around and around in a bigger and bigger circle to scrape the skin off," which sounds disgusting to me, but it's just another fact to him.

If I have to scrape the skin off hogs to be a man, I don't know how well I'll do.

According to the dictionary (yeah, I just looked it up) it says that, to be manly, one must possess "the virtues proper to a man as distinguished from a woman or child; chiefly, courageous, independent in spirit, frank, upright."

I think I'm usually frank and upright, if that means what I think it means, and I think I'm fairly independent, and I don't think I act girly; so that just leaves "courageous," and I'm pretty sure that's not me at all. I mean, if somebody was drowning, I'd try to save them, but I don't think that counts because I know how to swim.

Now, if somebody took a couple guns to work and started shooting everybody—a distinct possibility (I'm amazed it hasn't already happened, actually)—I can't imagine being that one guy who tackles the shooter. I'm pretty sure I'd be cowering under my cubicle, pretending to be dead.

One summer after little league practice—this was like fourth or fifth grade—these three brothers stopped me on my bike. The oldest was in high school, the middle one was in junior high, and the youngest was a year or two older than me.

They were standing in the middle of the street and I was just cruising along—doh-dee-doh—everything was fine, heading home from practice, and I tried to steer around these guys in my banana seater with the cool chopper handlebars, but the oldest brother shuffled over and put his hands out and just . . . stopped my bike by grabbing the handlebars.

They would've stolen my glove if Mom hadn't made me put my name on it with a big Sharpie marker; they took my hat instead. The next game, I was pitching and the middle brother was standing behind the backstop, wearing my hat.

I remember looking at him from the mound when we were ahead whatever to nothing, thinking, *You're on my turf now, beeotch.* But he was smirking back at me like, *Yeah, but you have to ride home sometime.*

Those guys are probably investment bankers or something now who know exactly what they want out of life, while I still feel like that stupid fourth grader who has to just stand there while three guys circle around me and steal my hat.

I don't know, I guess I just thought that things would be different by now, but they're not.

Dad took me to boxing lessons after that, but a few weeks later JoAnn started taking them, too. It's embarrassing to get beat up by your neighbor in front of everybody, even if she is three years older. So I never learned to box. And I never learned kung fu and I don't know how to wrestle or how to use a gun or anything.

I'm basically screwed.

There was this old movie on tonight—*Three Days of the Condor,* I think it's called—and this old spy guy tells this not-as-old spy guy that what he missed about the cold war was clarity of knowing exactly who the bad guys were and knowing exactly how to proceed from day to day.

That's me, exactly, except for the cold war part and the bad guy part and the spy part.

When my life revolved around golf, everything was simple. Would this make me a better golfer? No? then I wouldn't do it. Yes? then I would. Maybe? then I'd try it. I'd get up early every morning and work on my short game. In the afternoon, I'd work out and play a round. In the evening I'd go back to the driving range. Simple.

Now, it's like I totally don't know what I'm supposed to be doing from one day to the next.

What I need is some kind of computer program or an iPhone app that tells me what, exactly, I should be doing at this exact moment to become whatever it is I want to be. Like, maybe it'd start with you checking a bunch of boxes. Something like:

(CHECK ALL THAT APPLY)

- ☐ Airplane Pilot
- ☐ Bartender
- ☐ Fishing Guide
- ☐ Smuggler
- ☐ Professional Golfer
- ☐ All-Around Cool Dude
- ☐ Navy Seal Sharpshooter
- ☐ Good Cop
- ☐ Garbage Man
- ☐ Carpenter
- ☐ Artist
- ☐ Dolphin Proctologist
- ☐ Sleazy Politician
- ☐ Chinese iPad Factory Worker
- ☐ Masseur/Masseuse
- ☐ Smelly Biker
- ☐ Movie Theater Ticket Guy
- ☐ Porn Star
- ☐ The Guy Who Puts the Convenience-Store Sandwiches in the Little Plastic Triangle Things

- ☐ Car Mechanic
- ☐ Park Ranger
- ☐ Telephone Psychic
- ☐ Stripper
- ☐ Truck Driver
- ☐ Rock Climbing Instructor
- ☐ Farm Tractor Salesman
- ☐ Bad Cop
- ☐ Fireman
- ☐ Welder
- ☐ Florist
- ☐ CornNuts Distributor
- ☐ Sleazy Lobbyist
- ☐ Billionaire/White-Collar Criminal
- ☐ College Professor
- ☐ Fearless Adventurer
- ☐ Movie Star and/or Rock Star
- ☐ Kardashian
- ☐ Supervisor of the Guy Who Puts the Convenience-Store Sandwiches in the Little Plastic Triangle Things

And then it'd have another section where I could check the boxes for how much money I want to make and whether or not I want to get married and have kids and what kind of people I want to hang out with and how big I want my muscles to be and then, whenever I'd open it up, it'd tell me exactly what I need to be doing at that exact moment—what to eat, what to do, what to say—to become this ideal person in five or however-many years.

I would totally buy an iPhone just for an app that did that crap. But I guess I'd have to figure out whatever the hell it is I want to be or do with my life before it'd work.

Basically, I just want to be this guy with the charm of James Bond, the sheepish good looks of Matt Damon, the MacGyverishness of MacGyver, the inner peace of the Dalai Lama and the money of Warren Buffett.

And I want a healthy, fit body and a ton of women who want me for my brain but desire me for my looks.

And I want a car that doesn't need a coat hanger to hold the front bumper up.

And I want to ride motorcycles everywhere and be able to fly a plane without getting the crap scared out of me.

I want to be this guy that kids look up to and say, "That's the kind of guy I want to be when I grow up."

And I want to be hairier. I want to have facial hair and chest hair and back hair and I want to be able to grow a pony tail or shave my head if I want and have it cool either way because I'd have a kick-ass goatee to go with it.

And I want to be organized.

And I want to be able to check my computer program or iPhone app for right now at three in the morning and have it tell me exactly where I should be and what I should be doing and what I'll be doing tomorrow and next week and every single day for the next five years to get me to be exactly this guy I want to be.

I don't want to check it constantly, but I want to know it's there when I get off track. Like a GPS for your life. That's totally what I need. Somebody totally needs to invent that.

But it'd probably just tell me that right now I need to get off my ass and do something other than fantasize about some magical computer that will probably never exist.

July 10

God, I screwed up.

I mean, seriously screwed up.

I don't know what the hell I was thinking—or, as Mom would say, "You *weren't* thinking; that's the problem."

You're right, Mom. You're right.

But the more I sit here thinking about it, the more I wonder how anything could've turned out any different.

I mean, Regina shows up at my door with that long jacket with nothing but that little white silky thing underneath. And her hair was doing that sexy, kind of fifties movie star thing. Plus, she's got that pierced tongue, which I figured would be awesome, even though it actually feels like a ginormous wart, precisely where you don't want to feel a ginormous wart.

But I didn't know that at the time.

And each of her boobs must be at least as big as my whole entire head. How am I supposed to say No to that? I mean, seriously, I can't even imagine how any guy anywhere could've been like, "I'm sorry, but I think you should leave now," because that's so far beyond what my brain can even process as remotely possible. There's got to be somebody, though, who isn't gay, who could've told her No.

But what would I have done different?

I'd still answer the door, thinking or hoping that maybe Tanha didn't go away this weekend with Marpa after all—but then I'd open the door and it'd be Regina in that long jacket, saying, "L.J.! What're you doing here?"

"I live here," I'd still say, even if I was the kind of guy that things'd somehow turn out different for.

And then she'd still say, "Do you know So and So?" or

whoever she asked for.

I'd say "No" again, because I still wouldn't know whoever it was.

Then she'd still say that whatever friend of hers was hosting their monthly lingerie slumber party, or whatever she called it—some officialish-sounding name—but she couldn't find her friend's new house or something.

So that would've gone about the same.

The me who could somehow say No would've probably been less interested in the whole Tupperware-party-except-with-lingerie-and-a-sleepover idea than I had been (or maybe he'd be imagining lingerie pillow fights with ugly girls, instead of the frolicking *Playboy*-pajama-party-turned-*Hustler*-ish-pajamaless-party thing that I had in my head).

But the me who could say No probably still would've let her borrow my phone, because the me who could say No would still be polite and helpful or whatever. And then, when she couldn't get her friends on the phone, the better me probably still would've let her take her coat off.

It's not like I had a choice, anyway; she pretty much just said, "It must be eighty degrees in here," and then her coat was on the nail by the door before I could say anything and then she was standing there in that little white thing that was barely long enough to cover any of her important parts and, besides that, went all the way down to her two little dimples in the back and almost down to the tattoo around her little almost-outtie bellybutton in the front and I know the better me wouldn't have stared—or maybe he would've stared long enough to admire those mammongous bazoombas from an artistic appreciation point of view, but he probably somehow wouldn't have stared as long as I did.

I don't know what the better me would've said when she spun around and asked if I liked her outfit, because I thought I did this kind of nonchalant "Um-hmm."

And I thought I still played it cool when she was all like "Do you think it's too short in back? I want to show off my butt without looking slutty."

I just said, "No, no. It's fine. It's not slutty."

What else could I say? I mean, I guess I could've been all like Flanders on *The Simpsons* and kicked her out while I was quoting Bible verses, but that would've been rude, and the better me is definitely not rude.

Maybe I could've somehow stopped her before she took off those high-heeled shoes, but she kind of just put her hand on my shoulder and said, "I need to get these off," as she bent over.

I did say, "What're you doing?" actually, before she said she needed to take them off, but I didn't know what else to say. She was just bent over and those little spaghetti straps weren't doing much because I could see all the way down to her piercing and I was just like *Damn*.

I don't know about the better me, but all I could keep thinking was, What would it feel like to squeeze those ginormous, jiggly jombawongas?

I mean, I know that, technically, I'd probably already done that, but I was completely schwasted then and I didn't remember it. About all I remember from that night is rolling over into some sticker bush and getting escorted back to my dorm room by the campus security guy and him freaking out when he saw all the plastic palm trees I'd borrowed from Shively Dining Hall.

So when Regina was all bent over tonight, I couldn't stop wondering what it would be like to stick my head in between there and do the motorboat and maybe sort of almost suffocate a little. Are they as firm as they look? What would happen if I traced my fingertips all the way around? Would she squirm if I blew a circle around her nipple? What if I blew through a straw so it'd feel like real soft fingertips?

Maybe the better me wouldn't have been thinking any of that.

He probably definitely wouldn't have said, "I like your bellybutton tattoo," or whatever exactly it was I said, which led to the closer examination, which led to everything else, which led to me now freaking out more and more as I'm starting to realize how totally screwed I am.

I don't know what I'll do at work.

I won't be able to completely ignore her like I have been.

But if I act too friendly, then Tanha might wonder what's up.

Either that, or Regina will start blabbing to everybody and then Tanha will find out anyway. That would suck.

I wouldn't know how to explain that one. *Seriously, I just opened the door and she was standing there in a negligee thing and an overcoat and she had a pierced tongue and a little snake tattoo on her belly button.* How could I possibly make any of that sound good?

Plus, there's Chewbacca to worry about. Regina kept going on and on tonight about how frighteningly unpredictable Chewbacca is (that was how she put it, too: "frighteningly unpredictable"). Especially now that she's been doing so much crank lately.

A couple weeks ago, apparently, Chewbacca beat the crap out of some friend of theirs because she thought the friend was messing around with Regina because there were two big muddy footprints on their sidewalk.

So I was getting nervous as hell lying next to Regina, knowing that my front door was probably easy to break down and there was no quick back way out of my apartment. She tried to reassure me: "She only gets like that when she's drunk or cranked out."

But she'd just finished saying how Chewbacca is cranked out all the time. Right before the beating-up-the-friend story, she told me how Chewbacca spent the whole last weekend digging holes all through their landlord's back yard, looking for Indian arrowheads or some crap. Apparently that's what meth-heads do.

Regina tried telling me that I don't have anything to worry about because her loyalty isn't to Chewbacca (whatever that means).

But she said it like that'll only last for as long as I keep having sex with her. It's like I'm being blackmailed.

And if we keep having sex, Tanha will find out eventually.

Basically I get to choose between being hospitalized or losing whatever chance I may have with Tanha.

Screwbidy dewbidy screw screw me.

July 11

Overheard in the ATS parking lot after work:
The guy who's always smoking those clove cigarettes: Wow, so many stars!
Viking Boy: And so little time.

*　*　*

I can't believe how much food I just ate.

Tonight at work, somebody started talking about Taco John's, which got me totally in the mood for a beef burrito. My mouth was watering just thinking about it. So I stopped by Taco John's on the way home. I went inside because, when you've got a serious food craving, you want to make sure they get the order right.

When I went in, there behind the counter to take my order was Taylor, the girl who let me feel her boobies at work last week.

I was trying to be cool, even though the whole time I was thinking, *I touched your boobies, I touched your boobies.*

Finally I said, "I didn't know you had a second job. I haven't seen you in a while. Did you change your schedule at work or something?"

She said, "I got fired."

"What? When? Why?" Because if there's anybody who was an ideal ATS employee, it was her.

"They said I used 'inappropriate language on the call floor.'"

"Do you think this is because you reported Smeagol to H.R.?"

"Oh, gee, I don't know. It's possible, considering they hardly even pretended like it was a coincidence that I'd just reported him that morning."

I was just like, "I'm sorry." I'm the absolute worst person in the world at saying the right thing at the right time. I honestly don't know how I always have such good handle times at work.

I felt like I should say something, since I was one of the people who kind of encouraged her to report him, but I only encouraged her because I figured that's what I should do after she used my hands to demonstrate what Smeagol did to her.

In a perfect world, everybody would be able to grab anybody else's body parts whenever they wanted.

I don't even know what we talked about after that. We talked for quite a while, too, because I was the only customer in the whole place. I was pretty much just staring at her boobs the entire time. My mouth was kind of watering the whole time we were talking; I'm pretty sure it was from thinking about the burritos, though, and not her boobs.

Can girls tell when you're starting at their boobs, by the way? That's what I want to know. I mean, they have jokes about it on TV all the time, but can they really tell? I hope not.

There was just something about the way her little Taco John's polo shirt kind of hung down around her chest. I don't even know how to describe it. Like usually, a girl's shirt stretches across from the front of one boob to the front of the other so instead of two separate boobies, it always looks like one big bouncy bag o' fun.

But with Taylor's Taco John's shirt, I don't know if it was because it was kind of loose on her or what, but the shirt totally just slumped down against her chest between her boobs, so you could totally sort of make out the shape of each separate booby. It'd be embarrassing if she actually knew I was staring, especially considering she gave me all that food for free. And especially since she pretty much got fired because Smeagol felt her boobs. But I couldn't stop looking.

She gave me her phone number, though, so maybe she didn't notice.

* * *

I just checked my email. Besides all the junk mail—"You can make $6487 a month at HOME"; "Discover a new career as a Medical Imaging Specialist"; "Increase the thickness of your manhood"; "Please send me your bank account information so I can deposit this check for eighteen bazillion dollars"—I had an email from Regina and one from Tanha.

Tanha's was all like, "Sorry I didn't respond earlier—all your voicemails were in with my old messages and your emails all went to my deleted folder for some reason." Then she wanted to know if we could get together this week so I could help her study for her Spanish test "and maybe play some cribbage later." She had a smiley face and everything and then she signed it, "Talk soon. Love—Tanha."

I was really not looking forward to reading Regina's email after that, especially since it had that big red exclamation point marking it as important.

When I opened it up, though, all it said was, "Miss me?"

No. No I didn't.

I deleted it right away.

I don't get it, though. Just a couple days ago, it was like I couldn't get a girl to even talk to me and now it's like I'm suddenly Don Juan or Don Quixote or whoever.

Maybe I was giving off some kind of weird scent or something. I'm probably not anymore. Right now, I'm pretty sure I have beef burrito and Potato Ole's oozing from my pores.

Speaking of which, I think it's time to give birth to another politician.

July 12

Work tonight sucked. First of all, Tanha showed up with her hair half chopped off and messed up all Rastafarian-looking like Marpa's. That was a drag.

Plus, I've still got this ginormous hickey on my neck that still hasn't healed from last Saturday. Derek told me to think up the most ridiculous excuse I could think of—ideally one that doesn't involve anybody else having to lie for me—and then tell her that.

So I told Tanha I was driving to work with my head out the window and a big giant rock or bug or something hit me right in the neck. I was all like, "Does it look like a hickey? Adam said it looks like a hickey, but hickeys aren't that big, are they?" That kind of thing.

I'm pretty sure she believed me, because she didn't act weird at all or anything, so that was good, but I still felt like a total asstard. I just don't want to do anything to screw up whatever slim chance I might eventually have with her. She's so beautiful. And sexy. And smart. I know I could never find another girl anywhere near as awesome as her. I don't care if it'd be Jessica Alba on top of Vanessa Hudgens with some Brianna Frost thrown in, I'd still rather be with Tanha.

And here I am, getting ginormous hickeys from Regina on my neck.

So I had that to feel guilty about.

To change the subject, I finally broke down and asked her what it is she likes about Marpa.

She was like, "I've never met anyone who always says the exact right thing. This weekend he told me that I complete him."

"Like Jerry Maguire?"

"Who?"

"Nevermind."

"You don't believe me," she said. "I should probably get going anyway. My break's almost over."

"I believe you," I said. "Seriously. I totally believe you."

"Okay."

She had over seven minutes left on her break when she clocked back in. I pretended like I didn't know. I'm pretty sure that's not an awesome sign, though, that somebody would rather work than spend their break talking to me. So that sucked.

And then, right after I clocked back in, I got this call from this really *really* old lady who wouldn't stop crying. Her name was Ellen and she said she was eighty, but she sounded about eight hundred—no lie—but, every time I tried to get her date of birth, she started crying even more.

Finally I was like, "Ellen, what's going on?" all compassionate and stuff. Even though I'm not supposed to give her a reading until I've actually verbally verified that she's at least eighteen, that doesn't mean I can't talk to her.

In between sobs, she says, "My Ralph died. Nobody else will talk to me. Will you talk to me? Ralph died. I put on my dress, but that won't bring him back."

So anyway, there's about fifteen minutes of this. I find out later, when her grandson gets on the phone, that Ellen has a mild (?) case of Alzheimer's or dementia or something and, every couple months, she puts on her wedding dress and remembers that her husband died, like, twenty years ago. But to her, each time, it's like it just happened and she goes through that whole grief thing again and again and cries for three days straight.

It has to be the most depressing call I ever got. But her grandson, when he got on the phone, he was just like, "Meh, she does this every couple months. You get used to it," and then he started telling me his problems, which didn't sound near as bad as hers. He was kind of like, "Poor me, my grandma's annoying. Boo-hoo, I don't have a girlfriend," that sort of thing.

Then he sort of half covers up his phone and I hear him yell, "Oh my God! Grandpa's dead!" and then he starts laughing.

I was just like, *what the hell?* Then he told me he got the idea to do that yesterday when he talked to one of the other psychics—Adam somebody or something.

"Are you serious?" I asked.

Yes. Yes, he was serious.

When I talked to Adam about it I was just like, "Dude, what the hell?"

And he got all dickish about it, saying crap like, "You're always telling your callers to move to Alaska to find their soul mate, or that they need to make porn, or, 'watch out, an air conditioner is going to fall on your head.'"

How is that even remotely the same thing?

I just looked at Rob like, *Is he serious?*

But Rob said to me, "He's got a point."

I was just like, "You guys are both totally going to hell."

* * *

When I got home, I had this email from Regina, but I didn't know it was from her because it was from a completely different email address, so I opened it and it was like, "Artie hacked into my email and . . ." blah blah blah, blah blah blah.

Then she wrote about how, yes, she has multiple personalities, but it's not a "disorder" because there isn't one that's more dominant than the others. That's reassuring.

It just amazes me how completely she's deluded herself into thinking she's sane. I mean, she thinks she's normal and not crazy as hell, but she's got to be the craziest-ass chick I've ever met in my entire life. Depressed chicks I can sort of deal with, but this psychotic stuff is total bullcrap.

I'm totally applying for an assload of jobs tomorrow.

July 13

"Why do you want to work at Spring Orchard Communications?"

How am I supposed to answer that? Seriously. Am I supposed to say, *Because your name gives absolutely no indication that you're just another crappy telemarketing company? Because it's so much more rewarding to sell no money down real estate crap over the phone than it is to be a telephone psychic? Because I'd really prefer to make nine bucks an hour instead of eleven?*

I was just like, "I want to study business when I go back to college and I think a job like this will really give me a leg up." I actually said that, too—"a leg up."

He was like, "What kind of business do you plan on studying?"

"Uh, international trucking." He just looked at me like, what the hell? I just kind of shrugged my shoulders like, *You and I both know I'll never study business in eighteen million years.*

Then he went into the whole, "Where do you see yourself in five years?" crap.

I don't even know what I said to that. All I know is, whatever I said was complete bullcrap and it more than likely didn't make any sense whatsoever.

The interview pretty much went downhill from there. But, after it was over, I stayed and took a bunch of these tests, anyway (mostly because I didn't have the balls to just leave). There was a computer aptitude or something test, and a typing test, and one that was just . . . weird . . . one question—no lie—was, "Have you ever had a black, tarry bowel movement?" I think the answer options were something like a) yes, last night, b) yes, within the last week, c) yes, within the last year and d) never.

What the hell?

I didn't even read the questions after that. I just clicked the ovals as fast as possible so I could get to my next interview, which I figured had to be better.

It wasn't.

The next place was outbound telemarketing, which sucks enough as it is—I don't really like the idea of calling people, asking them to buy some crap they'll never want no matter how awesome the script is that I'm supposed to read.

But, to make matters worse, it wasn't even like a real telemarketing place. It was just a big room with a bunch of long tables and those uncomfortable-as-hell metal folding chairs with one of those old style telephones and a phone book at each chair. You actually had to go through the phone book and dial the number yourself and then ask if they wanted to donate to whoever they were supposedly collecting money for.

I can't remember what it was, but it sounded shady as hell.

I figured the third interview had to be better than those. The ad didn't say much, just that they were looking for college students and other go-getters who loved to travel, meet beautiful people, and make up to three thousand dollars each month. When I called the number, they wouldn't tell me hardly anything, which should've been my first clue. The guy was just like, "Come on down tomorrow at 2:00 and we'll be able to explain everything. The job is much too complicated to explain over the phone."

So I get there, and I'm sitting in this room with eight other guys who look almost as confused and way more go-getter-ish than me, and there's this guy up front, about our age, wearing a nice shirt and tie, checking his watch and chit-chatting all friendly with us. The guy sitting next to me said, "He'll be a used-car salesman in five years, guaranteed."

Then the guy up front looked at his watch and, at exactly

2:00—according to his watch, at least—he said, "William, go ahead and show these fine gentlemen what we do."

So William goes up front with this big book in his hand and says, "How many times do you find yourself without the answers to the questions you're looking for?"

On and on like that for, like, thirty minutes.

He never went right out and said it, but after a while it became painfully obvious that these douchebags want us to sell encyclopedias.

Door to door.

And not a whole collection of encyclopedias—no, no, no. Just one encyclopedia, with all the important information condensed into one convenient volume.

I was just like, first of all, I didn't know people still sold encyclopedias, or anything, door to door. And, second, even if somebody was stupid enough to let us in their door, they won't pay $139.99 for one book when they can get the whole entire internet for ten dollars a month. I mean, he's giving this spiel like he's never even heard of the internet.

And, third, you couldn't just tell us this crap over the phone? "Too complicated to explain over the phone," my ass.

All you had to say was, "Hey, we want you to sell over-priced, obsolete crap door-to-door to people who can't afford a computer or a bicycle or a bus pass to get to the library."

How complicated is that?

And you won't pay us, technically, because that would limit how much we can make. Instead, we get a commission for each condensed encyclopedia collection we sell, meaning that we have unlimited earning potential.

I was pissed. I was looking around the room, waiting for one of the other guys to leave so I could sneak out with him, but everybody just sat there like, I don't know. I don't know if they were scared to be rude, or if they were just in total shock that there's somebody stupid enough to think any of us would actually do that. There might've been one guy who was into it. Maybe that's all they wanted or needed, just one stupid guy. Whatever.

I just got up and left.

Car Salesman Guy tried to say something, but I just put up my hand. Kind of like *Talk to the hand*, which I've never done in my whole entire life. It would've been cool if people didn't stop doing that like eighteen million years ago. But I just put up my hand and left. And then a bunch of other guys—I don't know if it was all of them—walked out behind me.

I've never led a movement like that before. It was kind of cool.

Still, I was pissed. I was just like, *you made me drive all the way to Parkersburg for this?*

So, yeah, not the most successful day of job searching.

July 14

I had a job interview today at Advance Auto Parts and I kicked ass. I mean, seriously kicked ass. It was awesome. At the end, the guy was like, "I know I'm not supposed to say this, but we'll offer you the job after we check your references. I should get back to you this afternoon."

I was just like, "Thanks," and I gave him a firm manly handshake and I walked out to my car without tripping or doing anything stupid and I drove off without hitting any cars in the parking lot—I didn't do anything to screw it up, in other words.

I've got a new jo-ob! I've got a new jo-ob! God, I am so-o-o-o-o psyched.

I've always wanted to know more about cars and I can definitely do that there. He says they'll train me, so it's okay that I don't know a whole lot now. And everybody there was super cool. Plus, as soon as I get ASE certified, whatever that is, I'll be making the exact same I'm making now. And he said it doesn't take long to get certified and that they'll train me for that, too.

And I won't have to talk to crazy people on the phone all day.

And I won't have to deal with Smeagol or Liz or Regina or Chewbacca ever again for the rest of my life.

I won't get to see Tanha every day, which kind of sucks, but I basically only see her in the break room every now and then anyway. Plus, I'll help her with her Spanish, so I'll see her then—at least until she realizes I don't remember a single thing from AP Spanish. Basically all I know now is whatever's on *Dora the Explorer*. She said she made up a bunch of flash cards, though, so maybe I'll be able to fake my way through it.

I've got a new jo-ob! I've got a new jo-ob!

What has two thumbs and doesn't have to deal with the ATS bullcrap anymore?

This guy.

July 15

I just called Ryan at Advanced Auto Parts to see when I can start and he was all like, "We discovered a problem yesterday with the work references on your application."

I was just like, "What?" because I'm pretty sure I wrote the complete truth about everything on my application; that's why I was so psyched that the job was so perfect for me.

I said, "Did I write down a wrong phone number or something? Because I can get the right numbers for you today, if you need them."

He was just like, "Nope. I've got the right numbers."

He was kind of a dick about it, too, like I totally made up some huge lie on my application.

I tried to say something else, I don't even remember what, and he just cut me off and said, "We've already filled the position."

I don't know what that was about, but I guess I don't have a job at Advanced Auto Parts, after all.

I seriously don't feel like going to work today.

* * *

Normal bullcrap at work today. Derek was all freaking out because Smeagol threatened to fire him unless he handed over all the union cards or whatever that everybody already signed. But Derek never passed out any union cards. Derek hasn't actually done anything to get a union here except constantly complain that we need a union.

But when Derek told Smeagol that he didn't have anything, apparently Smeagol was all like, "We'll have to double-check your job application for any inaccuracies or inconsistencies and then, of course, we'll make sure to analyze your on-call performance to verify that you're the type of employee that's right for this company."

So Derek was all freaking out to me like, "You've got to help me, man. I can't afford to lose this job. I've got daughter to take care of."

I was just like, "I don't know how I can help, but I'll do what I can."

He didn't know, either.

One good thing happened tonight. I don't know if it was an accident or not, but when I got my last QA (perfect score, by the way, thank you very much) there was another QA sheet stapled to the first one. Sara did the one that got the perfect score, and Jacob did the other one, and it had PINs and notes all over the place, and it had a handwritten note on the top:

> Jacob—After listening to the tape of this call you scored, I can't find evidence of any of the violations that you claim to have found. With regard to the opening and close, please review your QA manual— these need not follow the precise wording as long as the required information is obtained from the caller. I could also find no reason for the PINs you assessed for Sincerity. Again, check your manual. Grading calls the way you graded this one would undermine the whole intent of the Quality Assurance system. In fact, your evaluation of this call might make one question your suitability for the QA team. I can't stress enough how important it is that this not happen again. Please speak with me if you have any questions. Thanks—Tim

So, yeah, I guess one sort of not sucky thing happened today.

July 16

I helped Tanha study her Spanish tonight (which basi-cally involved me holding up each flash card while she said what the word meant). Then we played Cribbage while we watched *Jerry Maguire* but she fell asleep before it got to the "you complete me" part, which is the only reason I wanted her to see the movie in the first place. But now she's all cud-dled up against me with her head on my lap, so it's all good.

I can't reach the TV remote without getting up and I don't want to get up because I'm scared it might wake her so I'm stuck watching this Time Life Music infomercial with Wayne Newton singing "Danke Schoen." He looks like this thirteen-year-old Italian Opie.

* * *

"After the Lovin'." I don't know who Englebert Humperdink is or was—I've heard the name; I don't know why—but he's got a look to him that makes you think he used to get a lot of lovin'.

The end.

* * *

She had this clump of hair kind of on her face, so I pulled it back behind her ear and then caressed her scalp a little bit.

Even though she's laying here with her head on my lap, I still want to get *closer* to her. I want to be inside her, and not even in a sexual way (though that would be okay, too). I want to somehow dive into those warm brown eyes of hers and melt inside of her so I can see out of her eyes and talk with her lips and step with her feet and feel with her fingers. I want to look in the mirror and see her face so I can memorize every little wavy filament thingy in her eyes and every little moist crease in her lips.

I want to see myself through her eyes so I can understand what it is about me that makes her smile or laugh or tell me about the girl who used to beat her up in fourth grade. I want to feel what she feels like inside when she's happy, or sad, or scared, or horny. I want to be inside of her when she smiles that coy teasing smile with her tongue poking into the left side of her mouth; I want to know if she does it on purpose because she knows how sexy it is, or if she doesn't even knows she does it.

Does she know how amazing she smells?

Does she know how beautiful and sexy and smart and funny and cool and amazing and awesome she is?

When she poked me in the ribs tonight, was that an invitation to poke her back, or was she actually mad that I beat her in Cribbage?

Does she know how warm and fuzzy and tingly it made me feel inside when she did?

What does she think about me? How does she feel about me?

Did she put her head on my lap because she wants me to do stuff like pull thin clumps of hair behind her ear, or because it's just comfortable?

Does she ever imagine being with me and loving me and living with me and having kids with me?

Does she want me to make the moves on her?

Does she want me to caress more than her forehead and her cheek and her neck?

Does she even know her hand is resting on my leg? Does she think about how close her head is right now to Sir Lancelot?

Does she like me as more than just a friend? Would she be here now if I wasn't helping her study for her Spanish test?

Will she be pissed if I start caressing and then rubbing

her arm and her shoulder and her side? Because I think that's what I'm going to do.

* * *

Crap.

About five minutes later—not even five minutes; it was as long as it took her to walk down to her car and drive off and then for her (the other her, the wrong her) to walk up here from wherever she was parked; before I even got the chain on the door latched—there's a knock on the door and so I answer it, assuming it's Tanha, but it's Regina, and the first thing she says to me is, "Happy to see me?"

I don't know if she says it because I probably looked all happy when I opened the door, thinking it's Tanha coming back to wryly say, "You know, I really don't feel comfortable leaving when I've lost so many games of Cribbage; maybe you'd let me have a rematch—in bed."

So I was probably—at least at first—looking all like I've got this scenario in my head of strip Cribbage with the shy, teasing compliments flowing into the gentle poking and tickling and those unrehearsed "I've-always-wondered-what-you-look-like-naked" compliments that'd get her thinking about being naked except, in my case, they'd be rehearsed as hell because I've been trying for two months to figure out the best way to phrase it to get her naked without sounding pervy and thus ruining whatever shot I may have had, so I'd probably just say something more about her eyes, if that's not too lame, or maybe something about how I love the way her hair's got that soothing fresh laundry smell, but I'd probably just suggest that the loser of the next Cribbage game gives the winner a backrub and then I'd lose on purpose and then I'd give a little platonic tug on her shirt and say, "Ooh, you should take this off so we don't get any oil on it," like I'm so concerned about the welfare of her clothes that any other advantages of her toplessness don't even occur to me, and then I'd gesture to her jeans and say something like, "If you take these off, I can massage your legs, too," or "Maybe you should take these off, too, in case I get sloppy with the oil" and then, after I work my magic, I'd slide up and whisper in her ear, "How am I doing so far?" and she'd make that "Mmmm" purring sound and then I'd move in for the friendly kiss that'd work its way into actual kissing that'd eventually flow into the caressing and stroking and nibbling and rubbing and licking and sucking thing and pretty soon she'd be holding my face between her warm wet hands and she'd look into my eyes and sigh, "Tell me you've got some condoms."

Yes. Nice image.

But when I realized it was Regina at the door, I don't know what my face might've looked like. Confused, probably.

And I couldn't tell from looking at her if she was pissed, or drunk, or horny, or what. And I didn't know if she had just been outside telling Tanha about what an asshole I am or if she had just hacked Tanha into little bits and tossed her into the Hocking River. She didn't have blood on her sweater, so that was good. (Her sweater looked kind of nice, actually, the way she was all poking out without a bra or anything.)

And then she says, "Take a picture, it'll last longer," as she walks in past me, and I can tell now that she's pissed and also, somehow—maybe she said something now that I think about it—that's she's been waiting in her car for the last however-many hours for Tanha to drive home.

And then she plops down on my couch like she owns the place, even though she's only been here the one time before, and she just blurts out, "I'm pregnant" and I totally feel like I just got the wind knocked out of me, without the falling flat on my back part.

All I could do was sit down on the edge of the couch—not too close—and think about how totally screwed I was.

Chewbacca will know the baby isn't hers—she's not that

stupid—and she'll want to kill me for sure. If she was ready to shove my balls down my throat when she thought Regina and I just kissed, she'll totally want to kill me now.

Crap.

And now Regina's in there, crashed out on my bed, probably dreaming about unicorns or something, while I'm out here slowly realizing that there's not enough weed in the world to calm me the hell down or help me think up a solution that doesn't involve my balls in my throat.

Crapity crapity crap crap crap.

* * *

Now that Regina's finally gone, I'm sitting here trying to figure out if I should be happy or relieved or pissed off or worried or what.

While I was out here, stressing out about Chewbacca cutting my balls off, Regina came out of my bedroom and she was like, "Ooh, weed," and she grabbed the pipe out of my hand and took a couple ginormous hits until she totally cashed the bowl.

I was like, "Should you be smoking that if you're pregnant?"

She says, all nonchalantly, "I'm not pregnant. I just said that so you'd let me in."

It seems like I should've been totally pissed right then, but I was too busy being super relieved. So I was pretty much just joking when I next said, "Is there anything else I should know?"

Apparently, Regina, is one of those people who can't help but tell the truth—the whole truth and nothing but the truth—when she's high. She was like, "You know that lingerie party last week? I made that up.

"And that girl, Melinda, who calls you at work all the time? That's me. I connected a cordless phone behind the cabinet in the QA booth and I call your extension from my car so all the calls show up as QA test calls."

"And you know those jobs you've been applying for? When they call at work, I tell them you never worked there. I told one lady you're on probation for child molestation."

"Why?"

"I don't want you to leave," she said, like that was a good enough reason. "Oh, and I know who your secret admirer is."

"Who?"

She didn't say anything at first—just did one of those eyebrow flicking things that can mean almost anything. Finally she said, "Me."

I must've had some look on my face because then she said, "That's not the reaction I was hoping for."

I don't know what she expected me to do or say. I was just like, "Is there anything else?"

"Yeah, but that's enough for one day."

So, yeah, I'm relieved that she's not pregnant, but I feel like she kind of blackmailed me into having sex with her again. I can't explain how she does it or what she says exactly, but she somehow hints like she'll tell Chewbacca about us if I don't have sex with her.

Not that I completely hate it, and I know it takes two to tango and all that crap, but as soon as I finish, I feel all sick and disgusted with myself inside.

I mean, God, she's just so incredibly annoying. Having a conversation with her is literally physically painful.

Like, tonight, we were just, I don't know, just talking. First we were talking about the music my landlady's been playing nonstop since forever, it seems like. Regina was all like, "That's the Amitabha Sutra," or whatever she called it. She was kind of know-it-all-ish about the whole thing, but I figured I don't know what it is, so maybe she's right. I didn't really care.

Then for some reason she started talking about Marpa

and his stupid karmic enforcement thing, which is a load of crap, if you ask me, but she thinks it's all awesome and he's all awesome and everything.

Okay, whatever.

But apparently, she knows some secret about him that involves me somehow, or about me that involves him. I don't know. She wouldn't tell me what it is. She just kept saying, "I can't. I promised. It was told to me in confidence, blah blah blah."

I hate when people do that. Why even mention it in the first place, other than to be an annoying assface? You could just not say anything instead of being all like, "Don't you think it's strange that his 'spiritual journey' of the last ten months has taken him from Spartanburg to Fairmont to Clearfield to here—all places with an ATS branch? That's all I can say."

So annoying.

Still, I was being cool. I was pretty much still ignoring her at this point, anyway.

But then somehow we started talking about I don't even know what, and I mentioned these Fossil Beds in Nebraska that we went to when I was little. I told her how they had all these prehistoric exotic animals that you wouldn't normally associate with Nebraska, and she wouldn't believe me. And I said they had rhinos—or hippos (I always get those two confused)—and zebras (which, it turns out, were some kind of prehistoric extinct striped horses instead of zebras, though a prehistoric extinct striped horse looks pretty much like a zebra to me).

She was like, "No they didn't. They didn't have rhinos or hippos or zebras in Nebraska; they're from another continent."

I was like, "Yes, they did." That was my whole point in bringing it up, actually, because I said I never would've imagined that they had such animals in the middle of America, of all places.

She was still arguing with me about it when we went to the kitchen to get some food and I was just like, *Who the hell cares?* but she was starting to piss me off, because she hasn't even been to Nebraska—or west of the Mississippi River, actually—so I go online and google it and go to the website and I'm like, "See? right there: a hippo" (or maybe it was a rhino—I can never remember).

All she says is, "But you said there were zebras and those aren't zebras; they're prehistoric extinct striped horses."

"You're missing the point. You said that there was no way that animals that are 'native' to Africa could've ever been in Nebraska and right here, in Nebraska, is a rhino" (or a hippo).

Now that I think about it, that wasn't even the point, either. The point is that we were having a gentle, relaxed, after-the-sweaty-stuff conversation and she turned it into an argument about details that nobody gives a rat's ass about. And she kept going back, pointing at the computer, saying, "You said there were zebras; those aren't zebras."

I mean, It's like, we'll be laughing and having a nice conversation and she'll be saying that Sir Lancelot is vag-tastic and everything and, just as I'm thinking, "Gosh, I don't know why I thought this chick was annoying; maybe I judged her too quickly"—at just the instant I'm thinking that—she'll do something to remind me why I thought she was so annoying in the first place.

Like, for example, apparently, I say, "Really?" a lot. I mean, I don't know how it is wherever she comes from, but in Cincinnati, it's a fairly common expression. Somebody says, "Hey, I've got two tickets to the Reds game Saturday," and you say, "Really?" Or somebody says, "Hey, they screwed up my paycheck again," or, "Hey, my pee tastes like blue raspberry Kool-Aid," and you say, "Really?" and the first person might say something lighthearted or even witty, or maybe just say, "Yeah," and then elaborate because that's what people do when you tell somebody something and they answer, "Really?"

Tonight, I don't even know what we were talking about or what she said, but I said, "Really?" and she flipped out. I mean, totally flipped out.

She was all like, "I just said so, didn't I?" and "Why do you make me repeat myself? You think I've got nothing better to do than constantly repeat myself when you're too lazy or stupid to figure it out the first time?" And she kept going on and on and wouldn't shut up, all because I said, "Really?"

I think I'm probably mad at myself more than anything.

I suck and I need another shower.

July 17

Holy crap, my arm feels like it's about to fall off.

Tonight at work, Derek asked me, "You're artistic, right?"

Apparently, I'd promised Derek that I'd help him forge a bunch of names on this union petition because if he doesn't give Smeagol all his names, Smeagol said he'd fire him.

I was like, "I don't know. I can doodle. Why?"

"What're you doing after work? Can you come over to our place and help me with some stuff?"

I figured this would be a sure way to keep Regina from coming over to my apartment again, so right away I said, "Sure."

When we get to his place he's got this pile of get well cards; the same get well cards that were getting passed around at work tonight with the note, "Our owner's wife, Mrs. Snyder, has terminal cancer. Please sign to wish her well. Make sure you both sign and print your name so Mr. and Mrs. Snyder will know who you are."

So anyway, my job was to copy all the signatures of the people we hate onto the "Yes I Want a Union" petition sheets so Derek could give them to Smeagol on Monday so he won't get fired.

The trick to forging a good signature is to follow their pen strokes exactly, and you have to do it fast, like you're actually signing it, so it takes a while to do it right. After a while, we got sort of an assembly line going; I was doing the signatures while Derek printed their names on the second line.

I was like, "Won't these people suspect something? Like, they just happened to sign these get well cards and two days later their signature just happens to show up on these things?"

"That's the best part. They can't fire you for signing a union petition—that's against the law. So they'll never mention that they even saw these signatures. If they fire them, they'll have to think of some other reason."

It took forever. We would've been done a lot sooner but, after we finished the first time, we realized that we used the same black ballpoint pen for every single signature, so we had to go back and redo a lot of them. We kept most of them in black and we did some in blue, and then a couple in red, a bunch in pencil and the rest in black felt tip.

So, anyway, that's what we did after work. We didn't finish until about four in the morning. I crashed out on their couch. Their baby woke me up at six. Mary was already awake and Derek was already gone at his other job, whatever that is. So I came home.

When I got here, there was a strange car in our driveway. There was just barely room for me to get around it to my parking space. As I went over to put an angry note under the windshield, I noticed that Regina was inside, sleeping. So as quietly as possible I hurried up in to my apartment before she woke up and now she's been knocking on my door for the last five minutes. I'm surprised the landlady hasn't come out to yell at her.

* * *

She stopped knocking; hopefully she's finally leaving.

* * *

Nope, she's still outside. Sitting on the steps in front of my door.

* * *

Now I hear her talking to Marpa.

July 18

We're all going to die.

That's all I know, or all I've been able to figure out.

Or both, actually.

It'll start with one of those innocent little not-even-one-Advil headaches that'll turn into a Slurpee headache that won't go away. Then we'll get a fever, a little scratch in the throat that'll turn into a can't-even-swallow-warm-tea sore throat, a rash on our stomach that'll spread across our body before it inexplicably disappears. Then our inner organs will turn to mush and then blood will ooze out of our ears and by the ninth or tenth day we'll be dead.

Or else we'll die in a car wreck.

Or a plane crash.

Or a train accident.

Or a house fire.

Or we'll have a heart attack, or a stroke, or cancer, or we'll get struck by lightning, or slip in the bathtub, or shake a Pepsi machine until it flops on top of us, or we'll get caught in an avalanche, or we'll survive after twelve days under an avalanche and we'll choke on our celebratory steak, or we'll get e coli, or swine flu, or monkey pox, or we'll bleed to death after getting our balls shoved down our throat, or we'll be an anonymous victim of some anonymous maniac, or we'll get wasted to ease the depression about the fact that we're all going to die and we'll pass out and choke on our own vomit.

We can lower our cholesterol and eat our vegetables and sprinkle soy nuts on our salad and take our vitamins and drop our daily deuce—we can spend our whole lives in a big padded fireproof, bulletproof, bombproof, Chewbacca-proof sterile bubble and avoid every germ and every accident and every catastrophe ever—and we're still going to die.

It sucks.

I don't really have a problem with not having a body and not being able to do anything—give me my bong and a bag of CornNuts and that's pretty much a normal weekend for me anyway—but when I try to imagine what it'd be like to be dead and not able to see or feel or to even *imagine* any more, that crap freaks me out and I'm totally not looking forward to it. And nobody ever talks about it so apparently everybody else is somehow cool with it. I'm totally not cool with it.

But no matter how much this inescapable inevitable fact of death lurks above me like some giant menacing lurking thing, and no matter how much I feel like I should be preparing for it somehow by, like, praying or meditating or . . . anything, the only thing I can think about lately is my penis.

It's taking over my life, and I want it to stop. It's got to stop. I don't know how to make it stop.

I know it's not my penis, per se. I mean, I remember enough from biology (or was it psychology?) to know that it's my brain that's causing all the trouble. Synapses firing and endorphins releasing and my sepatal pleasure center doing whatever it's doing. But as ineffective as my efforts to simply stop having sex have been, I can pretty much guarantee that digging into my hypothalamus with the corkscrew attachment of my Swiss army knife won't help. The problem is, I don't know what else to do.

Regina made me realize I have a problem. I try to avoid her at work and I don't answer my phone when the number says unavailable and I pretend I don't get the eighteen million emails she sends me every day, but then she still shows up at my apartment without any warning. Stalking me, basically. I don't know what to do about it. Stop having sex with her would be a start, I suppose.

But, holy crap, man. I mean, sex is fun. Seriously. It's got to be like the funnest thing in the whole entire world. With Ashley, it was okay, but nothing to write home about. Neither of us knew what we were doing and neither of us were all that excited about it (it was more fun to golf on an empty course, put it that way—and I don't mean that as a euphemism). But with Regina, it's like, it's way more fun than golf. I totally understand now why Adam's talking about sex all the time.

I want to say No to her, and I try, but then she sends an instant message that says, "What would it take for me say to Hi to Sir Lancelot right now?"

What am I *supposed* to say to that? I mean, I know there's that whole "eliminate desire" thing that Marpa always talks about, and I'm all for that, I really am; and if I could just figure out a safe, painless way to go about it, sign me up.

But maybe that's the point. Maybe it's not supposed to be safe or painless. Maybe that's why the path between fear and desire is a razor's edge, and not an eight-lane freeway.

But then I think about Irene saying how life's supposed to be easy and you should go with the flow and all that, and wouldn't the easiest thing be to just do the wild monkey dance with somebody who *really* wants to do the wild monkey dance with you?

When I think about karma and all that, I worry that all this love for me will be sucked up by somebody who I don't even hardly like, and then the person who I really do love will only want me for sex. But then I think, Would that be so bad?

Then I think that maybe it's not even about karma and it's all about the fact that Regina acts more and more crazy every time I see her. It's like, I have to watch *every single thing* I say or she freaks out. Just tonight, everything was going fine until I said . . . actually, I don't even know *what* I said, but she freaked.

I could see it coming with that totally pissed *I'm-not-*

angry voice: *Just because I'm reminding you that you have absolutely nothing to offer the world except sex, it doesn't mean I'm angry. And just because I'm telling you for the eighty-seven millionth time that the scars on your knees are ugly and your haircut's awful and your tattoo looks like it was done by some drunk blind guy, it doesn't mean I'm angry.* And on and on.

So I tried pretending that, just because I had my hands over my ears, it didn't mean I wasn't listening. Then she started throwing stuff at me. First it was harmless stuff, like my Nerf basketball and a pillow—stuff like that. But then it was like that got her into a throwing mood and she started in on the heavier, harder stuff. Like DVDs and books and her keys.

Once she chilled out, she was all like, "Sorry," and then she said she needs to throw things to "emotionally justify our relationship."

I was just like, *Wtf?* I mean, first of all, what "relationship"? Seriously.

That's when I really totally wished I didn't like sex. I mean, I've been trying to be gentle because I don't want her to go psycho and cry to Chewbacca or complain to Tanha about what heartless man-whore I am.

But at the same time I'm like, *How do I make her go away?*

That's why I think everything would be easier if I became a Buddhist monk or something. But when I have sex, I can't help but think that sex belongs somewhere in the middle path. Doesn't it? I mean, they had famous Buddhist guys who had sex, I think. The Beastie Boys have sex, don't they? And they're all about the Buddhism.

That should count for something.

Yesterday's quote of the day was from Mother Teresa that said, "let no one ever come to you without leaving better and happier," and it's like, what's more effective at making Regina better and happier than having sex with me?

Still, I don't know. I mean, I'd totally rather be with Tanha. Even though I know I don't really have a shot with her because she's with Marpa, I still don't want to ruin whatever tiny chance I might have by being with Regina. That's when I decided to end this for real. But then Regina looked at me with those big-ass bazoombas and she was like, "Is that what you really want?"

So then, I figured I'd end it over the phone. That didn't work, either. I've tried email. I've tried ignoring her. Nothing's worked.

I knew I was screwed tonight when she sent that instant message. It started out innocent enough; I'd just finished explaining why I don't like zoos when out of the blue she asked me the "What would it take" question. I instant messaged her back: "You could start by doing my dishes" (which she never did, by the way).

Then she tells me that, in a hundred years, we'll all be dead and none of this will matter anyway. And while she's detailing the Ebola virus and rattling off all these other ways we could hypothetically die, I'm thinking, "Doesn't our karma keep going even after we're gone?"

I mean, say I drive her nuts for however long, then when she's eighty, she finally takes her frustration out on her paperboy, then the paperboy puts a pile of flaming dog poo on the porch of some computer geek who never tips, then the computer geek screams at the mailman, the mailman climbs the clock tower and guns down some woman's new husband, then that woman grows old and bitter and all alone with a bunch of cats until she finally takes it out on her paperboy and it goes on and on and on and on.

All because I can't say No to sex.

So that's it. No more. I'm going into my bedroom and I'm going to wake her up and I'm going to tell her that we'll

never be having sex ever again.
Wish me luck.

July 19

Holy crap, work tonight was totally, truly awesome. I don't even know how to describe it. It was like, you know how it seems like there's always at least one little thing wrong with everything in the whole entire world—like even when something's awesome, there's always one little thing keeping it from being perfect.

Like, the filling inside of a Twinkie is awesome, but the cake part is kind of lame.

Or, like, Regina's got a great body with those ginormous perfect ta-tas—and she likes sex—but she's totally insane.

Or, like, work wouldn't be so bad if none of these annoying asstards worked here.

Well, tonight was like if they replaced the lame cake part of the Twinkie with something awesome, like more Twinkie cream. Like, my Twinkie fantasy of Twinkie cream filling inside Twinkie cream filling. Or like if Regina wasn't living with Chewbacca and she wasn't completely insane. That's what tonight at work was like.

It started out normal. But then, at about four o'clock, Liz sent Gretchen back to Smeagol's office. About five minutes later, Gretchen comes back all crying because she got fired. Then Liz sent another one back, and then another, and another. Smeagol fired almost every single annoying person at work tonight. It was awesome.

The best part was, every time another person was all sad about getting fired, Liz was all like, "If you were better at your job, you wouldn't have gotten fired."

So when Liz got fired last and came out of Smeagol's office all pissed off and crying, it was the greatest thing ever.

People were actually cheering when she left. Somebody

sang, "Ding dong, the witch is dead," and somebody else was like, "Nah nah nah nah, nah nah nah nah, hey hey hey, goodbye."

Best day ever.

I mean, when we were doing all the signature stuff on those fake union petitions, we thought there might be a chance that some of these people would get in a little bit of trouble—maybe start getting a bunch of bullcrap PINs or something—we didn't know that Smeagol would just go off and fire every single one of them.

Except for Regina. She's still there, so that sucks. We figured that must be because she works at the podium. It's not like you can give her a bad QA since she doesn't work on the call floor.

I don't know, maybe it wasn't completely perfect. I mean, it's still ATS, after all, and Smeagol's still the P.M. and Regina's still working at the podium, so it still sucks.

At least now, though, the suckiness has been dialed down a couple notches from twelve.

I mean, part of me feels like I should feel bad, but I totally don't. We only put the names of the super annoying fucktards on the list, for one, and it's not like we told Smeagol that he had to fire these people.

So, yeah, totally the best day of work ever.

*   *   *

Viking Boy's questions of the day: "Is the Buddha still alive or dead? Or both? Or neither? And why does Dora the Explorer have such a disproportionately large head when Diego doesn't?"

*   *   *

I've got a job interview tomorrow and I won't use ATS as a reference, so hopefully I'll get it.

July 20

Holy crap. I didn't think it was possible, but there's actually a job in the world that sucks worse than ATS.

I should've known the job would suck when the guy told me the longest the last five guys lasted was half a day, and the last guy quit after an hour.

There was this ad in the paper for an apartment manager, twelve bucks an hour plus free rent. I called him last night during my break and he told me to come by at eight this morning, so I did. Since the ad was for an apartment manager, I figured I had to look somewhat nice, so I wore basically the same business casual stuff I wear every day at ATS, except I added a tie to look professional.

That was my first mistake.

He told me to go home and change into something more comfortable, because the first thing I would be doing was mowing some grass. I figured, All right. I've been mowing lawns since like sixth grade; I've got this.

First of all, his lawn mower's a piece of crap. It took me, like, twenty pulls to get it started.

Still, that wouldn't have been so bad except what I had to mow was all the grass around these twenty little house-like apartments, each with their own lawn.

Which, also, wouldn't have been so bad, except nobody had mowed this grass the whole year. Seriously. I mean, you figure grass grows an inch or two a week and this grass was up to the tops of my knees. And I'm five-eleven. And my knees are pretty much where you'd expect them to be on a normally-proportioned person. So this was some tall-ass grass with the seeds all on top and everything. It sucked.

I couldn't mow like you normally would, just pushing the

mower forward, because it'd die every time and then I'd have pull and pull and pull on the stupid cord until it'd start again. So basically what I had to do, for nine straight hours, was tilt the mower up, push it forward about twelve inches, plop it down on that tall-ass grass, and then pull it back or tilt it back up real fast so the motor wouldn't die on me.

I mowed over so much crap, too.

Every so often, you'd hear this chunk-chunk-chunk-chunk when you'd plop the mower down and you'd see a bunch of pieces of whatever it was flying out of the hole on the side. I ran over a buttload of snakes and a couple unidentifiable small furry animals.

When I got to this one yard, though, it was the worst. They had a bunch of kids, so every three feet, I was running over something new. Barbies, Legos, a G.I. Joe. One of those cheap plastic soccer ball-sized bouncy balls like they have at Wal-Mart—that thing basically just exploded and scared the hell out of me. This little girl was crying after I ran over what must've been their pet of some kind.

I don't know how many times I had to refill that mower with gas. The owner guy had to come by with a new gas can, though, so it was a buttload of gas. Plus, the place in the lawnmower where the grass is supposed to shoot out kept getting all clogged up, so I was digging that out constantly, waiting for some mangled piece of metal to shoot out and cut off all my fingers.

Finally, at six-thirty, I was done, and I was totally ready to come home and crash out for the next three days.

But, no.

We had to go to take his plumbing snake to another one of his properties and unclog the toilet. That sucked.

I had to grab the twisting metal snake part of that beeotch and push it down while the old guy just stood there cranking the handle. That's where I lost all the skin on my hands. I mean, I had a few blisters from the nine-hour lawn-from-hell mowing marathon, but all the skin was still pretty much there. But this snake thing sucked. It was all wet, which made my skin soft, plus it was twisting and bending and pinching and just basically sucking ass. I tried using the gloves that he let me borrow since he didn't really need them to turn the crank, but the gloves kept getting caught in the little twisting creases or whatever of the snake. So then I just took them off; it's not like I had a whole lot of skin on my hands by then, anyway.

When we finally drove back to the first place where my car was, the old guy was like, talking about what a great worker I am and he had me drive his old beater truck back to the first apartments where my car was because, "I can trust you now that you're part of the family."

He's probably some old guy who's about to die and he's looking for someone to will all his millions to. The whole time he's talking to me about how I'm part of the family now and this and that, all I could keep thinking was, You don't want it to be me, dude.

Finally when we got back to my car, he was like, "Do you want me to pay you now, or will you be here tomorrow?"

I didn't have the heart or the balls or whatever to tell him he'd never see me again, so I was just like, "I'll be here tomorrow. Eight o'clock?"

"Eight o'clock."

Screw that.

I need a shower right now probably worse than I've ever needed a shower, but I'm totally dreading it because I have absolutely no skin left on the insides of my hands. Soap and water will burn like a monster mofo.

* * *

It's times like these that I think there must be a God because, seriously, I totally needed a bag of weed like nobody has ever needed a bag of weed in the whole entire history of weedom. And then, Poof! there it was, a tiny little dime bag sample from the Grab Bag, tucked away in a shoebox with my Mr. Bubble.

And I still wouldn't have found it if I hadn't decided to take a bath, and I wouldn't have decided to take a bath if that job today didn't totally suck. There were more coincidences that I forgot, but the point is, it seems like everything that happened led me directly to finding that secret stash. I needed to take a bath and a bath isn't really a bath without Mr. Bubble, right? So it seems like it was meant to be.

And not only that, but, if I still had this sample from the Grab Bag tucked away with the Mr. Bubble, maybe I've got the whole rest of the Grab Bag hidden away someplace where I'll find it when I really need it. That would be awesome.

For the first time in almost forever, it seems like, all is right with the world.

Enough talking. I'm going to fill up the tub and I'm going to get a Sobe green tea bottle and a hollow Bic pen and a bowl from one of my pipes and my Swiss Army knife and some bubble gum and some crushed ice cubes and I'm going to make an ice water bong and I'm going to get baked as hell and take a bath. With candles. Because that's how I roll.

* * *

Oh, yeah.

* * *

I want another hit, but if the bowl's empty do I want another one enough to get out the bag and load another bowl? Thank God! The bowl's still loaded.

* * *

I should totally take baths more often. Warm. Relaxing. The sides of the tub are cool on my arms.

* * *

Is this heaven?

No, it's Ohio.

* * *

Mr. Bubble kicks ass, but there is such a thing as too many bubbles.

* * *

Holy crap. I was just making a bubble snowman—a bubbleman?—when this loud crashing thump about gave me a heart attack. It sounded like the landlady upstairs dropped a bowling ball on the ceiling (her floor, my ceiling).

Now it's quiet enough again that I can hear my ink pen scratching across the paper. Plus, I can sort of hear my landlady's chanting music, but I can't tell if it's actually playing or if it's just in my head from hearing it all the time. "E-jean boo lawn chi wren ling Ming John she ah me toe foe you chew shin John Zen's eye Cheech in she wren John she zing booed yen Dow gee duh wan shin ah me toe foe."

Is there anything light enough to make Bubbleman's eyes and ears? And mouth and nose. Damn, I'm wasted.

* * *

If anybody ever dies from smoking too much pot, tonight will be the night.

* * *

Maybe if I had some food color (or is it called food coloring?).

* * *

Damn! Another big crash. What the hell? That definitely wasn't a bowling ball. I about dropped a log in the tub.

Whoa! Another one. Even louder.

It sounded like it was right outside. I'm trying to listen, but it's hard to focus; this weed came from the Grab Bag and it kind of hits you all at once.

It almost sounds like somebody is in my apartment. But that sounded the last time like broken glass. Or maybe now it sounds like broken glass. Or somebody walking on broken glass.

*   *   *

Either the landlady is making some kind of weird noises I've never heard before or somebody's in my apartment.

*   *   *

There's definitely somebody in here.

At first I thought it might be the cops—I figured the landlady called and said the guy downstairs had a big skunk in his apartment—so I sort of hid my bong (did somebody say bong? it's not a bong; it's a water pipe, for smoking tobacco, nothing else). Whatever it is, it's hidden behind the toilet now and it's all gross and covered with lint and cobwebs and tiny bug guts.

But if it was the cops, they'd knock first, wouldn't they? And they'd definitely be yelling. "Police! Get down on the ground! Now!" There's none of that.

Nobody's talking at all. It's like, whoever it is, they've been planning this for a while and so now they can just communicate with hand signals. It sounds like they're just walking around, grinding glass shards into my carpet and tripping over piles of clothes.

Does Chewbacca know where I live? Crap. She could if she really wanted to. It'd only take about two seconds online, probably. She'd maybe really want to. She'd definitely really want to if Regina told her that we had sex.

Would she do that?

Probably.

Crap.

*   *   *

Crap crap crapity crapity crapity crap crap.

*   *   *

I just threw the towel against the door, just in case you could see any candlelight from outside.

*   *   *

Chewbacca hasn't gone through my bead curtain yet, so she's still out in the living room, so it's possible that she doesn't even know I'm in here. She might not have seen my car, since I park down kind of behind everything.

Once she's through the bead curtain, though, it'll probably be forty-five seconds before she notices these other rooms back here, and then another forty-five seconds before she opens this door, which means three minutes until she finds me.

And then maybe—what? five minutes? two minutes?—before she cuts off my balls and shoves them down my throat.

That sucks.

* * *

I'm scared to move because I know she'd be able to hear me sloshing around in the water. I'm trying to write as quietly as possible.

* * *

Crap crap crap crap.

* * *

What sucks is, I don't have anything to defend myself with in here.

I don't think a bubble sword would be very effective.

I'm pretty sure Sir Lancelot would be no match for the machete or whatever Chewbacca's about to come after me with.

* * *

And I left all my clothes outside the bathroom door so I wouldn't get them wet. Nice thinking.

* * *

It sounds like she's in the kitchen now. It sounds like she's wearing cowboy boots.

* * *

Crap. This totally blows.
Talk about a buzzkill.

* * *

If anybody ever dies from having sex, tonight will be the night.

* * *

What the hell's she doing? Washing my dishes? But the water's not running.

* * *

Chewbacca. I can't remember what her real name is; I'm pretty sure it's not actually Chewbacca. I want to say Arnie or Archie or something, but those are guy's names, and I'm pretty sure she's got a girl's name, even though she looks like a Bruce.

Or a mean Bubba—as opposed to a happy-go-lucky, doh-dee-doh Bubba—actually she looks more like one of those flat-faced puppies with a Jay Leno chin and Michael Jackson nose and crazy Britney Spears eyes. Just wrong on so many levels. She definitely doesn't look like anything you'd attach a girl's name to.

Just go to ATS in Coolville and ask for Regina's big ugly partner who looks like a Wookie—that's her.

She was in the Army or Navy or Air Force or Marines or something. She just got back I don't know how many months ago from Iraq or Afghanistan or one of those places where they kill people in the bathtub on a daily basis, probably.

They live just south of Athens, I don't know the address. And I'm sure I threw away the directions. Township Road 57, I think. Turn right just past the bridge. Drive until you see my decapitated head stuck on a stick in the front yard.

* * *

Regina—I don't know her last name, either, or I can't think of it.

She's Chewbacca's crazy psycho girlfriend/wife/ whatever and she's been stalking me forever and I've been trying to avoid her while still trying to pretend like everything's cool, but Chewbacca still always looks pissed but I always figured her face was just ugly that way. But apparently it's not if she's breaking into my apartment.

If you find me mutilated in the tub, you'll know she's the one who did it: Chewbacca Somebody, from Athens, Ohio. Twp. Rd. 57.

First right past the bridge.

Decapitated head on a stick.

*   *   *

Now I just have to figure out where to hide this notebook where the CSI guys will find it but Chewbacca won't.

*   *   *

What the hell is she looking for? She's been in the kitchen for twenty minutes (maybe not that long) and she still hasn't come through the bead curtain to the back.

*   *   *

I guess I could spray her with this boysenberry gel candle.

*   *   *

I've got my fingernail clippers up in the medicine cabinet.

*   *   *

I bet that Jet Li or MacGyver could figure out a way to turn my fingernail clippers into an effective weapon.

*   *   *

Or my disposable razors, the contact case, the lighter, the ballpoint pen, these paper clips, the candles, incense burner and Softsoap.

MacGyver could make a bomb out of that crap, for sure.

But he'd probably use the stuff I wouldn't expect—toothpaste, Pepto-Bismol, vitamins, the roll of paper towels I have here for when I forget to buy toilet paper.

Yeah. Big-ass bomb.

That's what I need.

*   *   *

She's still in the kitchen.

*　*　*

Should I get out?

She'd hear me then, for sure.

And she doesn't seem to know I'm in here now.

She still hasn't gone through my bead curtain to get back here. That's when I'll know I'm a dead man.

She'll probably want to pig rape me with a broom handle before she brutally murders me. That'll suck.

*　*　*

The water in the tub is getting cold.

*　*　*

She's still in the kitchen. Maybe Chewbacca's so quiet because she smelled that nasty bowl in the sink and blacked out.

*　*　*

Or maybe it's Chainsaw breaking into my apartment to make up for all of his food that we ate. That would be cool.

*　*　*

Or maybe Chewbacca hired Chainsaw to break into my apartment to cut off my balls and shove them down my throat. That would suck.

*　*　*

It could be Regina, too. But if she's breaking into my apartment, that wouldn't be good, either.

*　*　*

Whoever it is, I hope they hurry up. My feet are totally pruney and this water's getting cold as hell.

It'd suck if I died of hypothermia.

     An Athens, Ohio, man died of hypothermia in his bathtub.

That'd suck.

*　*　*

Crap, I just realized that they wouldn't be able to arrest Chewbacca because I haven't technically seen her yet.

I'd just be a cold dead guy in the bathtub with his balls shoved down his throat. But I guess they'd find her DNA somewhere in the apartment.

But this is Athens, Ohio. The CSI budget probably pays for a Swiss Army knife, a used magnifying glass and a bunch of those paper strips they use to test the chlorine in a swimming pool. That sucks.

*   *   *

What is the proper amount of time you should stay in your bathtub after somebody breaks into your house? Because I'm freezing my ass off.

*   *   *

Now she's moving again.
Damn. Bead curtain. I'm dead.

*   *   *

God, I hate raccoons.

Stupid little fartmuncher about gave me a heart attack. The loud crashes earlier were him somehow smashing the garbage can outside against the window and then the cement block I had on top of the garbage can to keep him out fell in through the window, and then later he knocked over all my dishes in the sink. It was loud.

And then I couldn't get him out of the apartment. He wouldn't go back out the window. He just kept hiding in the back closet.

I finally had to make a trail of CornNuts out the front door.

*   *   *

I was too paranoid to sleep in my apartment, so I came here, to this Ramada Limited in Wherever-the-hell-I-am, West Virginia. Buford or Bluford or Bluefield, I think.

I still can't sleep. Even though I know Chewbacca more than likely didn't follow me all the way down here and, even if she did, she can't get in here without breaking down that big-ass door or scaling eight stories up the side of the building to my window, I still can't sleep.

I know I'm probably being way too paranoid. Especially since it's basically just a raccoon I'm running away from. But, I mean, if Chewbacca really is as crazy as everyone says, and if she's as cranked up as she apparently must be all the time, what's to stop her from finding my address somehow? Regina found it, so it must be possible.

And if Chewbacca gets "impulsive" when she's drunk, what's to keep her from impulsively coming to my apartment? And if she comes to my apartment, what's to keep her from breaking in? And if she breaks in, how the hell am I supposed to protect myself? With my three iron? I don't think so.

That's why I'm here. Sitting on the bed with the lights off and the volume all the way down on the TV, trying to chill out enough so I can get some sleep.

I'm hungry. I wish I had some CornNuts.

* * *

I had a million things I wanted to say when I went down to the vending machine for CornNuts and a Country Time Lemonade, but I got all paranoid on the way up here: what if Chewbacca's waiting for me when I get off the elevator? What if she gets on at the next floor? But then I figured it'd be worse if she saw me in the stairs because, at least in the elevator, you're going up to a floor and the doors will open and there's kind of a finality to an elevator ass whupping, like, *Okay, this is my floor, I guess I'm done beating you now.*

On the stairs, the beating would just keep going and going until, hopefully, the police show up. But then I realized that Chewbacca could stop the elevator and keep pummeling me—which I thought of before, but when I first thought of it, I figured that an alarm would go off and some security guy would be right there, but now it occurs to me that, even if there was an alarm, and even if the security guy did get right there and, even if he wasn't a donut-eating moron, nobody would be able to open the door and get in to help me for probably a half hour, at least, and by then I'd be a lifeless mass clumped in the corner, and Chewbacca would be wondering if she'd have a better chance to get away if she just finished me off and climbed out the top of the elevator like in *The Matrix* or if she'd hold what was left of my body in front of her to shield her from the police bullets.

That whole scenario was still playing out in my head as I nervously fumbled—like a scary movie asstard (totally like that)—to get the little credit card key thing to open the door.

And now that I'm back inside and there's no Chewbacca in the Ramada Limited closet or under the Ramada Limited bed or behind the Ramada Limited curtain or the Ramada Limited chair or the Ramada Limited bathroom door or the Ramada Limited shower curtain, I'm not even really hungry or thirsty.

I'm tired and my hands hurt like hell. That job today sucked royal ass.

July 21

They had this crappy Jet Li movie, *The One*, on last night where the bad Jet Li from one universe in the "multi-verse" was killing all the good Jet Lis from all the other universes.

I wish we had that. I wish there was another universe out there someplace where there's another me who doesn't keep screwing up, messing around with the wrong people and then getting so paranoid that he has drive far, far away just to get some sleep. Splurging on this Ramada Limited room with its Café Valet French Roast coffee and everything that smells like "citrus ginger" because (what the hell?) I might be dead soon so I might as well live it up while I can.

Maybe the other me could eat something besides CornNuts for breakfast because he didn't sleep through the complimentary breakfast like I did.

I'd like to trade places with him and say, "Here you go. Good luck!"

* * *

I just checked my email and there was an email from Regina that asked what would be a good time to come over. I emailed her back that today wouldn't work. I didn't mention that I wouldn't be there because I'm like, three hours away and that I was staying here at least another night.

She emailed me back like two minutes later: "Please please please let me come over. I'll make it worth your while, I promise. If I can't see you, I won't have anything to do but stay home and talk to Artie all day."

I don't know if she was trying to threaten me again, or what. I emailed her back: "You can come by at three if you want."

I'm kind of curious what she'll do when she gets there and I won't be around. Maybe she'll finally get the hint, but I highly doubt it.

*   *   *

I feel like King Abdullah or somebody.

First I spend the night in a big fancy hotel (or is it a motel?—people keep explaining the difference and I keep forgetting) that I can't afford, charging it on the credit card I forgot I had, and now I'm splurging on a big fancy lunch at the Bluefield Waffle House while the cars swish swish by on the dampish road. Sipping my vanilla cherry Coke and waiting for my Grilled Texas Bacon Chicken Melt Plate with my smothered, covered, chunked, and capped double hash browns, side of sausage and a waffle (because it doesn't seem right to not order a waffle at Waffle House, no matter how much other food you ordered).

Here comes Stacey with my food.

False alarm. I was here first, but this other guy got his food before me. That's okay. It gives me more of a chance to enjoy the ambience that is the Bluefield, West Virginia, Waffle House. And today is all about enjoying everything. The sprinkling rain outside. The yellow and red and the brown inside. It's all good.

I could get used to this life—sleeping in hotels (or motels), eating at Waffle House, not worrying about Chewbacca cutting off my balls and shoving them down my throat. It's nice. This day off from work is way better than yesterday, which was technically also a day off from work, even though I spent it mowing grass and Barbie dolls and assorted animals. I don't know if I can count that as work since I won't get paid because I'll never see that old dude ever again.

I forgot I left my phone in my car last night. I had a message from Tanha: "I was wondering if we could get together about an hour earlier for our study date—say, five-ish?

I promised Reverend Marpa that I'd be at his place at six for some big surprise he has planned for me."

I'm pretty sure that's not worth risking running into Chewbacca for, especially when I know that she's just getting together with Marpa later, anyway. If she's so excited to see him, he can help her with her Spanish. It's not like I'll ever be able to get her to *beba mi palo* or *chupe mi pito*, anyway.

So I don't know what I'll do all day, other than just chill out in my room and watch HBO until I've lost all sense of depth perception. I've seen billboards for at least three different strip clubs in town, but I don't have any cash or enough money to withdraw from an ATM to make it worth my while. I'm pretty sure I can't charge lap dances to my credit card.

Here comes Stacey—this has to be for me this time. Yes!

* * *

Dear Tanha,

~~This will sound crazy, but~~

~~I don't know how to say this, so I'll just say it~~

~~Remember how I said I never lie? I lied.~~

~~Remember when I told you I could never mess with a caller they way Adam and Rob do?~~

~~A funny thing happened at the Bluefield Ramada Limited~~

~~Let me start by saying I think you're the greatest.~~

~~Marpa doesn't really like you.~~

~~Marpa's only using you to get back at me.~~

* * *

Crap, crap, crap, crap.

I'm sitting here across from a cop in the customer lounge of Charlie Smith Motors in Beckley, West Virginia, with a ginormous bag of weed in my pocket, waiting for my car to get fixed enough so that I can drive it back to Athens. I told them I was in a hurry, but I'm totally hoping they get the cop's oil changed first because I really don't want to have to walk by him with this huge bulge in my pants.

And I really have to pee.

So now I'm just sitting here feeling helpless while this kid stares like a zombie at Curious George on TV. George was heading home from the market with some marshmallows, toothpicks and playing cards when he stopped to help a mama chicken get to her baby chickens that are stranded in the middle of a pond and I'm just sitting here hoping or praying or whatever that I'm not looking guilty or suspicious or anything other than focused on writing this paper for my history class (that's kind of the go-to vibe I try to give off when I want to appear innocent of everything).

An hour ago, I was just chilling in my room at the Ramada Limited, watching another crappy movie on HBO, when this instant message thing popped up on my computer. I don't even know why I opened it because I usually don't mess with stuff like that. I think maybe I thought it was from Tanha or something, because she said she wouldn't have access to her phone or email all afternoon, so I thought maybe she was using somebody else's email address.

But that doesn't make sense, now that I think about it, because if she doesn't have access to her own email, how could she have access to somebody else's email?

Anyway, I opened it. After a while, from the conversation, I finally figure out that it's Marpa's ex-fiancée. Her name's Samantha. Apparently, she's some porn actress out in California. I don't know how she got my email address—from Marpa or from somewhere online—but she got it.

We're chatting for a while; she says I've talked to her on the phone a couple times before, but I don't remember. After a while, we start to get more comfortable with each other and, for some reason, I feel obligated to tell her that Marpa's planning to get revenge on her boyfriend.

"I don't have a boyfriend."

"Your ex-boyfriend, then."

"Peter's the last guy I've really dated."

"Then whoever it was who got you to break up with him."

She said, "That was you. Remember? I called your psychic line. You said the Star card in my tenth position meant I should leave right away and move out here and get this job. Our apartment building blew up the day after I left. That's why I told you that you saved my life."

Finally, it starts to sink in. Marpa's whole karmic enforcement thing has totally been about me this whole time. I'm the one he wants to screw with. I don't know, I probably should've figured it out sooner, but I didn't.

Samantha said, "You knew that, right? Peter told me he had a party and you guys talked about it. He said you guys are best friends now."

No, we never talked about it.

So I've got all these wild scenarios in my head, trying to figure out what Marpa's been planning for his equivalent karmic adjustment. It must be something with Tanha.

The one I kept landing on was that he'll videotape her somehow—either having sex with him or in the shower or something—and then he'll put it on the internet. That's probably a best case scenario, though, knowing him.

I tried calling Tanha about eighteen million times, but she never answered.

I didn't want to leave a voicemail. I don't have a clue how I could explain everything on a voicemail without me coming across like a douche. Especially since I'd told her about eighteen million times that I would never mess with a caller the way Adam and Rob do.

She'd be like, "I can't believe you lied to me. You know I hate liars. You're no better than my ex-boyfriend." Then she'd start crying and say she never wants to see me again.

I didn't want to send her an email for the same reason.

That's why I dumped all my crap from my hotel/motel room into my car real quick and headed back to Athens. I figured if I hurried, I could get there before Tanha came over and I could stop Marpa from doing whatever it is he's planning to do.

As I drove, I kept trying to come up with some kind of note or letter or something to explain everything but, no matter how I worded it, it always just sounded messed up.

And then, I wasn't really paying attention and I guess I was driving too fast on the onramp and there had been a little rain earlier, which didn't help, and my stupid car spun around and smashed into the guardrail and blew out my tire and now my car's all messed up. It makes this chonk-chonk-chonk-chonk sound whenever I try to drive.

This guy in a tow truck happened to be right behind me and he hung around until I changed my tire to see if my car was okay.

When we took the spare tire out of the trunk, sitting in that little depression where the spare goes, was the Grab Bag.

At first, I was all super excited that I found it, since I'd been looking for it every-damned-where for-totally-ever, it seemed like, and part of me was kind of all proud of myself that I'd put it in such an awesome hiding place that even I didn't know where it was, and part of me was like, "Holy crap! I hope this dude doesn't realize that's a ginormous bag of weed and call the cops."

The tow truck guy was like, "Nice Crown Royal bag."

It was all flattened out and you couldn't really tell it was full of weed by looking at it, but I grabbed it real quick anyway and shoved it into my pocket. Now it looks like I've either got elephantitis of the nuts or a massive stiffy from watching Curious George make a bridge out of marshmallows, toothpicks and playing cards.

When we heard the chonk-chonk-chonk noise, the guy towed me here, where they told me I need a front control arm something or other that costs two hundred dollars, which is apparently half the price that the dealership would charge. And it won't take long at all, but the mechanic guy never did say how long "not long at all" is.

Until then, I've got to sit here with a big bulge in my crotch, hoping they finish in time for me to stop Marpa and hoping this cop doesn't ask me if the man in the yellow hat makes me hard or is it that little boy sitting in front of you or exactly what is your problem, son?

Screw me.

* * *

Holy crap, I don't know if I can come even remotely close to adequately describing what a messed-up day this turned into.

By the time I finally got back to my apartment, Tanha was already there, waiting at the top of the steps for me. She looked at me all surprised when she saw me walk up the steps.

"I thought you were already inside," she said.

"No. I just got here. Why?"

"It sounded like you were having sex. I didn't want to interrupt. I'm a little early, anyway."

The sex sounds picked back up after that and we both realized at about the same time that they were coming from Marpa's apartment.

Tanha walked over and sneaked a peak in his window. When she walked back over, she was like, "I think I'm going to be sick," so I let her inside my apartment real quick, but not before the landlady came out to yell at me that she's already called the cops because of all the crazy sex noises I've been making.

Tanha asked if I had any beer.

"No," I said, "But I've got some tequila." Then I showed

her the Grab Bag. "I've also got this."

We were going to light up inside, but you could totally hear Marpa's sex sounds through the wall, so we took the tequila and the Grab Bag and a blanket up to the roof where it was quiet.

Of course, at this point, I'm thinking everything is awesome. Tanha will break up with Marpa, he won't be able to make a porn of her and put it on the internet or whatever he was planning and, best of all, I don't have to tell her anything about any of this.

So we're talking, getting wasted, starting to have a good time. Tanha's starting to laugh a little. Every time I'd finish a cigarette, she'd want to flick it because she didn't know how.

It was turning into a nice evening. The sun was going down; it was going to be another blah Athens sunset, but at least the sky was clear and it was perfectly warm and not too humid. I remember even actually thinking to myself that I wasn't even worried about Chewbacca.

But just as I thought that, this minivan pulls up in the driveway right under us. I didn't recognize it from the top; it just looked kind of ratty and rusty with a big huge sunroof open in the front and it smelled like a nasty rotten egg fart. Then the driver and the passenger got out and I was just like, *Oh, crap!*

It was Chewbacca and Not-Ben.

Just as I figured, less than a minute later, I hear this *Bam! bam! bam! bam!* on what I'm pretty sure was my door.

"Regina! I know you're in there! Get out here! We need to talk!"

There's more pounding and yelling like that for a while before we hear the landlady's door open, and she's like, "What's going on here?" all pissed off that they're interrupting *Wheel of Fortune* or whatever. Then she said, "I've already called the police," but that didn't seem to matter, because right after that, there was more banging and Chewbacca yelling, "Regina! Regina!"

Then we heard Marpa's door open and Chewbacca was like, "What the hell are you doing? Where is he? I can't believe you. Whore!"

Regina yelled back, "You don't own me. And I'm not gay. I only said that so your douchebag friend there would quit hitting on me at work. Why do you think I've never gone down on you?" That sort of thing on and on and back and forth.

Chewbacca was still yelling, like, "Where's L.J.? I want to talk to him." Marpa must've finally come out then, because the next thing Chewbacca said was, "Who the hell are you? Who the hell is this? Are you having sex with him, too?"

About then a police car pulled up beside Chewbacca's van.

Regina told Chewbacca, "Don't yell at him. He only had sex with me to get back at L.J."

By then the policemen made it around the corner and they were like, "What's going on here?"

And so Regina explained everything.

Apparently, she'd convinced Marpa that she was my girlfriend so he'd have sex with her. And she had sex with him to get back at me. As she was describing Marpa's karmic adventures, and what I did to instigate the whole thing, Tanha was just looking at me with this look of—I'm not sure if it was horror or disgust or fear or revulsion, or some combination of everything—it looked like she just found out I was an axe murderer who liked to drown puppies in his spare time.

I don't know if it was because I was super high or what, but when I saw that look, and heard how Regina was describing everything, I just busted out laughing. I stifled it enough that the cops couldn't hear, but not enough that Tanha didn't notice.

I felt bad, because now she had this look of total disappointment on her face—way worse than any of Dad's disappointed looks—but I couldn't help it.

I mean, I told some complete stranger on the phone—somebody who'd never met me and didn't know anything about me—that her Tarot cards said she needed to move across the country to do porn, and she believed it. And she actually did it. And now everybody's making it sound all like I'm Hannibal Lector.

I couldn't *not* laugh at that. I'm pretty sure I would've laughed even if I wasn't as high as God. I still think it's funny. Maybe that's just me.

Tanha didn't see the humor in it, though. Just as I was in the middle of exhaling a drag from my cigarette, she punched me right in the nose.

Holy crap, talk about pain. That hurt in about a million different ways. First of all, my nose hurt way worse than I thought my nose could ever hurt. It was like sharp and stabbing and dull and throbbing all at the same time. Plus, when she hit me, my head jerked back right into the corner of the chimney.

That wasn't awesome.

And on top of all of that, the cigarette smoke I was inhaling went back into my lungs, I think, and up into my nose and into my eyes, so there was this whole burning sensation all up in my nose and my lungs, and I couldn't breathe and my eyes were watering like crazy.

For as long as I live, I hope I never experience that again.

Before she turned to leave, I held up what was left of my cigarette, even though it still had a few good drags left. I didn't really expect her to take it, but she did, and flicked it over the side of the roof.

I never saw it, because my eyes were all watered up, but I'm guessing it must've flown right in through Chewbacca's sunroof, considering what happened a few minutes later.

The first thing Tanha did when she climbed down off the roof was walked right over to Marpa, right past Chewbacca and the cops and Not-Ben without saying a word, and she kicked Marpa right in the nads.

The cops and everybody just stood there and watched her turn around out to her car and drive off while Marpa writhed around on the ground.

That was awesome.

Not long after that—before Tanha's car was even to the top of the hill—there was this huge ginormous explosion practically right under my head. When I looked down, Chewbacca's van looked sort of like a can of soda that you forgot to take out of the freezer. The roof was all peeled back and the windows were all blown out. The side of the cop car was all messed up, too, and that nasty egg fart smell was like a million times worse.

Pretty soon, the police start screaming into their radios, "10-80 at Hillview Lake! 10-80 at Hillview Lake!" while they're chasing Chewbacca and Not-Ben down the driveway and into the woods.

The landlady's freaking out because there's a ginormous hole in her dining room. I'm trying to pick up all my crap up off the roof as fast as possible so I don't have to breathe that nasty-ass air any longer than I have to. I was like, *Okay, Grab Bag, cigarettes, lighter, tequila, blanket—did I get the Grab Bag? yeah, it's in my pocket.*

It wasn't a super huge fire like you see on TV, but there was a buttload of this blackish brownish smoke. I don't know if that was from the chemicals or from the seats and stuff burning, or what, but it was nasty.

After the cops caught Chewbacca and Not-Ben, they made all of us leave so they could evacuate the area. And they evacuated the hell out of the place, way more people than it seems like they needed to.

All the hotels in town were full by the time I got there. Everybody else must've called ahead for reservations. I thought I'd have to drive all the way to Jackson, but then I saw this Budget Host place out toward Albany. It's okay, but it's no Ramada Limited. And it's a pain in the ass to get to; I passed the turn three times before I finally figured out how to get here.

So that was my day. Two different hotels, two nights in a row. I really am starting to feel like King Abdullah. Time to see what's on Skinamax.

July 22

Viking Boy's question of the day: "Is your soul the same as your body, or different from your body?"

* * *

Holy crap. The first five minutes of this call, I could barely get this guy to say two words. Now he won't shut up.

"When I come home from eight straight hours of dealing with customers who want to know why we won't take their bogus coupons, and cashiers who can't count, and delivery drivers who don't deliver, the last thing I want to do is come home and listen to her describe in minute detail every little thing that happened to her that day. 'We were driving to the store and this lady turned right out in front of us and I had to slam on my brakes or I would've hit her. There was this little bitch girl at daycare who kept taking Steph's toys. When I went to Kid's Closet to sell Steph's jumper, the lady would only offer me five dollars, so I took it to Toy Emporium and they let me trade it for fifteen dollars of store credit, so we got this Dora bike helmet with the elbow and knee pads.'"

I should probably be happy this guy's doing all the talking. When I got in to work today, it was like a ghost town. There's hardly anybody here. So of course we've been in queue all night. Finish one call, get another. Finish that call, get another. It's like working in a factory.

The only time it has let up was when Smeagol called me back to his office. I was sure I was about to be fired and, to tell the truth, I don't think I really cared. I figured Derek broke down and told him that we'd forged all those signatures on the union petitions and I was all prepared to laugh in Smeagol's face.

But when I got back to his office, he was like, "As you may have heard, we've been doing performance reviews the last few days and we've lost some people. Besides several TSRs, we've lost one QA and an interim floor supervisor and I'd like to fill those positions as soon as possible."

Every time I've been in Smeagol's office, he's been a total ass, so I didn't have my hopes up.

But then he said, "Your name came up as the best candidate to replace J.D."

"J.D?" I said.

"Jacob," Smeagol said. "Dover. Now that he's no longer here, we need you to move into the QA booth."

I was just like, "What happened?"

"Apparently, he got arrested. They say he and a friend had a meth lab in a van that exploded. That's not important. What's important is that you say Yes. You want the job, right? You'll make almost twice as much an hour, plus benefits and some decent performance incentives. Sound good?"

"Yeah."

"Good. You start tomorrow. Come in at your regular time."

Before I left his office, I was like, "Do you know who the new floor supervisor will be?"

"Not yet. Why? You know somebody?"

"I think Derek Reynolds would be good. He's—"

"Yeah, I don't know. We'll see. We've got a lot of good candidates."

So I'll be a QA. I figured I'd be more excited about it than I am.

And I'm usually more excited when I've got a nonstop talker on the phone, but this guy's just bugging me for some reason. He's going on and on and on about how his wife talks too much and how it's like going through a mentally exhausting three-hour gauntlet every night when he gets home from work and how it takes forever to get to sleep after that. He keeps saying I wouldn't understand since I'm not married.

I want to tell him to try doing it for eight hours every night while wearing a headset that pinches your ears so hard that it feels like your brains are slowly oozing out of your nose. But all I say is, "Yeah. Mmm-hmm, mmm-hmm" every few minutes.

Three more hours to go.

July 23

Kroger
When you want the best
* * *

Knight Transportation
* * *

Moonlight Mushrooms
Grown like no other mushroom
* * *

J.B. Hunt
* * *

Crete Carrier Corp.
* * *

Covenant Transport
* * *

SAIA
* * *

Bud Light
* * *

EPES
* * *

HeartLand Express
* * *

Schneider National
* * *

Air Ride Equipped
* * *

Dear Sobe Green Tea,

How did you get to be so awesome? You're like a little slice of heaven in a clunky, inconvenient, probably-not-BPA-free plastic bottle. You may not be a significant source of saturated fat, trans fat, cholesterol, dietary fiber, vitamin A, calcium or iron, but you're a significant source of joy in my heart.

I think about you way more than any person should ever think about a beverage—I can't help it. I can't help but daydream about that playful way you hide from me in the refrigerated beverage section, often, but not always, on the bottom shelf, never out of reach. Calling to me with your clear caramel color. "L.J.," you say. "I'm here for you." Tempting me with your sweet minty goodness. And then, once I have you, enticing and tickling and tantalizing my taste buds until I'm unable to do anything but drink all of you in, body and soul, while with my heart I sing, "You make me so very happy; I'm so glad I've got you in my car."

I love your invigorating aftertaste. It's way better than Sprite or 7Up or Sierra Mist—and don't get me started on that total crap Arizona Iced Tea—it has an aftertaste of ass compared to yours. If I ate a pile of dried horse poo and washed it down with a glass of turkey pee, I'd swear I just drank an Arizona Iced Tea an hour earlier. But it's not like that with you, Sobe Green Tea. With you, I feel like I just orally pleasured Vanessa Hudgens with a mouthful of Altoids. That's how invigoratingly fresh you are.

And what is that magical ingredient that keeps me nice and steadily awake without the rollercoaster highs and lows of caffeine? I'm guessing it's not the ginseng, because that total crap Arizona Iced Tea has ginseng, and it sucks at keeping me awake. Is it your guarana? Your rose hips? Your ascorbic acid? Whatever it is, it makes you the perfect drink for driving. You make 328.7 miles since my last tank of gas feel like a drive to the grocery store and you turn my every pee into a foamy work of art.

Oh, Sobe Green Tea, without you, I'd be hating life right now. I wouldn't be filled with this giddy excitement I feel. I wouldn't know the smell of newly mown grass, or the sound of a gentle breeze rustling the leaves of the trees. I wouldn't feel the warmth of the sun on my arms, or see the joy of a child playing with his puppy. Without you, my life would be a prison of fear, submission and repetition. Without you, I would be living a life of pain and regret.

But oh, Sobe Green Tea, why must you play so hard to get? You're the first thing I look for when I go into a convenience store. Do you know that? And so often you're unavailable. My every journey into the refrigerated beverage section is marred by a mix of trepidation and hopeful expectation as I wonder, will you be there? Why must it be like that? Why can't you always be waiting for me beside the Sobe Elixir and the Sobe Energy and the Lizard Lightning? Why do you make me drive from the Speedway, to that other place, to the Love's Travel Stop before I can have you and again feel your cool caramel caress against my lips?

That's all I ask, Sobe Green Tea. Always be there for me, forever. Please don't put these unreasonable limitations on our relationship. Don't ask me to call my favorite retailer and tell him to stock you. Because I won't do it. If you give me the same commitment that I'm willing to give you, I promise that I'll love you forever.

Thank you.

Sincerely,

L.J. Davenport

* * *

I'm counting down. In less than ten minutes, I'm supposed to clock in for my first day as ATS's newest Quality Assurance Specialist.

It's like an awesome job—almost impossible to pass up—sixteen bucks an hour, plus medical, dental, tuition assistance with supposedly no strings attached, plus all the free pizza I want every three months. Plus, I'm pretty sure it's a decent enough job that Mom and Dad wouldn't get on my ass for not doing anything productive. Plus, it's doing something that I can totally kick ass at.

So I don't know for sure what I'm doing here, lounging on this marble? granite? slab picnic table at this rest area in St. Clair, Missouri.

I went to my apartment last night after work. Even though the Hazmat guys were all done doing their Hazmat thing on Chewbacca's blown up minivan/meth lab, the power was still out and the whole place still had that nasty rotten egg fart smell. I threw all my clothes in the car so they wouldn't smell like Chewbacca, then I figured I should load up everything that was even remotely valuable, in case . . . I don't know. I was worried the police would search my apartment for some reason or the landlady would decide to steal my lava lamp and bead curtain, I guess.

I was planning to stay at some cheap hotel outside of town for a few days until they turned the electricity back on.

But I missed the turn to the first hotel and I just kept driving when I saw the second one. It was such a nice night— just the right temperature and just the right humidity for a relaxing, windows-down drive. And it was quiet and there weren't hardly any cars on the road until I got to around Jackson and then there weren't hardly any cars again until Cincinnati, and there weren't that many cars in Cincinnati, either, since it was almost two-thirty by the time I got there. And then, I don't know why, I drove to Fitzgerald's.

They were already closed, but there was a guy taking out the trash right as I walked up and he let me in to see Ernie and I sold him the Grab Bag and had a beer and then I drove another couple hours until I had to pull over and sleep, then I woke up, dumped a load, bought some Sobe Tea and CornNuts and started driving again until I got here.

I don't know what I was thinking. I mean, as I sit here now, all I can figure is that maybe I was worried that if I didn't keep driving I'd somehow end up back at work today and then I wouldn't get the eight attendance points for a no call-no show, and then I wouldn't have over sixteen points and then I wouldn't be automatically fired.

I'm still worried about that, actually, which is why I'm counting down the minutes until I'm supposed to clock in.

I mean, even though I know in my head it's physically impossible, I'm still paranoid that I'll be magically teleported back to work somehow. Like some weird something will somehow suck me through some wormhole or vortex or whatever and plop me down in front of the time clock right as I'm supposed to clock in. Or that this is just a dream and, any minute now, I'll wake up in the ATS parking lot with Smeagol knocking on my window.

That would suck.

But I don't know why I feel like that because it'd be the perfect job now. Besides the money and the benefits, all the annoying assholes have been fired. Except for Regina, but that's not even really a problem now that Chewbacca's in jail.

I was eavesdropping on a couple people in the break room yesterday and they were saying that the police charged Chewbacca and Jacob Not-Ben with all this crap like possession of meth, manufacturing meth, and third-degree arson, plus a bunch of other stuff which, according to them, is like five or ten years. And Marpa's headed back to Florida; he gave up his karmic enforcement thing after Tanha knocked his nads into next week, so it's like the ideal situation for me.

But still, here I am. Counting down the minutes. Enjoying the sunshine. Feeding CornNuts to a squirrel. Watching this little kid play with his dog while his grandma stares at me like she thinks I want to drag him off into the bushes.

And I just realized: for the first time in forever, it seems like, I don't hear the landlady's music in my head.

Two minutes.

Ha! Not two minutes! I just realized: since I'm in Missouri, my phone's showing the time for the central time zone, which means it's an hour later in Ohio than I thought it was, which means I was supposed to clock in fifty-eight minutes ago. Ha ha, haha.

Ha ha.

I want to jump up and click my heels together. I'd do it, too, if that old lady wasn't standing right there. I don't know why I feel like I accomplished something, but I do.

I've totally got Dora the Explorer singing in my head. "I did it! I did it! I did it! Yeah, oh, *lo hice*!

"I didn't do much except not go to work.

"I did it! I did it! I did it! Hooray!

"Now I don't have a job and I . . . don't know what rhymes with 'work'

"I did it! I did it! I did it! Yay!

"I sold the Grab Bag to Ernie even though he is a tool.

"I kept a little for myself because I'm not a total fool.

"I did it! I did it! I did it! I did it!

"It feels like a huge weight is lifted off my shoulders. And now instead of balls, I've got these huge brass boulders.

"Doo-dee-doo-dee-doo-dee-doo-dee-doo-dee-doo-dee-doo—I did it!"

Now I just have to figure out what to do next. I don't have a clue where I'll go. I don't know what I'll do. But I have enough money to last for a couple months. And, for the first time ever, I feel like I'm actually in control of my own life.

It's kind of scary.

ACKNOWLEDGEMENTS

I would like to thank the following people for their love, support, encouragement and help along the way: Rae-Fen, Tara, Del, Joyce, and the entire Sutherland clan, Robert Miklitsch, Zakes Mda, Darrell Spencer, Meagan Allison, John Beach, Emily Berry, Cat Crane, Mike Gossett, Katrina Hewitt, Caitlin Holbrook, Amber McMakin and, of course, James Taylor, Brian Tichota, Markos, Vodie and Woody.

ABOUT THE AUTHOR

Sherman Sutherland received his PhD in literature and creative writing from Ohio University. He currently teaches in Ohio.